The Sixteenth of June

A NOVEL

Maya Lang

SCRIBNER

New York London Toronto Sydney New Delhi

Scribner
A Division of Simon & Schuster, Inc.
1230 Avenue of the Americas
New York, NY 10020

First Scribner hardcover edition June 2014

SCRIBNER and design are registered trademarks of The Gale Group, Inc., used under license by Simon & Schuster, Inc., the publisher of this work.

For information about special discounts for bulk purchases, please contact Simon & Schuster Special Sales at 1-866-506-1949 or business@simonandschuster.com.

The Simon & Schuster Speakers Bureau can bring authors to your live event. For more information or to book an event, contact the Simon & Schuster Speakers Bureau at 1-866-248-3049 or visit our website at www.simonspeakers.com.

Jacket design by Evan Gaffney
Jacket art © Frank Ramspott/E+/Getty Images

Manufactured in the United States of America

1 3 5 7 9 10 8 6 4 2

Library of Congress Cataloging-in-Publication Data is available.

ISBN 978-1-4767-4574-9
ISBN 978-1-4767-4578-7 (ebook)

For all the readers
who never made it through *Ulysses*
(or haven't wanted to try)

Dubliners celebrate the 100th anniversary of "Bloomsday." That would be June 16, 1904—the day the [events in *Ulysses*] take place. And it's not just a Dublin thing—Joyce fans all over the world are celebrating the unique literary event.

—Lynn Neary, NPR *Morning Edition*, "Celebrating the 'Bloomsday' Centennial," June 16, 2004

The book is diffuse. It is brackish. It is pretentious. It is underbred, not only in the obvious sense, but in the literary sense. A first-rate writer . . . respects writing too much to be tricky.

—Virginia Woolf on *Ulysses* in her diary, September 6, 1922

The Sixteenth of June

Leopold turns the volume up as the hail comes down, as if he can drown out its sound, the thudding so loud that Nora worries the windshield will crack and across it a giant web will bloom.

She can see the cracked glass, the fingers spreading across the surface in a slow ripple. She takes a deep breath and tries to imagine something more pleasant. We are a happy couple under a shower of rice, she tells herself. Who knows? Such a moment could be lovely, a silent symphony of smiles.

Leo hasn't said a word about his grandmother since they got the news. There has been no reminiscing, no look of regret while knotting his black tie that morning. He had merely paused in the foyer before they left. "You okay? I know this is the first—" Nora had stopped him with her eyes. The first, the first. It is all firsts. The first meal at a restaurant since. The first movie since. And now this, coming full circle.

Ten miles of highway behind them, Philly's skyline lost in the rearview. Leo is relaxed beside her, in pilot mode. He adjusts the dials and knobs and vents, attuned to his instrument. Leo is most at peace like this, filled with the pure act of driving. He would make a happy chauffeur.

Nora leans back against the headrest. There will be no nap; she feels too frazzled. But she sees music when she closes her eyes, and this soothes her.

She has always been able to do this, ever since she was a girl. A better hobby than books because no one knows she's doing it. No one ever peeks over her shoulder to say, "'The Very Thought of You!' Is that the Ella Fitzgerald version?"

Black notes float across the white page. It is the opening riff, Ray Noble's score. *The very thought of you / And I forget to do / The little ordinary things / That everyone ought to do.*

She can tell how the notes want to play out, how they are hopeful, lifting up, an easy springtime swing. The song is flirty, but she wonders about doing it in B-flat, her voice molasses instead of a bird. Sometimes the thought of someone isn't delicate, feathered, about to take flight. Sometimes it is a weight, syrupy and thick—

Stephen fills the white bowl with hot water. He cups the bowl in his hands and carries it to his desk, where a mirror and razor lay crossed.

The razor has a tortoiseshell handle, the brush a head of badger hair. The set, wrapped in green velvet, was a gift from his mother. "Not the sort of thing I could have given Leo," June had said with her tinkling laugh. But he'd caught the look in her eyes just beneath the laughter, that uneasy, questioning look.

The thought of such a ritual brings comfort now. Stephen will need to gather himself today, as though he were in small pieces, a vase knocked over by a careless hand.

He sets the bowl down and perches the mirror against the wall, leaning it at an angle. He moves his books to the floor (how good it feels, to demote them to the floor!). And suddenly, when he sits, he is no longer in gritty, graffitied Philly, filled with kids on bikes, girls with braids skipping rope, looking too suggestive, too big, too knowing for their age. Just like that, he is transported to a different time, when men wore hats and donned violets as boutonnieres. When a shave did not involve cheap cartridges or canisters of foam.

Stephen picks up a washcloth and dips it in the water. 9:07 train, he remembers. But he wants time to slow, to not think about the schedule. He has the radio on in the background, the comforting sounds of NPR, and he will listen for some tidbit to pass along to Nora. The first funeral since her mom's. They will all be focused on themselves and the party tonight. Stephen will pass along a story to make her smile.

3

They are going through the news on the radio, the morning report, and he hears with a stir of annoyance that they are doing a feature on Bloomsday. Of course. He pauses, squeezing the washcloth over the bowl, listening to the woman's voice. She is in Dublin, the streets teeming with celebration, the drinking and reenactments in full swing.

He presses the washcloth to his face, breathing in its warmth. Time slows beneath its weight. The world always prods us to go faster, but it is a heinous concept, that faster is better. The sound of his computer dialing up said it all ("How do you not have Ethernet?" Leo would groan), like a village in Eastern Europe getting bombed.

Grandma Portman would have agreed with him. "There is no longer any downtime, *bubeleh*," she would have said. "Everyone is much too busy for it." When he draws the washcloth away, his face is flushed.

He touches the shaving brush to the tin of fragrant cream. The voice from the radio floats out to him. "There are still those in Dublin who neither like nor understand James Joyce," the reporter says.

Stephen smiles. Smart ones, he thinks, brushing the cream against the grain of stubble.

He clears a small path through the white shaving cream, watching his progress in the mirror. It is like shoveling snow, pushing these pathways clear. The handle of the razor feels substantial, cool in his palm.

Stephen pulls the skin of his cheek taut. He makes a small stroke by his sideburn, ensuring the rectangle of it is a clean line. He will enjoy this ritual, tuning out the radio until the Dublin report passes. He examines his face in the mirror and, satisfied, turns to complete the other side. He wags the razor back and forth in the bowl. The water obscures, turning cloudy and white—

"So this will be good," Leo ventures, lowering the volume. To his relief, they are making excellent time.

"Good?" Nora yawns into her hand. "You don't mean the funeral?"

"You'll get to see everyone. Sharon and her side. They'll all be there."

"Circumstances could be a little better."

"Whatever." He shifts gears, switches lanes. "Funerals can have an upside. Just think of it like a wedding without the chicken dance."

"Maybe. But no alcohol."

"No alcohol," he concedes. "This is true."

"Plus there's that whole deceased thing."

"There's that."

"Though maybe they're similar in other ways," she murmurs, glancing out the window.

Leo frowns, sensing his words about to get hijacked.

"No one really wants to be there, if you think about it," she pursues. "I mean, the bride and groom are happy, I guess. And the person who passed away would want a crowd. But no one wants to get dressed up. No one sees it as anything but an inconvenience."

"And here I'd been looking for the silver lining." He smiles to show her he means it lightly. She brings her hand up to her hair.

"You pulling?" he asks.

"No." She drops her hand to her lap. Her ring catches the light and winks at him. Emerald cut, color E, VVS1. A solitaire.

"We need some hair on that head for the wedding," he adds, and she laughs a little, despite herself.

This will be his task, such moments of small victory. Looking after Nora and shepherding her through the day, ducking questions about how they don't have a date ("Still!" he can hear them), while smiling reassuringly. A casual shrug as if to say, You know how it is, so busy. But we love each other and that's what matters. This to be exuded, his arm around her. Checking on his dad, making sure Stephen isn't being a snob at the service. "I'm writing my dissertation on Virginia Woolf's nose hairs," Stephen will announce. "Their contribution to literature." Making sure it all goes smoothly. Two hours to manage like a quarter-back on the field before returning to the car, gliding home—

One

―――

Leo wakes to the rumble of his stomach. He reaches for the button on his alarm clock, unsure why he bothers setting the thing when he's always up before it anyway.

He snakes out from under the covers and grabs his robe, an old flannel rag Nora has been threatening to toss. But he prizes it, even if it is tattered, linty, undeniably musty, not holding up well under assaults from the washing machine. A small hole has crept into the seam of the left pocket, so when Nora held it up and said in her I'm-trying-to-be-reasonable voice, "Leo, the thing *reeks*," he could only point out that another rinse cycle might kill it. L.L. Bean had stopped making them ("And there is a *reason* for that," Nora would say, eyeing it from her side of the bed), so a certain olfactory presence has to be tolerated. He couldn't admit it to her, but he has come to feel the robe is his morning companion. Old and loyal, it sits waiting for him by the foot of the bed, eager to be put to service. A sort of sartorial dog.

He pads into the living room and reaches across the counter to set the coffee brewing. This is his routine, his morning lap: wake, hit the alarm, slip from the bedroom, an a.m. assassin. Follow the curve of the breakfast bar, start the coffeemaker (another device he beats to the punch), and smack on the lights of the guest bathroom.

Only here, under the bright flood of fluorescents, does he begin to feel awake, as though the series of moves that brought him to the white bowl (whose seat he is mercifully permitted to leave up) were performed on autopilot. Leo plunges his hands into the water at the sink before it has a chance to warm.

His morning is predictable, unassailable. Even today, a familiar dilemma awaits: There is the gnawing in his stomach and the reality of the dormant kitchen, with only himself to fill the gap.

Every morning this comes as a quiet devastation, for certain promises had been made when they first moved in together. "You'll have such a sucky commute," Nora rued as they unpacked boxes. "I should, like, make breakfast for you."

"You're a night owl," he pointed out.

"I don't mean *every* morning. But I could whip up something on weekends. A big scramble or a quiche, that'd be easy enough."

He was so touched by this vision, so moved by the portrait of domesticity she painted, that he'd given an embarrassed shrug and mumbled, "That'd be nice." Instead—and he sees this now, with the wincing clarity of hindsight—he should have pounced on the offer, taken her up on it right there. But he was like a virgin being offered a blow job, too startled by the offer in its wondrous generosity to accept. He should have held her to it when he had the chance, cementing it into their routine. Because now, after living together for so long, the thought of making him breakfast would cause Nora to double over with laughter. He didn't know it then, but the terms get set at the start.

It doesn't matter that he is the breadwinner, the majority owner in the franchise of their domestic life. The person who, for some time (years!), has posted the rent and slipped the credit card onto the bill at dinner, shielding the amount from her eyes. And he does it, waking hideously early, so that they can have this urban loft that she had loved. A place near Rittenhouse, she'd said, because she wasn't quite ready for Philly's outskirts.

And in exchange, in exchange, would it be so much to ask? Not to whip up a fresh plate of eggs for him each morning or anything like that, though some vestigial part of him toys with the image occasionally: Nora in an apron, a floral counterpoint to his flannel robe. Leo understands this is off-limits, not to be considered. But if even the weekend quiche is impossible, would it be so much to have her there with him? If she could just *be* there, perched at the counter on a stool, what a luxury that would be.

Instead, the specter of her promise taunts him each morning. *There is no quiche for you in the fridge,* the empty kitchen seems to gloat, and he feels her words sail away all over again. "Remember that time, how you said . . . ," he might begin, but she'd scowl and shoot him that look, that look that said a thousand things (How could you? How dare you? Are you thoughtless, insensitive, a caveman?) in one bullet of a glance.

The kitchen is gray, quiet. He pauses at its threshold. Speckled Formica masquerades as granite; linoleum sits underfoot. A stem rack above the sink allows inverted glassware to drip directly into the basin below, and this detail, of all things, had sold Nora on the place. "That one with the stem rack," she said fondly when they were deliberating between apartments, no matter that he could've installed one in any of the contenders for all of twenty bucks.

When they signed the lease, he figured the kitchen presented an opportunity. *Potential,* in the jargon of real estate. They had the option to buy, which he assumed they'd promptly do, never imagining that five years of rent would go down the tubes.

His plan had been to put in new countertops. Quartz seemed like a good bet; granite was surely on its way out. Stainless steel appliances, maybe one of those wine storage units his parents have, glowing blue. The investment would be worth it. Apartments in the building were getting snatched up and the market was bulletproof. His dad would nod approvingly, eyeing the finished reno. Would nod and say, "Smart move."

Of course, the ideal apartment would be in a building that solved the whole breakfast conundrum. Leo pictures a buffet, maybe like a grown-up dorm. Newspapers in the corner, one of those conveyor belts where you stick your tray. Enter, eat, leave.

As it is, the common space of the Club Room at 2400 Locust sits untouched, the oversize couches and mounted flat-screen getting traffic only during tours, future residents imagining parties that never actually take place. Why not have a breakfast plan instead? It could be pitched to the working crowd, the commuters and consultants and corporates like him who share the elevator, waiting for the doors to open so they can resume scrolling on their BlackBerrys. Nothing fancy, just a way to help the early risers tackle the morning. Genius.

Because no one should have to do this. Stand there unshowered, unshaved, trying to figure out what to *cook*. Only after having coffee and breakfast does he feel capable of making coffee and breakfast. And he can never bring himself to down a bowl of cereal or one of those protein bars.

"You're like a Brit," his mom likes to say when he piles on the eggs and sausage at Sunday brunch. He ignores her, not wanting to encourage her Europhile moments, but the truth is that he'd loved London. He'd stopped there on his way to see Nora when she was studying abroad. He'd crashed with Geoff, a friend doing a semester at LSE—the kind of thing his parents had hoped he would do ("LSE!" his dad had boomed. "I did a year there, you know." Yes, Dad. We know).

He liked the city more than he thought he would. People had warned him about the food, but he liked that, too. Bangers and mash, black pudding. There was no freak-out about cholesterol, fat. They ate with relish the inner organs of beasts and fowl. Ate it without apology. Between the pints and the fry-ups, Leo felt a heightened sense of manliness. Soccer—football—was not muted in the background so that your girlfriend could talk to you and test your levels of eye contact. It was on full blast, all eyes fixed its way. The women talked to each other or were fans themselves.

He watches the coffeemaker speculatively, the pot still empty, a few dribbles collecting at its base. It is a relic, black plastic, a freebie from when Nora signed them up for a coffee subscription service. It claimed to have an "auto pause" feature so that you could pour while brewing, but whenever he tries that, it keeps right on going, the drips hitting the vacated plate with a hiss. They should register for something better, if he can ever get Nora around to registering. Maybe one of those espresso machines, shiny and chrome, a Ferrari to greet him in the morning.

He tugs open the fridge door, breaking the hermetic seal of the cushioned rubber, and spots the eggs hiding in the back—a day past their date but surely fine. He grabs the carton along with the package of bacon, squishy and cold. He'll make a scramble, maybe adding the Chinese sausage left over from last night, sweet and toothsome. Two kinds of pork at breakfast! Stephen would be disgusted. Stephen, too filled with ideas to ever need food.

He starts the bacon in the cast iron skillet. Nora never touches it, put off by the fact that you aren't supposed to wash it. "No soap?" she asked, incredulous. Her pots and pans are scrubbed to a mirrored finish, gleaming as they hang above him on the pot rack. The skillet, meanwhile, sits out of sight in the cabinet, the bastard child of the kitchen. It is unsightly, barnacled; Nora is right that the kitchen looks better with it hidden. Still, he has a soft spot for it, for all the dorm rooms and camping trips it's seen him through. You're no city boy, it rasps.

The flannel robe gathers about him loyally, warm.

The cat interrupts his thoughts, pressing his leg. A dramatic stretch—her back foot lingering in the interstice between steps—before she goes in for the head-butt.

"Maria," he greets her, leaning down to scratch under her chin. She purrs, the sound traveling up his hand.

Nora had adopted the cat after she graduated, naming it after some opera singer. He was in Boston at the time, a year of school still left. "I figured she'd be good company," Nora explained. "It's weird, being here with everyone gone." By everyone, he knew she meant Stephen. Leo couldn't tell what bothered her more: her mother's illness or her best friend's absence. Still, he'd taken the cat as a good omen. A pet was surely a sign of hope.

"Breakfast?" She cries, delighted, leading the way to her bowl. Clever girl, he thinks. They understand what we say better than we understand them. He pops a piece of sausage into his mouth after feeding her and glances up at the kitchen clock. 7:12. He saunters over to the bedroom door.

"Hungry?" he calls out. He hears stirring, the rustle of bedcovers.

"Mnnn." A noncommittal grunt. Not hungry, he decides.

"Tea?" he tries.

Another grunt, more affirmative.

"Tea it is," he tells the cat, who mews in response.

He returns to the skillet and presses the bacon. One of the world's best sounds, surely. He cracks three eggs, tossing the shells into the disposal. He shoots, he scores! He fills the kettle with water even though it will take a small eternity. Nora will smile from beneath the covers when she hears its whistle.

The service starts at ten, so they should leave by eight thirty. Nine at the latest. But he planned an early start, figuring Nora would insist on her time alone. And this way there will be no tensions, no bickering. He won't have to consult his watch and then the kitchen clock, muttering, "Christ, Nora, traffic!" He'll go for his run and maybe even enjoy it, not wondering why on earth she felt the need to banish him from the apartment.

The eggs lift their milky-white edges from the skillet as they set. He shovels the whole mess of it onto a plate, the sausage lumped in with the eggs, the bacon like a carpet beneath. The plunge of his fork releases the yolk in a bright yellow stream. Nora has probably drifted back to sleep, but soon the kettle will sound its opening notes and the white mountain of duvet will stir.

He glances at the phone mounted on the wall. His parents were probably doing their own version of this routine a few blocks away on Delancey, nibbling egg whites and toast. It's ridiculous that they're still hosting the party. "But this is what he wants," Nora murmured last night over dinner. "Your dad loves Bloomsday. It's his thing." Maybe. Leo doesn't understand the party during a normal year, let alone this one. "Of course that's what he *says*," he replied. "He just doesn't want to disappoint my mom."

His dad isn't the type to make a fuss. This is what he nearly told Nora, that his dad isn't the type to let a funeral get in the way. But the words had stalled on his tongue, some instinct preserving him.

He won't call home now. It's far too early. But maybe he'll swing by on his jog. He usually defaults into tourist mode, chugging past Independence Hall and Penn's Landing, as though his feet can come up with nothing more original when left to their own devices. Today he will stop by Delancey, his father passing him that look, the one reserved just for him. Not of pride, exactly, but of recognition. My son. Stephen would never think to check on their folks.

Leo will assemble breakfast for Nora the way she likes, tea and toast on that silver tray. It's warped, a flea-market find, but it makes her feel special. He'll take the paper with him into the guest bathroom, this time more content, sated after his meal. Linger pleasantly as his bowels release, the ripe perfume of the morning rising to greet him, the world spread before him in black and white: sports section, tech news, headlines. A second bathroom could be the thing that saves relationships.

When he hits the streets at a steady clip, the owner of the corner bodega will nod at him, his Korean eyes quiet, kind. Flowers set out in white buckets, dripping onto the sidewalk below.

He'll leave the tray with a note (*See you in an hour. Love, L*) and then shut the door behind him. Twisting the bolt so that Nora, hearing its click, will know she has her time. And, with luck, they will be on their way.

Two

___

Nora reclines on the couch, her hands crossed over her stomach. She tries not to think about how she must look with her head propped on the pillow. Hannah Portman was probably being arranged into a similar pose at that moment.

"I think it's the wrong one who's gone, if you want to know the truth." Her voice sounds shaky. Starting is always the hardest part. But she is here to air her most toxic thoughts, to let them out. "If there were any justice in the world, it would have been him. Instead there he is, alive and kicking, never an illness of any kind. Though he likes to complain enough."

Her heart is at a trot and she breathes to steady it. "My dad thinks they're snooty. Leo's parents, I mean. When he first heard about the annual party, he just about fell over laughing. But my mom—I think she understood. The thing about Michael and June is that they have these rules. And, yeah, June comes down hard on people who never got the manual. But no one in that house ever yells. There's something to be said for that.

"I'm supposed to be doing more with my life. It's what my dad says. 'Got into Yale, and for what? All that debt, for what?' But I'm the one with the student loans. It's not like they're his problem.

"I get it from other people, too, even if they don't come out and say it. Like my program director." Although, in a way, he'd said exactly that. "You were not born to be a teacher," he told her crossly at graduation. "Why are you throwing your talent away?"

"Stephen, too. It's obvious he hopes I'll go back to opera. He'll be embarrassed for me when I get introduced around today. Almost thirty, giving voice lessons. A lounge singer.

"Meanwhile, Stephen has this total attitude with teaching. He calls his students morons. He thinks his parents are pretentious, but who is he to call anyone a snob? Why begrudge people their hobbies?" She feels where her thoughts want to take her, the justifications and rationalizing. Pulling your hair out isn't normal, she knows. It's no hobby.

"With today . . . it annoys me, I guess, that I'm so aware of it. Everyone else at the service will be thinking about their own shit. How they need to go to the supermarket, the emails they need to write. And I envy them. They don't get what a luxury that is, to be bored at a funeral.

"My mom's funeral wasn't exactly official. We had people over to the house, like a morose party." Nora thinks back to that afternoon, neighbors milling about the living room. "We should've done something nicer. But my dad—" He told Nora about the arrangements before she could object. "Those funeral homes cost a fortune," he grumbled, and she was too exhausted to fight him. "My dad had the last say. So there wasn't even a eulogy." There was only the cardboard box of ashes sitting unceremoniously on the coffee table. The box was long and rectangular, as if it might be holding a pair of boots.

Nora lifted the cover after everyone left. The ashes were coarser than she expected, gritty and uneven. The lack of uniformity alarmed her. She touched one of the shards through the clear, thick plastic and felt a strange urge to pocket it. She replaced the lid hurriedly, appalled by her own desire.

"So today, it's not like it's the same. I didn't really know Leo and Stephen's grandmother. I saw her at Delancey a couple of times. I swear the woman never said a word. She just sat there. I once told Stephen it was like she'd been taxidermied. He got so mad at me— maybe the maddest I've ever seen him.

"Anyway, it's not like today dredges up all these *memories*. It's not like I'm going to stand there and have it all come flooding back. Part of me is curious to see what a real funeral is like. I'm sure Michael and June shelled out for it. And I've never been to a synagogue before." Nora frowns. Will there even be a burial? It's what she has been picturing, a stately cemetery scene, but suddenly she isn't sure. She should ask Leo, though he might not know. Only Stephen had converted.

"I couldn't sleep last night, so it must be on my mind." Couldn't sleep and had pulled, but she doesn't say it. "The thing I can't figure out is if it really bothers me or if it's just *supposed* to bother me. There are these times when her being gone comes up for real." Like when Leo had proposed. Nora couldn't call the one person she most wanted to tell; she didn't want to call the one person she had left. "But there are other times where it comes up in a fake way. Like I'm supposed to be thinking about it. Like it's my duty.

"It's not that I imagine her doing all these mother/daughter things with me. I don't know that she would've taken me wedding dress shopping, for example. That wasn't like her." Nora pictures her mom at the kitchen table with the bills and the mail, stapling things, highlighting things, an office manager to her core. She would tap the papers when she was finished, the corners perfectly aligned.

"Grandma Portman died suddenly. She was old, but it happened fast. And I wonder what that's like." Nora's eyes roam the ceiling. There is a pattern, fifth tile up, second across: a woman in profile. If she stares at the tile long enough, her face comes into focus—the hook of her nose, the broad plane of her forehead.

"They used to call it a nadir," she remembers. "After a course of chemo, the cell counts would dip. That was the medical term for it. I kept waiting for someone to be like, 'I know, I know, poor choice of words.' Like it isn't bad enough you're going through this awful period, but then they have to come out and call it that? It's like if they were to call chemo 'suffering.' Or cancer 'that sucky thing.' 'What does she have?' 'Oh, that sucky thing of the liver. But we're treating it with suffering.' And the worst part is, soon enough, you're nodding along. Because you've forgotten that the word once meant anything else. You forget the nadir isn't temporary. It's now your whole life.

"I guess you can't go through all of that without getting used to it. She had so many trips to the ER that we stopped freaking out. How awful is that? We should have freaked out every time. But that tenth emergency—it can't feel like the first.

"Michael and June got the one phone call. They never had to go through what I did. My mom got diagnosed my sophomore year. That's, what? Seven years of phone calls."

Nora shakes her head. "I guess, at a certain point, my mom and I sort of drifted apart. Leo and I had that amazing summer together. It seems so ridiculous that I did that. She'd just been diagnosed. There I was, gallivanting around—" She stops. It's what her dad would say. "There you go, gallivanting around! A selfish girl." "The truth is that it was hard to be around her. She used to joke that cancer was like a mistress. I didn't know what she meant, but maybe now I do. She couldn't be with her kid with the mistress in town.

"I stopped knowing how to hang out with her. I didn't know how to *be*. I tried to make myself useful. I took her to chemo a few times, but she didn't like anyone else driving her car. 'I have those mirrors set just right,' she'd say. Then we'd get there and she'd sit in her chair with her magazines. She never wanted ice chips or a blanket—she got annoyed if you offered. So I just stood there, not knowing what to do, feeling like I was in the way.

"The stuff she complained about was minor. There was this nurse she thought was rude, this black woman with long fingernails. I hated it when she complained about her. I thought it was racist. 'Those damn fingernails,' she'd say. 'It can't be hygienic.' 'Cut it out, Mom,' I'd tell her.

"Maybe I was preparing myself for it. I don't know. Maybe I latched onto Leo and his family because I knew what was coming. Maybe that's why no one talked to Grandma Portman. Maybe you disengage without realizing it because some part of you knows."

Nora nods at the ceiling, sees the words before her, the truth of them. "Everyone thinks the past is the nightmare, that I just need to wake up from it. But the past isn't the nightmare at all. It's the present that threatens to consume you. Because at least in the past I had her.

"I don't know what to do with myself. Every day, I have this feeling of not knowing what to do." Nora stops, swallows. "It feels like I'm in a swimming pool filled with tar, with a three-hundred-pound backpack on. It takes everything I have just to stay afloat. And I don't know if that's okay. Do you fake it more? Fake it less? Does 'fake it till you make it' work?"

Her fingers find the couch beneath her and probe its surface.

"Then there's the wedding. It's always *there*. Even at the funeral today—a funeral, of all places. Everyone will look at the ring and ask if I have a dress." Nora bites the hard ridge of her cuticle. She feels a sharp peal of pain as it separates that isn't altogether unpleasant.

"I guess the whole time she was sick, I fooled myself. You tell yourself these things, like, 'Oh, it's not *cancer* cancer.' What does that even mean? And you see her not looking great, but she looks that way for months. So you forget that she once looked any different.

"Meanwhile, there's the hospital stuff around the house—the beige water pitcher, the pink kidney-bean thing. You hate that stuff, but it comes in handy. Maybe that's a mistake. Maybe you should never let the kidney-bean thing into your home in the first place.

"I still try and fake myself out. Like I'll put off paying my credit card bill—which used to drive her nuts—so that, for a second, I can hear her getting upset about it. 'You paid your MasterCard bill yet? It's the second already! You can't leave it till the grace period, Nora.' I do these things to bring her voice back for just a minute.

"Anyway. The time it hit me, I think for real, was when I went to call her. I want to say it was the night of her funeral, but I could be wrong. It might have been the next day. Those first few days were a blur. But here's what's funny: I picked up the phone because I wanted to tell her about how weird the funeral had been. That's what was running through my head.

"I was in the middle of dialing when I stopped. It's like that feeling people talk about with phantom limbs: that used to be there, but it's not anymore. Like a tickle from what's gone.

"And later, I think a few hours later, I dialed anyway. I guess I wanted to see what would happen. Like there was a chance I'd imagined it all. And before I could confirm it by looking around the room and seeing the flowers or my dress, I dialed.

"I heard it ringing on my end. Doesn't that mean it has to be ringing somewhere else? I never found out what happened to her stuff—her cell phone, her purse. I imagined her phone lighting up.

And it seemed, for just a minute, that someone would answer. That someone would have to.

"It rang and rang. I didn't even get to hear her voice. She was one of those people who never recorded a message. Thought it was silly. So there was just that automated one. You know, where it goes, 'Hello. Please leave a message after the tone.' That was when I realized: from now on, I'd be talking into space."

Three

___

S tephen wonders if he is supposed to bring a date.

It hasn't occurred to him until now, standing on the train platform, his umbrella aloft. Surely it is a foolish concern, one his grandmother would have batted away, but new couples have been cropping up everywhere. Getting coffee, doing laundry, crossing streets. Errands and tasks that hardly necessitated company were no longer being done solo. "Stephen!" his friends chirped, looking up brightly from their lattes and shared laundry stacks.

He knows to expect it at the party tonight. "Anyone special these days?" they will ask, elbowing him. But it dawns on him that he'll probably get some jabs at the funeral too. "A handsome guy like you," they will say, frowning. "Isn't there anyone in that department of yours?"

Until recently, dating had felt like a casual game of musical chairs. If you sat for a moment, it was only to get up again. But then the pace had quickened, his friends scurrying to grab their seats. And then not budging, evading his glance. Stephen was the last man standing. "Well, of course we've all been playing," they seemed to say from a seated repose, Leo and Nora studiously looking away. "Didn't you know?"

The spring issue of the Yale alumni magazine, which he had flipped through last night in a fit of insomnia, confirmed that this was not the work of his imagination. There were the weddings, not tucked away at the end of the class notes, but right up front for all to see. Fellow alumni in attendance were dutifully listed, the names, nestled between commas, like ducks waddling in a row.

He recognized some. Their names looked strangely official now, as if they bore no relationship to the classmates who had barfed into bushes and staggered home from strange beds at dawn, who had skipped 11:00 a.m. classes because they were too *early*.

Any subsequent nonmatrimonial updates, on the heels of such ceremony, felt lacking. He scanned the notes hopefully for word of some exotic exploit: a kooky fellowship in Vienna, a Peace Corps update from Nepal. Perhaps a documentary filmmaker mucking about in Sudan, or even an athletic triumph to confer glory (a classmate had been drafted by a professional soccer team a few years ago and there had been a stir). But if there was any mention of quirky adventure, it was alluded to in the past tense: "After a brief stint running a microbrewery in Portland, Paul Yu is in his first year of medical school at Columbia." People, the class notes informed you, were growing up. Paul Yu had come to his senses.

Stephen had sighed and put the magazine down. He used to take pleasure in the class notes, sometimes reading them right by the mailbox. People were backpacking through Thailand, mountaineering in Chile, and he could picture them in their jewel-toned parkas. Some had consulting jobs; others were pursuing musical theater or teaching English in Japan. It all felt transient and silly, like playing dress-up.

If his own situation felt a little less adventuresome, it was mitigated by what he read. He couldn't contribute stories of building wells in Nigeria, but he could joke about his unwashed roommate, Andres, who smelled permanently of wet wool and goat, or his Marxist professor who decided to conduct an experiment of the proletariat by having his students grade themselves. These were the ridiculous tales of being twenty-two and twenty-five, of being in that happy, malleable phase of postcollege life before everything set in the gray cement of adulthood.

True, he was a little more mired than his friends, ankle deep while they went globe-trotting and job-hopping, but he didn't mind. Indeed, he took pride in it. He was the only one he knew who had gone straight to grad school from college, even using the summer after graduating to take intensive German.

His ego (*das Ich!*) rallied around his work ethic. He was the most on track of his classmates back then, and he felt the pure certainty of an evangelical Christian politely declining booze and drugs. Poking his head out from his cave in the quarterly glimpse afforded by the class notes, he would return to his studies feeling gratified.

And when he occasionally attended an alumni event, the *Yale Connect!* postcards coaxing him out, he saw his success reflected in their faces. "You're in a PhD program?" they would ask resentfully. "And you're in your third year already?" He would feign embarrassment, nod at the floor.

He had been impressive for a solid stint there, a postcollege golden era. But then news of grad school acceptances started trickling in. Someone had gotten into Princeton, he would see with a frown, and he had to soothe himself with reminders that he was in his fourth year, coursework completed. ("I got an incredibly generous offer from Penn," he imagined himself saying to the Princeton snot, with the barest suggestion that he'd been lured away from Harvard.)

Then he was in his fifth year. And his sixth. Any lead he had felt squandered. How quickly he had gone from being the early bird to the dawdler. "You're already studying for comp exams?" had once been uttered aghast in bars. Now it was a cheerful "Still working on the old diss, eh, Stephen?" with a buck-up tone of pity.

And that was it. The *already*s! had turned into *still*s? The exclamation points, those jealous stabs of hysterical punctuation, had rounded into questioning sneers. It was no wonder he had let the spring issue of the alumni magazine sit untouched. Who needed to see the news trumpeted of more nuptials and neurologists? Their degrees trailed behind them like shoes from a rear bumper. Gone was the playful sense that their activities might be abandoned for more hip pursuits. Paul Yu & Co. were in it for good.

"You are almost thirty now," his grandmother had observed on Tuesday. She said it wistfully, and Stephen felt caught between the troubling possibilities that she was either reminding herself of this fact, to ground the balloon of her wandering mind, or was reminding him. And so he had held his tongue rather than reply—as he normally would—that he knew his own age perfectly well. He nodded in polite agreement, as he did that whole afternoon.

He shifts his umbrella to the other hand. Gone now.

Just days ago he had stood in her room. Days, hours. How many minutes had it been?

Standing by her bed, he had felt paralyzed, unsure if he should attempt a final good-bye. Would it offend her? Would it diminish her chances? So he had remained mute, not realizing he would regret what he didn't say more than what he did.

She had likely taken his reticence as a sign that the end was near. Michael and June visited that same evening, and he imagines them standing by her bed with bowed heads, deferential at last. In death, you were a victor.

Then there was the place itself. Pine Grove. They probably all have similar names. Shady Oaks. Cypress Point. Maple Valley. Nursing homes and country clubs like to affiliate with trees. But there was a dignity there, the kind of hushed reverence he normally associates with libraries and museums.

"Not too shabby, eh?" Grandma Portman had prodded, watching him take it in when he first visited. It was the week after 9/11. He had decided to check on her after learning that his parents had no intention of visiting.

He lent his grandmother his elbow as they strolled the grounds. He had been expecting a dilapidated building that smelled of antiseptic, threadbare common rooms emanating despair, but this was more like college, with its sprawling campus and tennis courts. They stood together on the crest of a gently sloping hill. "It was good of you to come, *bubeleh*," she said, squeezing his arm. They gazed at the weeping willows, the IN MEMORIAM benches beneath. Stephen, touched by how pleased she was to see him, felt bizarrely close to tears.

"God, it's so scary," Nora had said of the attacks. "I was worried my mom's chemo would get disrupted, with all the chaos at the hospitals."

"Right," he replied awkwardly. Nora had tunnel vision. Not even those towers could get her to look up from her mother's sickbed.

It occurred to him, standing on that hill, that he hadn't confided in Nora in weeks. He had fallen into the role of listener. He didn't fault her for being preoccupied with her mother, but selfishly, he missed her. She was becoming less available to him as a friend, and he sensed her fading in some way he couldn't pinpoint.

Meanwhile, his grandmother seemed so delighted to have him there. He remembered her as being stern when he was a boy, but any trace of severity had vanished from her face, softened by age. And then there was the matter of the new head bob.

It was probably involuntary, some sort of neuromuscular twitch.

Her head went like a basketball at times: nod nod nod. It must have been uncomfortable, but she said nothing of it. Stephen had come to see her, and that was all that mattered, yes? Her head bounced along in agreement, all the repressed affirmations from a lifetime released at the mere sight of him.

So he walked with her, dutifully following her. Down the hall, through a glass atrium, the corridors drenched in light. He felt a strange sense of familiarity, as though in a dream.

His plan for that visit had been to make a quick escape. He would make sure she was okay and deposit the box of cookies from Metropolitan Bakery. "I have office hours at four," he had warned her. But sitting there, the grounds stretching past her window in a vista, he found himself settling into his wingback chair. He talked with her about the events of the past week, how angered he was by the politicians and the talking heads. "I was born in New York," he said. "And here are all these people in Texas and Alabama discussing it like it's their tragedy. Like they're allowed to speak for the victims!" She nodded sagely.

They continued talking, their discussion lightening as the sky grew dark. He told her about teaching, that sea of alien faces smirking at him. How they fidgeted, turning in papers that were a collective atrocity. And this at an Ivy League school! Next he was going on about his committee, the fatiguing levels of ass-kissing its members required. He felt as if he were getting a degree in babysitting, in appeasement, in coddling. "Stephen, don't you have office hours?" she interrupted, glancing at the clock. "No one ever comes anyway," he replied hastily, reaching for a cookie. He thought he saw a momentary gleam in her eye, but she said nothing, her head bobbing away.

And so what began as a pleasant surprise of a visit, a that-wasn't-so-bad sort of visit, became a routine. He went monthly at first, then a bit more often. Until finally, by the time Leo and Nora got engaged, he was going every Tuesday, a ritual as comforting as attending synagogue.

He told himself he was being a good grandson. Responsible. Slightly heroic, even. But when he purchased his ten-trip ticket at the urine-scented kiosk, he didn't feel the weight of obligation. Grasping that ticket, he felt free.

He looked forward to the meditative rocking of the train. He had come to know its rhythm: the particular place where the electricity might cut out for a moment before surging back; the moment when the train left the rickety tracks of Thirtieth Street and picked up speed. The conductor, punching tickets as he teetered down the aisle, always nodded at him in recognition.

With each stop, the town names rang out overhead: *Chesssssssst- nut Hill! Noooooorristown!* This bellowing struck Stephen as quaint, a throwback to an era of transport involving steamer trunks and porters. By the time Pine Grove's stop approached, a feeling of good- will found its way to him and he felt lighter, jauntier.

There was none of that buzz in the air at Pine Grove, the inces- sant hum of reachability. Around him now, the commuters thumb- ing their phones seem tethered to some invisible force, as though at any moment the great cord of connectivity might give a tug and yank them off the platform. The *Times* recently ran an article on the growing number of people who check email first thing in the morning. It was a rising demographic, he read. He pictured Leopold scowling at his phone while shuffling to the bathroom in that foul old robe.

It was the sort of thing he could have shared with his grand- mother on a typical Tuesday, a normal Tuesday, when he hadn't been informed by phone that she likely only had twenty-four hours left. She would have sighed. "We are becoming half-robots," she would have said knowingly.

Pine Grove offered him a respite. Each time he walked along the gravel path to its campus, he would be reminded of a leafy sanctuary: college, Central Park. The rush to pair off, to win—it all fell away. No one was in a panic to get to that last chair before the music stopped. No one was in a rush at all.

Today, it is all different: a new train line, a strange set of names clacking on the signboard. Vendors at coffee carts parked along the platform dole out coffee and plastic-wrapped bagels in a steady stream. Accustomed to the station's sleepy noontime calm, Stephen feels unnerved by the harried morning bustle. It occurs to him that he will miss the ritual of his visits as much as he will miss her.

He enters the train after everyone else. The car smells of baked damp, black umbrellas drying at the feet of their owners like small dogs. A heavy spatter hits as the train lurches forward. The weather forecast, following the Bloomsday report, had mentioned the possibility of hail. Stephen takes comfort in this. The skies should darken for Grandma Portman, a terrible morning to atone for their terrible mourning.

She had gone more gently than he would have thought possible. No battles or resuscitating. "As little suffering as we can hope for," Miriam Maxwell, Pine Grove's director, had told him, and he understood that he was supposed to feel grateful.

"Tickets!" the conductor cries.

It was Miriam who had called him on Tuesday morning. Stephen was groggy when he answered the phone and felt a second behind everything she said. "Twenty-four hours left?" he repeated. "How could you possibly know that?" Yet he registered her calm, the quiet space she gave him on the line, and realized she must make these calls often.

He still didn't believe her when he went to Pine Grove that afternoon. His grandmother had never fully recovered from the embolism, but just recently he had thought that she was starting to look better. She had died at dawn on Wednesday, alone.

The conductor looks menacing as he comes forward, snapping the jaws of his punch. The expert commuters all have their tickets out, badges of veteran experience. Stephen unfurls the receipt of his one-way peak fare, a scroll with a hieroglyph of symbols. He'd been informed at the information desk that his ten-trip ticket couldn't be used. Four unpunched slots remain: [7] [8] [9] [10]. He'd never imagined that he might not use it in its entirety. How long will it sit now in his wallet, a reminder?

The conductor swipes his receipt, punches it, and walks off with it in hand, muttering, "Tickets! Tickets!" Stephen does not have a chance to object, to ask if he will need it later, much less to inquire—as he had planned—if cabs are available at his stop. The synagogue is three miles from the station, he had been told.

Next Tuesday, he reflects. Tuesday will be the longest day.

A rustle of paper from the man seated beside him, scrawling away on a yellow legal pad. Stephen watches him, his pen flying. Stephen needs for the ride to be productive. He knows this but resists it. He hates toting around his briefcase on the day of her funeral.

But life didn't stop for her. His EGL 220 class had continued, Stephen standing in front of them on Thursday (yesterday! Just yesterday) feeling drained. The show must go on, he had thought, leaning on the lectern.

He could have canceled class; no one would have faulted him. But he's been putting in the bare minimum as it is. His lectures have grown shorter. He grades hastily. Paradoxically, this has resulted in his students' perking up, deciding he isn't so bad. The less of himself he puts into the class, it seems, the more they like him.

His briefcase holds a thick stack of Milton essays in one compartment and a thin sheath of dissertation notes in the other. It isn't a choice, really. He can't bear to face his proposal. He isn't sufficiently caffeinated, adrenaline-charged, amped. It will likely sit untouched until the last possible moment: 2:00 a.m., the night before a meeting with Stuart, nervous energy flooding his system as he curses himself for having neglected it.

His efforts thus far have yielded little more than multicolored stickies in various books. *Reading 1922: A Return to the Scene of the Modern* had achieved the status of a sea creature, teeming with colorful protrusions like a coral reef. Meanwhile, titles flit through his mind, which he jots down in his notebook. Long paragraphs should be filling it. Instead he has single lines with clumsy edits:

The Caves Behind the Characters: Interiority in Virginia Woolf
The Unwritten Novel: Subjectivity in Woolf (and Eliot?)
The Parallax View: The Subject's Gaze in Woolf and Eliot in Modernism

Stephen isn't clear on what the parallax view is, but he had spotted it while skimming Žižek. Citing Slavoj Žižek makes him feel brave, those Eastern European consonants, with their feel of currency. Žižek: *cha-ching*! The snappy syllables make Stephen a theorist, one of those hip academics who wears Doc Martens and participates in protests.

Stephen's dissertation will involve Virginia Woolf. This much he knows. Increasingly, there is Freud, creeping in like a draft from a window, but Stephen does not mind. There is poetry in the Freud, and his German is finally coming in handy.

The rest is up in the air, a nebulous mix that makes him feel as though he is trying to capture the weather in a net. He has moments when he thinks he is onto something. These occur late at night, his mind igniting, surrounded by books. It is a heady feeling, thinking he has the thread of something, that he need only hold on. "So, too, Woolf implies with all fiction writing: our subjects always escape,

leaving us only with the truth of our impressions." *YES!!!* he writes
in the margin. He goes to bed exhausted but satisfied, relieved that
he has made some progress.

But in the morning, he cannot decipher his notes. "The novel
is always unwritten, coming apart," reads one sticky note. What
on earth does it mean? None of the previous night's understanding
comes back to him. *The Writer as Reader in Modernism* has been
added to his list of titles. He is embarrassed by his chicken scratchings, by the spark he felt. Who will ever read these words? What is
their point?

Across the aisle he notices a woman gazing out the window as
they bump along. She wears a wool coat, and her toddler leans
against her, on her way to sleep. The girl's shoes point up at the
ceiling; she is small enough that her legs don't meet the seat's edge.
Her hair spills across her mother's coat, laced with static. A folded
stroller sits on the luggage rack above them along with a patterned
diaper bag.

A bump causes the electricity to flicker, and Stephen realizes he
has been staring. Always this. Watching people around him and
wondering, wondering instead of working. But the woman gazing
out the window captivates him more than anything in his briefcase.

Stephen's work does not call out to him in this way. It does not
speak to him of secrets and stories. He wonders about the woman.
He imagines a divorce, something that makes her look away rather
than stroke her daughter's hair. To know more about her would be
to have some riddle solved. An unwritten novel is in each of us,
Woolf would say.

The people at the funeral today will smile blankly if he tries to
explain any of this. They will remember the term papers they wrote
in college. They will think what he does is frivolous.

Stephen sighs and unclasps his briefcase. For the first time, the
legal-pad activity pauses. He can feel his seat companion take in

the rubber-banded stack of essays, surveying them with interest. Teacher? Writer? Stephen is glad the top essay has *Professor Portman* typed in the upper-right corner.

He will grade the papers as quickly as he can, a benevolent line at the end of each with some mix of positive and negative to indicate the tip of the grade. He will put his head down, mirroring the intense concentration of the man beside him, and work until the name of his destination rings out.

At the synagogue he will embrace his parents and pay his respects to his grandmother. Only you, he thinks. Only you knew how much I will miss you. He bows his head for the grandmother he has lost. As if it is not for some part of himself, too, that he mourns.

Four

S even years. Nora gazes out the window, watching the trees roll past.

Saying the number aloud that morning had come as a shock. How had she lived through those years without ever doing the math? Of course it was seven, but it had somehow felt like one, darkening until the lights went out. She and her mom had been stranded on an island, the tropic of cancer with its thickets of growth, while for everyone else life continued, unerring and plain.

Does knowing the number help? Do you have to feel the slap a thousand times to grow numb to it? The words of the song come back to her. *The very thought of you / And I forget to do / The little ordinary things / That everyone ought to do.*

Leo signals for the exit ramp.

She'd started with each of the shrinks optimistically, coming home and telling Leo that this one, this one seemed promising. Leo was intent on being supportive. "This is something you need help with," he said earnestly. She couldn't tell if he meant the grief or the pulling, or something more broad that couldn't be named.

Leo's form of therapy is action: pickup basketball, a project around the apartment. "People get too stuck in their heads," he likes to say. She studies his profile beside her: black hair, brown eyes, stubble visible even at this early hour. Stephen has June's fair elegance, but Leo is stockier, resembling neither of his parents. Like the car he drives, he is a dark horse.

"A jet would be more fuel efficient," Stephen remarked the day Leo got the keys. Leo had saved for the Escalade since college, dreaming of its acquisition, and he made everyone come outside to admire it. "A lease!" June exclaimed. "Who leases? I still don't understand why you won't let us help." How quickly that check would have been written, her manicured hand drawing the orange Hermès checkbook from her desk drawer. But that wasn't Leo. He waved off his mother's offer and turned to Stephen. "My guess is you'll be bumming rides within a week."

When Leo looked at the Escalade, he didn't see a gas-guzzling SUV. He didn't see a car bigger than their city needs. He saw the achievement of his own industry, his drive summed up by what he drove.

When something truly bothers him, he polishes his beloved car, parking it by his parents' place on Delancey so that he can use their hose. He doesn't mind the pedestrians walking by as he waxes the black finish to a mirrored shine. "Hey," he says, nodding, working the rag in circles as though he is the neighborhood bartender. People always smile and nod back, pleased by the industrious man taking such admirable care of his car.

And it works for him. When he returns to the apartment, Nora can tell some change has taken place, as though he is the one who had been buffed and cleansed, his troubles shed in the gray water running down the drain. He comes through the door whistling, and it seems impossible that anything had ever bothered him at all.

She sees the same expression on people's faces when she performs with Carol's choir on Sundays. Everyone emerges from the pews looking renewed, reconnected with some vital impulse. It is the feeling she hoped the shrinks would bring. She imagined returning from one of those appointments lighter, unburdened. "Hey, you," Leo would say, surprised. She would smile back, happy to feel some of the weight lifted.

"We'll be there in a minute," Leo announces. They are following the main road, historic and quaint, a Pennsylvania town rooted in time.

"I forgot to ask you before," she says, turning to him. "Will there be a cemetery?"

"Hmn?"

"With Jewish funerals. I wasn't sure what happens."

"A burial," Leo replies. "There's a family plot, where my grandfather is."

"And no one at the service knows. About the party tonight, I mean."

Leo checks the rearview. "Well, they haven't been invited. Sharon and those guys. They wouldn't get it, you know?"

Nora can hear the internalization of Michael's words, the loyalty of son to father, and she softens. She is too hard on Leo sometimes, critical when she doesn't need to be. It was sweet of him to put out breakfast like that, on the nice tray. "He's good to you, that one," her mom once observed. The plastic kidney-bean receptacle sat beneath her mom's chin, holding the thick bile she brought up. "He'd rub your feet every night if you asked." "Mom!" Nora had protested, embarrassed, but she knew her mom was right.

Leo hadn't seemed like the doting type when they started dating. "A *frat* guy?" her roommate, Claudia, asked incredulously. "You're dating a frat guy from BU? That's a total party school." "Whatever," Nora replied. "It's not like it's serious."

And it wasn't, at first. Leo was an experiment. It was her sophomore year. Sophomore slump, they called it. Little did Nora know that her life would soon be getting upended. When her mom got diagnosed that spring, the thought of having once craved adventure made Nora laugh.

She'd met Leo the summer after her freshman year. "Take the train into Philly!" Stephen had urged over the phone. "It's a cultural mecca out here compared to Union." She went to see him in early August, a sweltering and humid weekend. She set her bags down in the foyer, craning her neck to take in the grand sweep of staircase. "Holy shit," she whispered. "This is like Wayne Manor." A round table in the entry held a spectacular arrangement of white tulips, curving haughtily toward her. Nora felt a pang of trepidation and wondered whether the clothes she'd packed were nice enough. And right at that moment, Leo came crashing down the stairs in a ratty T-shirt and gym shorts. "What's up?" he said, passing her, head-phones over his ears.

"Off to the gym again," Stephen murmured. "His home away from home."

"You didn't say your brother would be here." Cute, she thought appreciatively, watching him lope out the door.

"That's because I wanted you to come. Leopold is like the miss-ing link to the Neanderthals."

Nora barely spoke to Leo that weekend, seeing him only in pass-ing—on his way to meet friends, heading out to play basketball. He had long, dark lashes and a bright easy smile, with a confident ease about him. He wasn't intimidated by his older brother and barely seemed to notice her. A jock, she figured.

That fall, Leo came down to New Haven for a concert. "Phish," Stephen informed her. "God help us all." The three of them met for drinks, crowding together at a bar. Nora sensed Leo's interest from across the table, a flicker of it undeniably there. Stephen was a ju-nior, she a sophomore, Leo a freshman, and she imagined them as Russian dolls, nesting inside one another. A perfect fit.

"So you're a singer," he said when Stephen got up to get the next round.

"Opera."

"Any shows coming up?"

"Sunday, actually."

"Sunday? Like, this Sunday?"

"Yup."

"As in, the day-after-tomorrow Sunday?"

"That's the one."

"Well. How 'bout that." He grinned at her wolfishly, and Nora felt a thrill travel through her. She began to wonder if he'd known about her performance all along. If maybe he'd noticed her that weekend in August after all.

"I could date him," Nora mused to Stephen that night as they walked back to campus. Stephen rolled his eyes, not thinking she was serious. Sunday, when Leo came to her show, she knew she hadn't been imagining it.

She sang as she always did, immersed in the piece, aware of the audience only vaguely. "You must feel them," Renata Scotto advised imperiously. "Without being controlled by them." But after the lights came up, she sensed Leo watching. She felt his gaze in the roses at her feet.

He sought her out in the lobby. "You were incredible," he breathed. She smiled. Stephen, beside him, frowned.

"Nora, he's a *freshman*," Stephen told her later. As if she didn't already know.

Leo was supposed to be a fling. But he had surprised her. Leo was like that dress you tried out on a whim, expecting it to be all wrong, only to find with a shock before the mirror that it worked.

One weekend in November, a few weeks later, he came down to visit her. She returned to her apartment from the music library to

find dinner waiting: spaghetti, meatballs, garlic bread, and choco-
late cake for dessert.

"You did all this?" She stood in the doorway, still in her coat, the
cramped kitchen emanating warm, delicious smells.

He smiled, drying a pan.

"This surprised me," she confessed after the meal, the two of
them lingering at the table. Claudia was at the library, studying for
an exam.

"Why? Because guys don't cook?"

"No. It's just—I know you never had to. That you guys always
had this stuff taken care of for you."

"Yeah, well . . ." He made a face. A white taper jammed into an
empty beer bottle started to drip wax onto the table. Leo fingered it,
rolling it into a ball. "There was this restaurant back in the city—in
New York, I mean, before we moved. We used to go down to it like
it was an extension of the apartment. It was this little Italian place.
We knew the waiters, the maître d'. We always got the exact same
thing. And I hated it.

"When I got to college, it was like I could finally do stuff on my
own. Cooking, laundry. I'd literally never used an oven before. How
weird is that?"

Nora regarded him. "What made you want to?" Truthfully, this
side of Leo made her uneasy. She sometimes wondered if Stephen
might be gay—her tall, handsome friend, perpetually unattached.
Coming home that night to the sight of Leo with a dish towel over
his shoulder, she felt a pang of concern.

"Because I don't want to live like that," he said flatly. "Dependent
on everyone for everything. It was a weird way to grow up, in Manhattan. My dad grew up without much. Not, you know, rich. And
the stories he'd tell, about never wearing nice clothes, or having to
eat leftovers all week—it sounded nice."

"Being poor?" Nora stared at her empty wineglass.

"No," he said, refilling it. "Being *normal*."

Stephen had described Leo as if he were Homer Simpson: a beer-loving, doughnut-eating relic whose oafish ways were as much a source of chagrin as they were comic fodder. But watching him, Nora understood that his family had him all wrong.

After dinner, he came around to her side of the table and knelt by her chair. He took her face in his hands and kissed her, gently, differently from how they had kissed before. He gazed at her, as if to say, Now you know me. And then he undressed her, his movements tender, both of them caught in a spell. They made love right there, the candle still going, its wax pooling on the table. They didn't even bother locking the door or thinking about her roommate. Later, Nora was never able to look at that creaky chair the same way.

They didn't leave a single corner of that apartment untouched. The bathroom, with its filthy bath mats. The kitchen, against the refrigerator. Even on campus, that time in the garden, the lilacs all around. Leo wasn't her first—there had been a couple of guys her freshman year—but he was the first one who knew what he was doing. The first who made a study of her body.

"Here we are," Leo says beside her, yanking on the parking brake. Nora starts. "You okay there?"

She nods and looks up. The synagogue is brick, squat. It is more modest than she was expecting, a housewife in an apron instead of a supermodel, soaring and tall.

"Hang on a sec." Leo frowns. "Looks like I missed a call."

She tries to recall when they last made love. It has been longer than she would've thought possible, back when they knew how every night would end. "Let's never become one of those couples," she once told him. "Those boring, sexless couples." He had nodded fervently, the thought unimaginable to them both.

He must miss it. But how to have that conversation? "We used to—" she might begin, but then what? She would find herself at a loss, unsure how to proceed, not wanting to put him on the spot. Their old life was on the other side of a chasm. To allude to it only emphasized how far it really was.

If only she could find the right words, but they remain out of reach. Even with Michael today. What words are there? "We're both motherless!" Or "Welcome to the club!" These are not the things to say, even if they are true.

She looks out across the parking lot, where two smokers linger. Maybe there are no perfect words. One of the smokers takes a deep, long drag. Maybe that's the point.

"Ugh," Leo mutters, snapping the phone shut.

She turns to him. "What was that about?"

"Stephen. Did he tell you how he was getting here?"

"He took the train. I thought you knew."

"Well, he's not here, apparently. My mom left a couple of voice mails. Like they don't have enough to deal with today."

Nora is about to reply that she's sure Stephen is on his way. But then she sees a familiar figure emerge from a taxicab, a green-and-orange vehicle in the circular drive. Stephen holds his briefcase and an umbrella (not a collapsing one, she notes, but a full-length one with a wooden handle, which is so exactly Stephen). She has a fleeting impression of Dick Van Dyke in *Mary Poppins*—that tall, lanky frame—and half expects him to kick his heels together. A giggle escapes her.

"Oh, he's right there. No harm done." She turns to open her door, eager to see her friend, but there is a muted series of clicks. The door resists her, unyielding.

"Did you just lock me in?" She turns to Leo. "Seriously?"

"Just listen for a second, before you go running out. 'Stephen,

Stephen!'" He dons a shrill voice and does a silly wave, a young wife running to greet her man back from the service.

Nora folds her arms across her chest. You aren't attractive when you do that, she wants to tell him. That high-pitched-voice thing.

"The two guys smoking are Mike and Jon, by the way. Sharon's kids."

"Oh! Your cousins!" She squints at them, having mentally filed them away as strangers. One has a goatee and unruly sideburns; the other has large, black disks tugging open his ears, visible even at this distance. "And those two are definitely related to your dad?"

Leo smiles. "Mom always says they brought the wrong one home from the hospital." Nora has in fact heard her utter this very line; June treated the subject of her in-laws like a used tissue. Still, it is a shock to see them. The contrast to Michael, clean-cut and sharp, couldn't be more pronounced.

"Jon works at a CVS. Mike—the one with the goatee, named after my dad, actually—has a record. Drugs, I think. There was a call once, in the middle of the night." Leo squints, remembering. "They both live at home. And you should be forewarned that Sharon is, er, living large these days." He holds out his hands to approximate her girth. "George—her husband—he's a good guy, though. They've been married like ten years now. He's a car salesman."

Nora feels a momentary layer of warmth. The warmth is a picnic blanket opening in slow motion. She watches as it comes to rest, unfolding before her. Flaws, she thinks happily.

"And this is why you locked me in? For an overview of the family?"

"My dad—he told me that Stephen was visiting my grandmother. Like, a lot."

She hears an edge in his voice and waits for him to continue.

"I swung by Delancey this morning. I guess my dad saw the visitor log when he, you know, signed her out or whatever. Stephen's been going to see her for ages. Every single week without fail."

"Okay."

"He never said a word about it to any of us. We didn't have a clue."

Nora can hear the question coming like the approach of a missile, its quiet whistle parting the air.

"He ever say anything to you?"

Nora watches as the two guys stab their cigarettes out. A spark of ember arcs out from a shoe, showering orange.

"Nora? Love?"

"No," she says, turning back to Leo.

He nods to himself. "Okay." The missile falls away, called back home. "It's just—it's so *weird*. I don't know why he'd keep something like that to himself. Let alone why he'd do it." Leo shakes his head. "My dad said she might've modified her will. She met with her lawyer a couple of months ago. Not that it matters. I mean, she wasn't loaded or anything. And, you know, it's her money. Obviously."

Nora nods. What bothers you isn't the money, she wants to tell him. What bothers you is the secret. "I'm sure Stephen wasn't trying to hide anything."

Leo frowns.

"He definitely wouldn't have wanted her money."

"I guess we'll find out Monday," Leo replies.

Nora glances out the window. Stephen is holding the synagogue doors open, indicating for his cousins to go forward. "Why not just ask? Pull him aside before the service. Clear the air." But she knows, even as she's suggesting it, that Leo will do no such thing.

"I'm not supposed to know. My dad said not to mention it, that he doesn't want Stephen feeling spied on."

"But the point is that you *do* know. You can't pretend you don't."

"He's the one who decided not to tell us."

"He started it, you mean?"

"Listen, if it happens to come up—"

Nora shoots him a warning look.

"You don't have to raise the subject or anything. But, you know, if *he* were to bring it up, on his own—"

Nora realizes there is a lock button on her door. She reaches for it.

"Well, don't go telling him about this."

She looks at Leo, exasperated. This is his specialty, this particular form of unreasonableness that strikes him as perfectly fair. Asking the unaskable of her, but then refusing to ask perfectly benign questions of anyone else. How come Stephen gets the kid gloves while she gets the land mines?

Something in her look gets across, for Leo nods and says nothing more, hitting the unlock button.

The two shades of black she wears are not the same. She realizes this stepping out of the car, the cloud-filtered light illuminating her outfit. Her dress is a wool sheath that has proved too useful. The jacket, meanwhile, purchased for auditions, is silk. It has been sitting untouched in the closet and is fresher, nearly shiny, like paint that hasn't yet dried. She had thrown it on just before leaving the apartment.

June will notice, she realizes miserably. What had seemed like such a clever solution to the predicament of a chilly morning now strikes her as foolish. She wonders if she should leave the jacket in the car, though it's probably inappropriate to enter a synagogue with bare shoulders. Etiquette is etiquette, she decides, resigned to her two-toned fate.

"Always have to leave everything to the last minute," her dad would say with irritation.

June had no doubt consulted the weather ahead of time, laying her outfit on the bed. "Make sure it gets steamed," she would have instructed, and Carol would have held up the wand of the garment steamer as it issued its great, hot billowing clouds.

Inside the synagogue, it is warm and dark, redolent of wood. Leo steps forward to don a yarmulke, provided by the temple in what strikes her as a thoughtful gesture. The yarmulkes look like black Pringles, nesting in a concave stack.

"Any sign of June?" Stephen asks, materializing beside her.

"She's probably looking for you," Leo retorts.

"Your mother had some calls to make," Michael intones from behind. "Hello, by the way." He leans in to hug his sons and to kiss Nora on the cheek. His normally bright eyes look a few notes quieter, laugh lines more visible because they are not in use.

Michael has close-cropped salt-and-pepper hair and strong, angular features. He is one of those men who cause women to look. Nora has seen it when they are out at dinner, waitresses and wives glancing at his gold wedding band with regret, then looking at June appraisingly. Men took in his black, rubberized watch in lieu of a Rolex and saw a man who had confidence without conceit.

"We've been wondering about you," Leo says pointedly to Stephen. "No one knew where you were."

"Ah," Stephen replies. "Judy the Cruise Director. I forgot to sign in."

Leopold's ears ignite.

"You took the train?" Michael asks pleasantly.

"I took the train." Stephen wriggles his briefcase for them as though it were a prop. "Too much work. Papers to grade, research to do. If only the world stopped for death."

"Indeed," Michael says.

"Has June been a nutcase this morning?" Stephen inquires.

"This is a busy day for your mother." Michael straightens Stephen's lapels, giving them a tug, perhaps more firmly than necessary. "A long day for everyone." Here, a trace of his usual spark, his eyes musing over the day that awaits them.

"The Dow is up," Leo offers.

They all turn. His eyes are focused on his phone. Michael goes to say something but stops. The comment sits in the air like a fart.

"I'm so sorry for your loss," Nora blurts out.

"Thank you," Michael replies. "It was kind of you to come."

They make their way down to the front of the room. There are pews, just like at a church, and Nora registers this beneath the lash of self-chastisement ("I'm so sorry for your loss?" Really? That was the best you could do?) hissing in her brain.

"She's probably on the phone with the caterer," Stephen mutters at Nora's elbow. "Instructing them to churn the butter by hand."

Nora smiles. "Party planning until the very last second. The devil is in the details."

"That it is."

"I'm worried I don't match," she confesses as they sit down.

"Mourning is no time for vanity. You show respect by not being particular in your dress."

Nora takes this in and wonders if it is a tenet of Judaism or one of Stephen's aphorisms. I should make a collection of his sayings, she thinks to herself. Though she isn't sure his words have done much to reassure her, particularly when she sees June coming down the aisle.

June is resplendent, even in grief—her blond hair perfectly coiffed, her makeup flawless and just so. She air-kisses her sons and nods at Nora, glancing over her outfit before taking a seat next to Michael. She wears a chic pantsuit, the jacket fitted; there is no doubt as to its inky shade of black. Stephen's asceticism dissolves before its glory.

The rabbi enters the room and Nora watches the rows of yarmulkes pivot. Conversations come to false conclusions and the background hum quiets. Leo is in the midst of showing Michael his new phone, the Palm he just purchased at Best Buy. "Cingular," he says. "I wanted to show you the other night. But, you know, the timing."

"Right," Michael replies, his eyes on the rabbi.

The rabbi makes his way around the coffin. It is hard to believe Grandma Portman is inside. A closed coffin, thankfully, though how do Michael and June know it's the right one? Had they been shown the body before the service, the rabbi opening the latches like a sommelier presenting a fine wine?

A prayer commences in Hebrew. Stephen follows along on her left while Leo remains silent on her right. Nora has been acutely aware of Michael these past few days. But it occurs to her that if what Leo said about the visits was true, it is Stephen who grieves the most.

A week from now it sprouts open, she should tell him. A month from now and you're dealing with it like it's the first time. The box you put the person in holds nothing. You end up carrying them around with you.

Meanwhile, people share their silly notions. "Time helps," they say. "I know exactly," they say. The polite response—the only response—is to pretend such words have meaning. Feign gratitude, if you can muster it.

At the end of lessons, the moms sometimes grab Nora's hand to examine the ring. "Are you *so* excited?" they gush. She can see the visions of bridal shops and calligraphic flourishes pass before their eyes. She can see them remember their own excitement. It gets transmitted through the grip on her forearm, the pressure too firm. Meanwhile, her students say nothing about death, nothing about marriage, their eyes darting up to hers only briefly before retreating to their sheet music. And for that, she is grateful.

Growing up, Nora never daydreamed about her wedding. She was never one of those girls. Even when she performed at weddings in college, she didn't give them any thought. There was that lovely one where she did the Bach cantata in the family's backyard, sheltered by the trees. Still, she didn't think any of it would apply to her—that she would be on the other side of things one day, hiring rather than being hired.

Not that it matters much. June will commandeer the planning, slowly wresting it from her. There are probably clipboards and files waiting in her office, organized in meticulous rows. "We'll release doves in honor of your mother," June will say. "Or perhaps sound a silver bell in remembrance. What do you think, Nora?"

They sit back down in the pews. Nora adjusts her skirt and realizes that Stephen was right. Gray, black. Who cares?

The rabbi pats his pocket for his bifocals with a distracted air, an accountant about to review forms. She realizes, before he begins, that he will do a bad job. He probably has a template on his laptop, "Deceased, Female," and simply fills in the name. Copy, paste, print.

"Hannah Portman was a woman who loved art," he begins. He seems surprised by the words, pausing over them, as though reading from a novel, the strange book of someone's life. Nora feels Stephen stiffen beside her. "She was actively engaged in the community. She loved her family deeply. This was clear to those who knew her." The rabbi scratches his nose with a gnarled finger, its knuckles oversize with age.

"She is survived by her son, Michael, her daughter, Shannon, and five grandchildren." Leo snickers over the gaffe. Nora nudges him to be quiet.

Stephen is sitting very still, his hands clasped. He had never talked with Nora about his grandmother, but maybe the rabbi is getting it all wrong, each word a wound. Michael and June and Sharon might not have known how Hannah Portman spent her days—if she read books or played bridge. If she gossiped with a group of friends or kept to herself. "My grandson is engaged!" she might have said. "A lovely girl. Used to sing opera."

Maybe Grandma Portman did love art, or maybe that was an embellishment from the rabbi. Michael and June might have hinted at it, suggesting he mention it. They probably wanted to imagine Grandma Portman at a museum, gazing reverently at a painting. No one wanted to think about life's banality at its end. No one in a eulogy ever said, "She watched TV with the volume on too loud. *Wheel of Fortune* was her favorite."

Nora got the impression that Grandma Portman had been dumped off at the nursing home, unwanted furniture shoved into storage. "You're living a life of leisure there," Michael had teased. Meanwhile, he and June grumbled about the bill. "You'd think Sharon could at least *offer*," June once said hotly.

Glancing around the synagogue, Nora realizes there are no floral arrangements—no enormous bouquets of lilies gathered in remembrance. No programs placed at intervals along the pews. Maybe no one gets an elaborate funeral. She imagines June shrugging: "Why put on an event for someone who can't appreciate it?"

Nora shifts in the pew. She remembers how Grandma Portman used to sit alone on the couch during the rare family gatherings. Once, at Yom Kippur, Nora had braved that upholstered island and joined her. Nora's tentative "How are you, Mrs. Portman?" had been met with a lightly accented "Oh, fine, dear. Just fine." Then they had watched the room in silence, sitting as though before a play—June zipping around, making the final adjustments, Michael selecting jazz on the audio system. Leo finally called out, looking for her, and Nora tried to hide her relief as she slipped away.

No, she hadn't gotten the impression that Hannah Portman was a woman who loved art. She didn't seem especially grandmotherly either. It was hard to imagine her knitting baby bootees, cooing over a bassinet. She seemed like a woman who had perhaps seen too much. A woman exhausted by the long life she'd led.

Perhaps Grandma Portman had felt out of place at Delancey, uncomfortable around the bold, expensive artwork on the walls, the intricate rugs. Looking at June—too tall, too thin, too made-up— she might have wondered why Michael hadn't ended up with a sweet dental hygienist, a Moira or a Debbie. A nice Jewish girl who would pump out kids and bake cakes. Grandma Portman might have imagined them together in the kitchen, sharing recipes, laughter, prayers. When she thought ahead to old age, she probably never imagined such silence.

Nora never stopped to think about why Grandma Portman sat there, withdrawn. What if she dreaded their too-perfect get-togethers? Maybe she longed for the return to the nursing home, where she could finally relax. She'd call up a friend so that they could watch *Wheel of Fortune* together, clucking sympathetically when the black bankrupt sign hit. They would trade stories about the strange creatures their children had become—their modern, complicated lives.

Nora should have made more of an effort with her. She should have confessed her unease that day, sitting down next to her. "I'm always worried I'll spill something on this couch," she could have said. "And, my God, the rugs."

Maybe Hannah Portman would have stirred from her reverie and looked at her anew, this bushy-haired girl who could do more than sing. "I didn't grow up like this," Nora could have added, because Hannah Portman might have just assumed she had. Those Yale kids, such snobs.

Accustomed to being ignored, Grandma Portman might have enjoyed having an audience. "In my time . . . ," she might have started, because wasn't that what old people were supposed to say? Yet Nora has never heard anyone actually say it.

Grandma Portman could have recounted a story from when Michael was young, a boy in Brookline. How she watched for him through the window, waiting for him to come home from school, the plate of cookies already out. And then looked on as he did his homework, clutching his pencil too tight. So smart, she might have said. Even then, you could tell.

They might have taken a liking to each other, she and Grandma Portman. The two of them were the only ones who did not zig and zag, but watched it all from a remove.

Maybe that was why Stephen had visited her—because they both felt like outsiders. Maybe no one feels as if they belong in this family, even the people in it.

Nora should have made some fractional effort with her. Who knows what it might have yielded? Instead she had ignored her, too caught up in her own troubles. She'd made a snide joke about how Hannah Portman resembled a taxidermied animal. And she had said it to the person who loved her most.

She feels for Stephen's arm beside her, touches it. I am the one who's stuffed and fake, she wants to tell him. She thinks of his weekly visits to the woman they had all ignored and feels a swell of feeling for her friend. I'm so sorry. If she could say it in Hebrew she would. May peace find you, Stephen.

His hand folds down, finds hers. And here you must comfort me, she thinks. On top of it all, you must comfort me.

Five

L eo reaches for a white paper plate, using his thumbnail to separate it from the stack. People stand in groups around him in the synagogue's basement. The burial had taken less time than he imagined. Who knew funerals were so fast? This business of death is efficient.

But this is the type of thinking that would make Nora and Stephen wince. They think he is a heathen for not dabbing his eyes and staring off in regret. Only a barbarian consults his watch at a funeral. Only a barbarian is tempted by the food.

The buffet table bisects the room. Black trays with clear plastic lids display their contents: smoked fish, pasta salad, sandwiches. A catering company probably has an in with the synagogue. Shivah trays. So good, you will die. Leo disguises his laugh by coughing into his shoulder. Aunt Sharon must have made the arrangements. His mom had glanced at the table, her lips pursed in disapproval.

Leo reaches for a sandwich, a cross-section of turkey and lettuce and tomato speared with a toothpick, green plastic wrap on its end. Is it decorative? For safety? Did that little bit of green protect you from the toothpick's point? He contemplates this, about to take a bite, when he feels himself being watched. He looks up. What? he thinks, as Nora meets his eye accusingly.

Nora's eyes flash their code. *Memo to Leo: Be the hero. Don't eat the hero.* He drops the sandwich like a dog.

The morning has been filled with such rebukes. How Stephen and Nora carried on at the cemetery! Murmuring to each other, eyes lowered. Their gestures composed a ballet, a great performance of propriety. Meanwhile, he watched as Nora tugged at her outfit during the service, so anxious to get everything right. Arms crossed? No, better straight. She darted nervous looks at June, attempting to mirror her movements. And what was so respectful about that? The dead don't care if we slouch. But there Stephen and Nora stand, so upright and stiff, too pious for food.

Leo has given in to their small demands, not minding the way anyone else in his position might. Whether you stand straight or talk in a hushed voice at a funeral is meaningless. But not causing a scene? That, as they say in the MasterCard ads, is priceless.

The dead probably want us to do whatever we think offends them. Eat, cough, laugh. The dead probably long for such acts. All those stirrings and scratchings—glorious when you can no longer do them. These are the fidgets and falterings of what it means to be human. When we are most ourselves, our faulty selves, and finally relent.

"Go ahead," the dead might say. "Let one rip."

In the far corner, Nora and Stephen stand huddled together. Their friendship bobs between them like a current, keeping Leo at bay.

He feels a tap at his arm. Magnified eyes under oversize glasses, and what can only be a wig, sitting at an angle that is just slightly off.

"A sad day," the woman remarks.

"Thank you for coming," he replies, holding out his hand. "Leopold."

The old lady comes up to his elbow. She takes his hand using just her fingers, the pressure nonexistent.

"Oh, I know who you are. I saw pictures." She shows no sign of relinquishing his hand, and he has the strange feeling of having loaned it to her.

"You're from Pine Grove?"

She nods. "A couple of us came over. The shuttle made a special trip."

Perhaps at a certain age, he reflects, you dispense with names.

"But where is Stephen?" She peers around the room.

Leo gestures with his free hand and she follows his gaze. Stephen and Nora have been joined by another old-timer, a fluff of white hair over a stick of a body, like a Q-tip.

"There he is!" A smile breaks out across her face. Her lips are frosted pink, a horror against her yellow teeth. "A wonderful grandson, to visit so often."

"Right," Leo mutters.

"I don't mean it that way. You kids are busy with your own lives. She knew that." The woman brushes away the thought. She has pink polish on her nails, which appear large and rounded, like coins. "It's just that those visits meant a lot to her. She kept to herself, you know. But when Stephen was there, she'd light up. A kind soul, your brother."

"Oh, sure."

"Well. Our condolences for your loss." The woman pauses, nods. "She will be missed." With that she begins shuffling down the buffet.

Leo feels the faint trace of her fingers, his hand finally released. "Our condolences," she had said. Was she speaking for the lot of them, a bingo club or mah-jongg group? Was she their ambassador? Or had she once been married, her husband now gone but still causing her to default into an automatic *we* after so many decades together? Maybe she was the resident busybody at the nursing home, the one who kept tabs on everyone and attended the funerals. Grandma Portman had probably frowned at her pink lipstick and nails, her ridiculous lopsided wig.

Grandma Portman was impassive. Leo couldn't tell if she enjoyed seeing them at Delancey or if she didn't want to be there. He wouldn't have been offended if it were the latter; he simply wanted to know, either way. It was her inscrutability that bothered him.

Stephen probably knew the answer. Who visited a nursing home like that? Monthly would be one thing, but weekly! Stephen probably wanted to live out there, where his old-man wardrobe of cardigan sweaters and houndstooth blazers would fit right in.

For months, Stephen claimed to be too busy to make it to Sunday brunch. It usually ended up being Leo and Nora and his parents, a strange double date, Nora so sullen that he had to work extra hard to cover for her. Leo didn't mind. But the whole point of brunch was for the family to be together. What good is living in the same city if you never see each other?

"Work," Stephen always said apologetically when he begged off. Like he knew the meaning of the word. Yet he'd found time for Grandma Portman. Leo imagines Stephen doing the rounds, making balloon animals and performing card tricks. He imagines Stephen being greeted with applause.

He should've asked that old woman about Stephen's visits. But what would Leo have wanted her to say? Why Stephen visited so much? What he and their grandmother had in common? Leo pauses, considers. Why he kept it a secret, really.

It wasn't something the woman could have explained. Stephen wouldn't have told the residents he was there on the sly. Sitting in the common room, he wouldn't have said, "This is just between us here, okay?"

"You should ask him," Nora had said in he car. Couldn't ask him at a funeral, though, he wishes he'd replied. That'd hardly be appropriate. Or: You ask him, if you think it's so easy.

Leo drifts to a corner table with soda bottles. The plastic cups are cherry red and lined with bright white, the kind they used for beer pong back in the day. How happy the frat house had felt, always full, bustling with life. Leo used to make the guys laugh by collecting the cups after a party and drinking their contents.

He pours himself a Coke and takes a sip. Talk: as if that would mend matters. The carbonation offers its sharp bite.

"It's better, I think, that we not say anything," his dad had declared that morning as Leo stretched. His dad was the true runner, with muscular calves that bifurcated like the halves of a heart. Leo used to try to build his up when he was in high school, doing calf exercises on the stairs, until it occurred to him that—as with so much else in life—he hadn't inherited his father's genes. No amount of work could give him what nature had withheld. "Sure, Dad," Leo had replied. His dad nodded, knowing he could trust his son.

There is valor in letting things slide. This is what Leo has learned from his father. It is why his mom gets her way with the remodels and shopping sprees, why she gets to have the party tonight. We look the other way in love.

Leo glances at Stephen and Nora across the room. Leo believed her when she said she hadn't known about Stephen's visits, but she also didn't seemed surprised. "Aren't you offended?" he wanted to ask her. "Don't you think it's strange? He's supposed to be your best friend!"

But some part of him thinks that Nora is sympathetic to secrets.

She first told him about the pulling a few weeks after her mom's funeral, leading him into the bathroom. "Look," she said tearfully, parting her hair in the mirror. He knew, before he turned, to brace himself—that whatever this was, it wouldn't be good. He kept his face still as the shock ran through him.

The bare spot was the size of a quarter, white scalp visible through fine tendrils. It wasn't like a bald spot on a man, but horribly unnatural looking, like a face without a nose. He kept his breathing steady, the lightbulbs over the vanity gaping. Then, meeting her eyes in the mirror, he took her into his arms.

There was a name for it. Trich-something. Whenever he types the first few letters into the search engine, the computer supplies the rest. A trick, he always thinks. It fooled you, duped you. You lived with it every day without knowing it was there.

Nora's pulling is like an addiction, a dark secret they gloss over. What bothers him is not the strangeness of her desire to pluck herself clean (did it have something to do with her mom's chemo? He'd hoped one of the shrinks would ask) but that because of it, he has to tiptoe around her. He isn't supposed to ask about it because there's always the fear of making it worse. "You pulling?" is the most he ever says. Two words. "You tired?" "You hungry?" "You pulling?" He utters them casually, not really thinking it helps—surely she does it in private, at night—but because it helps him. Those two words were like a release valve letting out steam.

Nora was horrified when he told his family about it. It didn't matter that the websites specifically recommended family support. "My parents are sophisticated about this stuff," he assured her. He refrained from voicing his surprise that Stephen hadn't already known. Because shouldn't best friends confide in each other?

Apparently not. Apparently Stephen and Nora didn't talk about reality. "You want to come with me to Pine Grove today?" "Nah, I'm planning on pulling out some more of my hair." Theirs is a different model of friendship, one Leo cannot grasp. Where it is perfectly understandable to have surprises surface. Where it is okay to have kept things hidden all along.

"Nothing ever happened between us," Nora told him early on. "Just so you know." Leo was relieved to hear it. Stephen and Nora had been best friends since her freshman year. It was hard not to imagine a drunken night, a onetime hookup they vowed to forget. "I know all about the appeal of upperclassmen," Leo teased. "I fell for one myself." Nora gazed back at him, her eyes level.

Nora wasn't Stephen's type, anyway. Occasionally he brought a date to a wedding, always a ridiculous model type, an art-history or French major who made June's nostrils flare with jealousy. Nora was pretty—brown hair, green eyes—but unthreatening. She was pretty in a way that drew you in rather than turned you off.

Stephen's girls knew their beauty. They were like ostriches with their long, skinny legs, parading around on high heels. They wore plunging necklines to reveal bony torsos. Their hair moved in sheets. They were delicate creatures, used to getting their way. Stephen's indifference posed a challenge to them.

"He's never said a word to you about it?" Leo once prodded. "About what?" Nora asked. "His love life! Why no one sticks!" Nora shot him one of her looks, protective and fierce. "That's his business, Leo," she said firmly.

Maybe. But when you keep your business a secret, it becomes everyone's business. It becomes the thing people worry about, the elephant in the room.

And that's what Nora and Stephen share. They are the kids at the playground who go off by themselves, whispering behind a bush, refusing to play with everyone else.

That would be fine if they made their reasons clear. But neither of them feels compelled to explain their behavior. They don't mind leaving puzzles in their wake. "Wasn't the whole point for you to do opera?" Nora's dad had said when she graduated. Nora glared at him, but Leo felt a twist of sympathy for the guy. Leo knew what it was like to be on the outside, scratching your head.

Leo's job, like a janitor's, is to push along, never asking questions or complaining about the messes. Never mind that he wants to be a source of support. Your problems are my problems, he wants to tell Nora. Your skeletons are my skeletons. That's what love is.

They rely on him to remain steadfast. And how they take him for granted, their beloved dope! They don't see the gift of his predictability. They've never had to worry about him or been thrown for a loop.

His parents do it, too, teasing him constantly. He is goofy Leo to them, with a humdrum job and a love of sports. They depend on him for it, but turn up their noses as well. Leo is like the corner Wawa: unexciting, but convenient. Always available.

Growing up, Stephen had been a vortex of need. From as early as Leo can remember, the family catered to Stephen, shaping itself around him. He fought with their parents often, hiding out at the Strand on weekends. He wrote poetry and tacked his dark creations to his bedroom wall. He pierced his ear in high school, a silver loop in the cartilage, up high. And didn't that mean something, depending on which ear? Or was that only for earrings that went through the lobe? Their parents stayed up late conferring about it, wringing their hands. Leo made himself a promise to never cost them sleep.

Teachers used to call home to make recommendations about this gifted, brooding boy. Stephen wasn't like the others. He wasn't like the preppy kids at school who took Ritalin so that they could stay up late studying, twitching with ambition. He wasn't like the usual misfits—the theater nerds and tech geeks. Stephen was a scholar, the teachers agreed. Michael and June fretted over their delicate bird—asthmatic, astute—while Leo played with his LEGOs and joined lacrosse.

Leo didn't mind. He didn't care, even back then, that the attention was on his brother. He admired him, the way Stephen got those awards: best essay, best science project. Then puberty hit, and frail Stephen began to grow. Girls turned their heads. Guys looked at him grudgingly. Leo was relieved for his brother, suddenly tall and handsome, no longer a target in the halls.

Stephen never seemed to notice him back. Not when Leo made the basketball team ("Aren't you too short for that?" Stephen had asked). Not when he got elected class representative. And certainly not after they moved to Philly, with Stephen halfway out the door to college.

If Leo was the puppy of the family, Stephen was the cat, regal and haughty.

Then the three of them had that summer in Philly, and everything changed.

The funny part was that Leo had by then given up on the idea of being friends with his brother. His freshman year, he'd pledged Pi Kappa Alpha. "You're such a Pike, dude," they told him. Brotherhood, he realized, could be found in other ways.

These guys appreciated him. They noticed him. They *loved* him. His unwavering normalcy was no longer a weakness, and Leo felt more sure-footed. He might never be a bigwig like his dad, and he wasn't book smart like his brother. He didn't have his mom's looks or care about her frilly world of privilege. But, for the first time, he felt like those things didn't matter.

Going into that summer, Leo was focused on Nora. He was thrilled that she was staying at Delancey, that they'd get to spend more time together. He accepted her close friendship with Stephen. There was no point in objecting to it or acting jealous. That would be, as the Pikes liked to say, a dick move.

So Leo played it cool, tuning them out when they went on about Yale, mentioning shared profs and friends, dorms and events whose names Leo didn't recognize. He smiled and sipped his beer, pretending not to mind.

What he didn't expect was for the three of them to find a dynamic all their own. Philly seemed to open up for them that summer. They ventured to neighborhoods he hadn't known about in high school: the narrow strip of bars on Sansom, the little pockets of Old City. They would meet for happy hour at the Nodding Head or a picnic at Rittenhouse Square, crowding together on a blanket. Leo realized that he and his brother were finally doing that elusive, brotherly thing of hanging out without its being a big deal. Trivia night at the corner bar, karaoke at the place on Chestnut, Nora bringing down the house with a roar. Even a baseball game once, a season opener, Phillies vs. Braves, the three of them sharing a bag of caramel corn.

Leo felt some part of him stir that summer, some missing piece click into place. That summer felt golden and whole. He worked for a software company during the day and came home to Nora at night. They hung out with friends and went to bars. The difference was that Stephen was with them, too. Leo saw a glimmer on the horizon. This was how life could be.

When their exclusionary bubble reared its head, Stephen and Nora laughing at some inside joke, Leo reminded himself that they'd been friends before he entered the scene. They talked like he wasn't there because it was their habit. He shrugged it off and issued a smile.

Just as he did today.

Stephen and Nora liked to play Mr. & Ms. Etiquette, policing his uncouth ways, but they never thought about how they could be inconsiderate, at times rude. Not to a bunch of strangers they would never see again, but to the person closest to them.

Memo. He feels it coming from across the room. *Do not belch and then blow out your Coke.*

His own parents aren't so particular. His mom, itching to get back to the city, will whisper to his dad at the earliest possible moment. His dad will nod while looking out at the room, a politician getting input from an aide.

His parents wouldn't care if Leo ate sandwich after sandwich.

They wouldn't care if he left early to squeeze in some work at the office. Nora fears them too much, convinced that the right combination of outfit and makeup and conversational morsel will produce some effect on them. But maybe that's how girls are, always trying.

His dad is the last person to sweat that stuff. He did the prayer thing because it was how he'd been raised, but it wasn't some display of reverence, the way it is for Stephen. When his dad surveyed the room, it was to check on Sharon, to make sure he had talked with each person there. His dad understands that funerals are a time for family, a time to gather the people around you—not to prove how devout you are.

Follow-up memo to Leopold: phones are to be put away.

He slips his Palm back into his pocket. It makes her less anxious, he figures. So he resists the urge to scroll through his email—a workday, his in-box piling up, a mountain to conquer later. Resists checking for pregame updates. (Malone out with his knee!). A travesty that Game 5 is tonight, tip-off at nine, the heart of the party, with an upset in the air. How could you not root for Detroit? The city of underdogs. He won't be able to sneak up to the TV without his mom tearing him a new one, and his dad isn't a basketball fan. "League of thugs," he always says when Leo mentions the NBA.

Leo has resisted other things as well. "Nice out here," he'd wanted to remark that morning as they glided through the suburbs. The trees looked like broccoli. The potholes disappeared, the road smooth beneath them. He wanted to suggest a quick detour to look at houses, imagining which one might someday be theirs. But Nora's face had been set, her eyes distant, and so he had refrained. He let her have her space, just as his dad was letting his mom have the party. Because that is what you do.

It is enough for him, what he has. He gets impatient sometimes, wanting to run out into their future, because he can see it waiting— the house, the lawn, the tricycle resting on the drive. They aren't ready yet, he knows. The hiccup of the past few years—well, who could have seen that coming?

And so he must be patient, bide his time. Try not to let those thoughts creep in when he worries if there will ever be a wedding. Of course there will. The doubts materialize when they're out like this, at a social event, when he can feel people look at them and wonder.

"No date yet?" Aunt Sharon had said, eyeing him, hefting her mass up the hill after the burial. She was wearing a muumuu that his mom had smirked at. "Well, what's the rush, anyway?" She lit a cigarette, pausing to exhale through her nostrils. "It's better to wait. You kids are too young."

Twenty-seven isn't young, he wanted to retort. And who was she to be giving advice? None of his friends are married yet, true. Dave had howled in protest when Leo announced the engagement. "You're in your prime!" Dave had said, aghast.

They didn't see that waiting was pointless. Because if he and Nora want the house, the kids (three, he imagines, playing out different combinations of boy/girl), they have to start taking steps. He isn't supposed to mention it, but Nora's birthday is approaching in August, her twenty-eighth. And after the wedding, the honeymoon (Hawaii, he imagines, lush and warm, too hot to quarrel; lethargy; flowers of idleness), she will be that much closer to thirty.

It's just a matter of time, he always tells himself. He has to be patient and not press, be patient and seem unconcerned. It is what the Pistons have been doing, defense beating offense, patience beating pizzazz. Hold back, wait. The meek shall inherit the earth.

He is part of a delicate operation with Nora that he himself barely understands. Is she better? Recovered? Not worse? It is a complicated dance requiring him to tread lightly, so lightly, on the balls of his feet. He cannot worry about his game plan, about the points on the scoreboard, because then any momentum will be lost. He has to bide his time, feel out Nora's rhythm. The pesky questions must be kept at bay. Stephen had started hanging out with him, after all, just when Leo had stopped caring.

That is the economics of life, the market of the heart driven by supply and demand, just like everything else. When you want too much, too openly, life sees your hunger and contracts. You have to conserve your desire, hold it close. Not mind as time unfolds, testing you. Not mind the sparseness, the seeming lack. No roses without thorns.

Six

P enny for your thoughts," Stephen says.
  "I thought they'd be worth more," Nora replies drily.

They are sitting in Leopold's black vehicular behemoth with the doors thrown open, the day finally having shed its damp chill. "Presumably a penny meant more back then. That saying goes back to the sixteenth century, at least."

"God, how do you *know* this stuff?"

"Comp exams." The image of the volume floats up to him. Blue cloth, letters in gold. A compendium of proverbs through the 1500s.

Nora used to go for walks with him when he needed a break from studying. "Slow down!" she would yelp, his feet on pace with his thoughts. The streets felt surreal after so many hours at his desk. These people don't have to study, he would marvel, staring at the slow trickle of West Philly—old men shuffling along, young mothers corralling their children. The hypnotic swirl of the striped barber's shop pole on the corner, curving red, then blue. How distant it felt, a life outside of books.

Nora's shoes now sit abandoned on the floor mat. One foot dangles out the passenger side, the other folded beneath her. "They should adjust for inflation," she muses. "'Ben Franklin for your thoughts,' maybe."

He arches a brow for effect. "Is that your two cents?"

She groans. "Awful!"

"I wonder, actually, how much it would work out to."

"The kind of question your dad would love."

Nora is right. His dad would relish the merging of economics and English. And the mileage he would get from it! "Currency was actually a precious metal back then," Michael would expound at cocktail parties. "Worth its weight in gold."

"Hopefully he'll be okay tonight," Nora adds.

Stephen snorts. "Don't you start. Tonight was his idea, though everyone acts like he's falling on his sword."

But she had been there, just days ago. Wednesday, the news of Grandma Portman's death still raw, Stephen's head whirling that the nursing home had predicted it so accurately. How did they know? ("An event like a pulmonary embolism—it's debilitating to the body at that age," Miriam Maxwell had reminded him gently. Yes, yes, he wanted to tell her. You've been telling us that all along. But it wasn't supposed to actually apply.) Just as he was feeling a wash of regret, thinking that they should have done more for her, that maybe they could have prevented her death, Michael looked up from the dinner table and announced the plan to move forward with the party.

"You're not serious," Stephen sputtered.

"This," Michael said calmly, "is my choice to make."

All right, Stephen thought angrily. We'll have the precious party and pretend. Leo was eating noisily, paying them no mind, while Nora sat staring at her plate.

"Is there a reason," she'd asked hesitantly, "why the funeral can't be Saturday?"

Michael explained about the Sabbath while Nora reddened, mortified. Meanwhile, it was never even suggested that the party be moved. God forbid Bloomsday be celebrated a day late.

"I know it's what he said," Nora says now. "I just wonder if he's in shock."

Stephen watches her and sighs. She was probably imagining Michael going through what she had, as if we all process loss the same way. You give him too much credit, he wants to tell her.

It was Nora who had shuddered at the cemetery when the earth hit the coffin. Michael stood with the shovel as though posing for a photograph, his expression stoic. Did he feel powerful in that moment? Was there some relief—perhaps even pleasure—in finally burying his past?

"She wouldn't have minded," June had said at the dinner table, dabbing her mouth with a napkin. "Can't you just hear her? 'No, no, don't cancel for me. You go ahead with your plans.' In a way . . . ," June tested the thought before speaking it. "In a way we will be honoring her, doing exactly as she would have instructed."

Stephen felt aghast listening to these self-justifications. But after hiding his visits to Pine Grove for so long, how could he speak up? He sat there silently, poking at the oily flesh of his salmon, tasting only his own cowardice. At that moment, had she begun to rot? Could she sense his final betrayal from the grave? But Grandma Portman was probably used to it. He pretended not to know her when she visited Delancey. He was no better than the rest of them.

"*Shivah*," Nora says, interrupting his thoughts. "Isn't that Indian?"

Stephen smiles.

"Oh, you laugh! But how am I supposed to know? You'd probably tell me about some Judaic-Hindu connection."

It is good to see some color in her face. All day she has been drawn, pale, as though someone took a remote control and dimmed brightness, color, volume. Meanwhile, Leo had introduced her around as if it were the county fair. "Any day now!" he said, nudging her, as though she were a blue-ribbon pig ready for slaughter. "Any day!"

"And how are you holding up?" Stephen gives her a sidelong glance. He doesn't need to say it.

"I don't know. Fine, I guess." She flips the visor down to examine her reflection. "I talked about her funeral this morning for the first time. So that's a sign of progress, right?"

"This was with your shrink?" Stephen knows that Nora has been seeing someone new. Ben Franklin for your thoughts indeed. "What did he say? Or she?"

"Nothing. He's not really one for saying much."

"Ah. A talk therapist." Stephen wonders if he is a Freudian, one of those who sets you on a divan and makes you face the other way. "Freud used to dispense cocaine to his patients, you know. He administered it through the gums. Loosening the lips, so to speak."

Nora laughs. "I was definitely not snorting coke."

"Can you imagine? There were probably a bunch of addicts wandering through Vienna, twitching and scratching themselves, wanting to pull their hair out." Stephen hears the words come out before he can call them back. He stops, horrified.

"You'd build a loyal client base," she says lightly. "A high referral rate, I imagine."

"I'm so sorry, Nora. I didn't mean—"

"It's okay." Stephen feels the air between them settle. "I don't know if anything helps, honestly. It's not like taking a car in to the mechanic. 'We got it! Problem solved!'" She wipes her hands clean, and her voice sounds uncannily like Leo's: cheerful, upbeat.

"Maybe it's something you always battle. There are people who fight depression, anxiety. They find things that work."

"But nothing works! She died almost a year ago. A whole year! And here I am, barely holding it together. Sometimes I worry it only gets worse."

"Who's to say there's a time limit on grief? Maybe you have to feel worse before you can feel better."

"I just—I keep waiting for things to feel normal again. But what if they never do?" Nora gazes out the open car door. "Honestly, the only time I feel like myself is when I perform. Which is weird, right?"

"I've seen you sing. The place could catch fire and you wouldn't notice."

Nora laughs. He remembers first hearing her, in his room at Branford. He had heard her voice coming through the pipes, but when he opened his door, there was nothing. Some sort of trick of sound, the strange acoustics of the old dorm. He wandered upstairs, ducking a Frisbee, the blast of the Spice Girls, a group of freshmen dancing in their pajamas while laughing hysterically. Turning a corner, he finally heard a trickle of her undulating soprano and followed it to its source. He stood in her doorway, watching. The sheet music was spread before her, though her eyes were closed.

She paused to make a notation with a pencil from behind her ear. He cleared his throat. "Too loud?" she asked, unembarrassed.

"You're amazing," he blurted.

She laughed.

"It sounds familiar." He gestured toward the score.

"*Lakmé*," she said, pencil in midair. "But stolen shamefully by British Airways. You've probably heard it in their commercials."

Just like that they'd become friends. Stephen doesn't remember what came next—how that conversation led to another, whether they had dinner or went for a walk. He cannot recall what followed. But the memory of that pure soprano pouring out of her—that memory arrests him still.

"It makes sense," he adds now. "We find comfort in the things we love."

"Like writing?"

"Ugh. Don't ask."

They haven't talked about his proposal. He's been skipping Sunday brunches under the pretense of work. Meanwhile he paces his room, sitting at his desk only to stand again. Once or twice, a thump has come through the floorboards, broom against ceiling, the downstairs neighbor telling him to quit it.

Maybe it is how his grandmother feels: trapped one floor beneath, haunted by the racket above. Is there rest in death, or does the noise continue? Apparently the hair and nails continue to grow, not having received the message to stop, the cells oblivious.

Stephen feels Nora eyeing him. He sighs. "It's just—it's like putting the cart before the horse. You can't state what a project is about before writing it. You write to figure it out. The proposal is this weird parlor trick: summarize your dissertation ahead of time! It's like trying to describe the child from the womb." He catches her smiling. "What?"

"I was counting the analogies. Three so far. Anyway, I know you have some sense of your topic. I've heard you talk about it."

"Not enough to fill thirty pages."

Meanwhile, his adviser has been encouraging him to incorporate *Ulysses*. "Your project would be incomplete without it!" Stuart said. "Especially if you're discussing the parallax view. Besides which, your parents would be thrilled." "It's bad enough they named us after the characters," Stephen replied. "Just be glad they didn't go with Dedalus," Stuart pointed out. "But there is a Dedalus!" Stephen informed him. "That's what they named the golden retriever. He shits on the kitchen floor once a week." At this Stuart had laughed, laughed in such a way that Stephen knew he had just bought himself another month.

"Oh, fuck. Stuart."

"Excuse me?"

"I'm just remembering—my adviser. I think he's coming to-night." It seemed unavoidable at the time. "So tell me," Stuart had said, "do your parents have anything planned for the big centennial?" "Your invitation's already in the mail," Stephen had replied smoothly, making a mental note to have his mother send one.

The part he hasn't told Stuart is that other doubts have been arising as well. "Do you ever worry that this stuff doesn't matter?" Stephen wants to ask him. "Do you ever wish you did something normal?"

"You'll be fine, you know," Nora remarks. "You always do this."

"Do what?"

"Work yourself up. Get all agitated. Wring your hands."

Stephen is about to protest that he isn't "all agitated," but then looks down to see himself wringing his hands. "This is different. It's not just the proposal. I'm having doubts about the whole enterprise."

"Meaning?"

"Meaning I wonder about all of it. If I should be doing something else. The thing about grad school is that you need to be committed. I started out so focused. But now—it feels pointless."

He thinks of the woman on the train, consumed with her own worries. He thinks of his cousins working minimum-wage jobs. George, his stepuncle, had made an effort to ask about his teaching. George listened, nodded. "She's better where she is," he said after a pause, as though seeing straight through to Stephen's grief. George always had an eye for suffering.

"No one else seems filled with doubts," Stephen continues. In his department, his peers seem like they are on autopilot. Emily, a pale Victorianist, writes long comments on her students' papers while sipping tea composedly by her enormous potted fern. Marisel, a plump

Latina, prattles on about cosmopolitanism in her too-tight jeans, her cellphone occasionally working its way out of her pocket from the sheer thrusting force of her backside. Josh, perpetually clad in ironic T-shirts, is a skittish fan of the postmodern novel. All of them feel like walking clichés. And what would that make Stephen?

He cannot bear the thought of being a stereotype. The worst part is that Leo would agree with him. "What good is something unless it improves people's lives?" Stephen could ask, and Leo would look relieved that his brother was finally talking sense.

Leo's eyes glaze over when Stephen talks about his research: "I'm trying to think about a theory of subjectivity in Woolf. Characters are always displacing themselves. They shuttle between past and future, caught in a memory but then thrown into the present, as though at any instant—" And Stephen will feel the image come over him. As though at any instant we are a handful of leaves, scattered by time.

But then he'll sense his brother stifling a yawn. You see! he wants to cry. You're doing it now! Here, but elsewhere. Standing here, listening to me, but imagining the emails you need to write, the wedding venue you want to show Nora. Who knows where people go off to in their heads? Thoughts intrude. A conversation is no simple thing. We are in a thousand places at any moment.

If Leo was haunted by past or future, he didn't show it. "Maybe people aren't so complicated," he'd say. "Maybe it's just you."

If someone asked Leo what he did for a living, he would smile. "I'm an IT consultant." With just the right touch of modesty he'd describe how he was a manager, running through the "workplace solutions" his firm offers.

Ah, the person would nod. Yes, I see. Leo's job fit into something broader, was part of an apparatus, a complex machine of interlocking parts. He went out into the world and contributed to it, producing software so that other companies could use that software and perform better. Products and efficiency and lives were improved, jobs begetting jobs, the furnace of the American economy burning to keep everyone warm.

How is what you do work? This is the unsaid question people direct Stephen's way. He isn't a coal miner or a surgeon. His father had an impressive career in finance. His mother, for all her faults, bore children. What is Stephen's contribution?

"You don't feel you are accomplished?" Grandma Portman had asked, listening to these questions and peering at him.

"I don't feel like what I do matters."

"Ah. Well. I was a housewife. When we compare, no one holds up. 'So what' is an annihilating question."

That was the thing about his grandmother. She could hit you with a line like that and stop you cold.

"You give yourself too hard of a time," Nora says beside him. "If you find something you love, that's enough."

"*I* give myself a hard time?"

Nora smiles.

Soon, the synagogue basement will empty. He and Nora had snuck out. She had a spare set of keys for the car in her purse.

He didn't need to give Nora an excuse to leave, but the trays of cold cuts and the two-liter bottles of soda had done it. The tacky supermarket food. He knew his parents were preoccupied with the party. But when he saw that afterthought of a spread—which they would never have permitted for something that mattered to them— he understood their heartlessness.

"Life is strange," he says, folding his arms across his chest. "I bet my grandmother never imagined ending up in Pennsylvania, of all places. How does it happen? You have such dreams when you're a kid. And then you find yourself teaching some idiotic composition class, grading papers on the train."

He recalls that book of proverbs with its blue cloth. The sayings it tracked weren't necessarily elegant or clever; they were simply what had pervaded. "Do people end up doing what they love? I'm not so sure. And why is that? It's as if life comes preprogrammed. We seem to go with the defaults, even if it means being miserable." As though when reaching for words, we can only grasp at what's already there: grasp at straws, offer pennies for thoughts. As though life would not meet us if we were to leap.

But Stephen cannot bring himself to say more, to follow the path of his thoughts. Not today.

The idea had come to him after his last visit with his grandmother. He could go to New York.

It was a preposterous idea, but it had taken up residence, and he found himself returning to it. He began to wonder about writing his dissertation from afar. You can write anywhere, he realized. It was such an obvious thought, but it had never occurred to him before. He could email Stuart his chapters, take the train in for meetings. Why not? What was keeping him in Philly? The only person he would miss was Nora.

Then another, more dangerous thought entered his mind. She could come, too.

Oh, it was unthinkable. He could never do such a thing, could never even suggest it jokingly. But it has become a daydream, one that's startlingly vivid. He can picture the two of them in a small apartment, more cramped than the one he is already in, but somehow more charming for it. He imagines clacking away at a typewriter with a mug of tea, a scarf around his neck. He imagines Nora coming home from auditions. He imagines her practicing with her sheet music, a pencil behind her ear.

"It's better not to think too much," Nora remarks. He turns to look at her. "I know how that sounds. Maybe it's Leo's influence, what he would say. But me and you—we think everything to death. You can sit around contemplating life forever, but meanwhile it continues. So you might as well have chosen something and made the best of it."

A ringing endorsement for marriage. But Stephen has vowed since the engagement to keep his mouth shut.

He knows he will lose her, too. She will go out to Ardmore or Gladwyne, one of those bucolic suburbs Leo loves. She will end up locked away in her "might as well."

When Leo lays out his visions for them, Nora never frowns or looks away uncomfortably; they never fight over their future, so far as Stephen can tell. It is endearing to hear Leo describe it: the house, the oaks, the hairless limbs of toddlers in a blur of motion. He speaks of it with a grin, knowing that he is signing them up for a certain kind of chaos. "Three kids?" June had said, stricken. "Really?"

But Nora doesn't see that the vision rests on her back. Leo will continue with his job, continue bathing his beloved car. His commute will be easier, his life generally improved for the addition of wife and house and kids. He'll watch sports and hang out with the guys. Nora will be the one forced to sacrifice, subtly at first, the water getting incrementally warmer until it is at a boil.

We stake our place in this world. Isn't that what Grandma Portman had been trying to tell him? "To be a housewife is to become the result of everyone else's decisions," she had said.

It is what he feels happening around him, their choices narrowing. It all got decided somehow, fate urging you along, daring you to accept its nudge.

When he tries to hint at some of his doubts to Stuart, his adviser merely nods and says, "Just so, Stephen. Just so." Just once, Stephen wants Stuart to pause, to clear his throat. To say, "Well, of course, you don't mean that now, do you?" He wants Stuart to remove his glasses and look at him, frowning. Instead, Stephen's every concern is deemed proof that he's in the right place. Stuart often had a nostalgic smile playing about his lips, as though recalling his own similar frustrations. If Stephen were to tell Stuart tonight that he wants to drop out, Stuart would probably nod, bemused, and say, "Well said, Stephen. That's exactly *it*."

Hannah Portman had never set foot in Pine Grove before living there. She was shown a brochure; her tour of the place had been on move-in day. Had it felt like this? As if the person assuring you your doubts were for nothing didn't know you at all?

It is difficult to heed the warning bells. How much easier to just go along and agree. To watch the trajectory of the ball long ago set in motion and see where it will land, as though you are not the product of its outcome. To watch as though you have no hand in your own life. As though the only words we have available to us were written long ago in a blue book. As though we cannot make our own stories, decide our own fates.

Nora has already given up auditions. Occasionally the audience at Manning catches a glimpse of her soaring vocals. They freeze, startled, before whooping and clapping. Stephen has come to hate these moments. That's a world-class voice, he wants to yell. Meanwhile, Leo beams, proud of his girl. It isn't Leo's fault. He's always been clear about what he wants. No one can accuse him of disguising his desires. But Stephen has come to understand the lure of complacency. And there Leo is, encouraging Nora to settle down. Encouraging her to settle.

It all starts with a choice. "A girl, a girl. What did I know?" his grandmother used to say. Regret was a luxury. She didn't have time to question her decisions. It was Poland. It was 1939. She and her new husband fled, embracing each other instead of their doubts.

His grandfather came to America first, securing them a house. God, Stephen thinks. Did she ever pick out a place of her own? That house. Then the nursing home. Probably the coffin. Did she ever have a say?

Once it starts, it's hard to choose differently. His grandmother had made a decision, a choice that probably felt harmless at the time. A kiss, nothing more, a girl wanting to see how it felt. Hannah Portman had stepped up and closed her eyes, perhaps not so much choosing as giving in.

He looks at Nora beside him. It's not the future we should fear, he wants to tell her. It's ourselves.

It almost makes him laugh. I too, he thinks. I too am a reluctant bride.

Seven

———

"At least the wind's died down," June observes. "I was worried at the cemetery I'd come undone!"

Nora takes in June's blond helmet, streaked with highlights of ash and honey. That chignon could probably survive gale-force winds. June tilts the Escalade's side mirror to survey herself while Leo winces.

The family had converged around the SUV. "There you are," Leo said lightly, coming over to Nora's side of the car. She ducked to put her shoes back on, telling herself there was no reason to feel guilty. It wasn't as if she and Stephen had been making out in the backseat. When she straightened, Leo gave her an inquisitorial look. Any luck? his eyes asked. Nora raised her mouth to his ear. "I tried the dental tools. Even the bamboo splinters. But nothing! He's not talking."

"We have to remember to save the paper," June adds.

"For the obituary?" Stephen asks. "It was in yesterday's *Inquirer*. I already clipped it."

Nora had spotted it, too, scanning the paper over breakfast.

80

There was Hannah Portman's name, the serifed font skeletal and scythe-wielding. Nora's eyes lingered on it, thinking how strange it was to have a person's life reduced to a few words.

"No, I mean for the feature." June unfastens her clutch. "We talked to Tom."

"The feature?" Stephen repeats.

"Tom?" Leo inquires.

June brings out a tube of lipstick. *YSL*, the letters say, gleaming in gold script.

"Thursday was just the obit," Michael explains. "This will be a longer piece memorializing her. They're running it in the Sunday paper."

"An article? There will be an *article* about her?" Stephen stares at his parents.

"It's a profile," Michael says calmly. "We wanted to pay tribute."

"A shame it comes too late for the party," Stephen mutters. "Would've made a lovely favor."

June glances up from her application of lipstick. "We thought you'd be pleased." Her lips are rubies, glistening and red. Stephen looks away from her, shoving his hands into his pockets.

"Tom Laughlin," Michael says to Leo. "He heads the Arts and Culture section. Great guy."

They have a few minutes before they need to head back to the city. Michael and June's gray sedan sits several spaces over, its hue the same color as the sky: luminous, mercurial. "What a waste," Nora's mother would have admonished. "What good is an SUV if you don't fill it?" Nora imagines June sandwiched in the back of the Escalade, straddling the hump and looking put out, her black heel tapping.

"We've been thinking about placing an ad in the *Inquirer* at work," Leo comments. "Reaching out to more local companies."

"Talk to Tom tonight," Michael suggests. "He was saying it's been a record year for ads."

"Good for them." Leo nods. "It's the ads that sell a paper. That's their whole revenue stream."

That and weddings. Leo has a special "Weddings" edition from the *Inquirer* hidden under his side of the bed, tucked away like a dirty magazine. Nora had flipped through its lists of vendors and pointed advice for couples. "Dear Philly Bride," she imagined Leo writing, chewing on his pen. "My fiancée has a bald spot and is in protracted mourning for her dead mother. Is there a veil you'd recommend?"

"The whole family can be in the paper!" Stephen chimes in brightly. "Parties, deaths, software. A cornucopia of Portman news."

They ignore him, but Nora wouldn't be surprised if it actually came to pass. She can envision a write-up of the party: "Bloomsday Celebration Draws Elite Crowd." Delancey had once been photographed for an article on interior design. Maybe the newspaper would recycle the handsome photograph they had on file, Michael and June standing by the staircase, looking elegant and refined.

"Those two are like celebrities," Nora's mom once commented. Nora had laughed, but it was true in a way. Michael and June were so accustomed to a life of glamour that a tribute to Grandma Portman in the paper probably felt sincere to them. Nora can picture them in their master bedroom, June applying face cream. "We should commemorate her somehow," she would say to her reflection. "Maybe a piece in the paper?" "Perfect," Michael would reply. "I'll call Tom."

It would never have occurred to them to mourn privately, as Stephen wished. Michael was probably relieved to call Tom, to have a to-do list, spreading his grief outward. Maybe this is Nora's problem, that she holds her grief in, internalizing it, rather than distributing its weight.

"The new book is coming out," she remembers suddenly. "Is that next week, already?"

"Tuesday," June affirms, capping her lipstick.

"Sweet of you to remember, Nora," Michael says. "It's an exciting moment for the author. Nothing like that first big review!"

Nora sees a defiant pride break across his face. One day his company will make the front page: "Local Press Makes Waves."

Michael was formerly a funds manager in New York. Nora doesn't understand these financial jobs, all so abstract and vague. "What exactly is a hedge fund?" she once asked him cautiously. But she was lost immediately in Michael's explanation, the terms dizzying. "He stayed away from the shrubs," Stephen liked to joke. "Avoided the trellis."

His specialty had been selling short. Which, if she understands correctly, meant that he bet against the market, anticipated declines. "But how does that work?" she persisted. "How do you profit from a decline?" "You can profit from anything," Leo told her. "My dad just saw things that other people didn't." "But isn't there an ethics to it, a problem of conscience?" "How do you mean?" Leo asked. "Because if you think something's going to go down, you're betting on people losing money." Leo had smiled. "A lot of it is through derivatives, love," he said reassuringly. "Meaning what?" "Meaning that it's all Monopoly money anyway."

It makes Nora's head hurt to think about such abstractions: buying and selling not objects, or even slices of companies making those objects, but *ideas*, all of it speculative, notions and forecasts factored into algorithms. What was it like to trade in intangibles?

When Nora sings, she feels it in her body. People treat the arts as if they are obscure, finance as though it is concrete, but she has always thought it is just the opposite. Music is visceral. People respond to it right away. "You were so moving," people will say after a performance, and Nora likes to think she has actually moved them, the sound waves traveling from her mouth into their bodies and causing an internal shift.

"It's not so complicated," Michael told her of his work. "I just looked the other way. It's hard to stand out when you're all looking at the same data. So I started looking down when everyone else was looking up." He shrugged, as though describing something simple.

All she knows for sure is that he had done spectacularly well. He'd made enough that he could purchase the town house on Delancey, that dignified strip of privilege, and have his wife renovate it extravagantly. Enough that he could start his publishing house without worrying over whether it would be profitable. "Small presses usually aren't," he said, his eyes twinkling.

Dubliner Books had put out a few chapbooks of poetry, some experimental fiction, and now this biography. "You should have an online presence," Leo urged. "Not just company information, but actual content, like online poems or whatever. People could read this stuff from their phones."

Michael smiled tolerantly at the idea, but Nora senses a different a side of him is nurtured by publishing. He often appears at brunch with ink stains on his fingers. "You're just getting in the way over there!" June chastises. "As if you're a tradesman!" After the table is cleared of dishes, he spreads sample layouts across its surface. "Which one do you think, Nora?" he asks, indicating with a tilt of his head for her to come over. The surprise of his kindness never wears off.

Nora suspects that Michael thrills to the tangible nature of publishing. He is like a farmer, cultivating books in lieu of crops. He shares stories of his labors on Sundays, regaling them with tales of the printing machines and drawers of type.

"Wait, they do it by hand?" Leopold once asked, incredulous. "Surely there's a better way."

But Michael had chosen to work with that particular letterpress company because he was charmed by its approach, its dedication to the art of printing. The company is owned by a woman, Helen, in her twenties. "Just out of art school, all on her own," Michael marveled. He was filled with admiration when he described her. "How quickly she does that job. Practice makes perfect. Seems to see with her fingers." Leo sulked when Michael sang her praises, a jealous pet forced to watch another animal get rewarded.

The printing company operates out of an old warehouse down by the river. "You should hear the racket!" Michael likes to crow. Nora imagines it is the great clang of productivity—people making actual *things*—that he fell for, so different from the hustle of Wall Street.

Michael gazes at his finished products reverently, a boy beaming over his latest creation. The first chapbook of poetry was an eyesore, a ghastly shade of gray with a dark-purple font. "I now have a say in color," June says airily whenever the books are brought out.

"You'd think you'd have more sympathy for the guy," Nora once remarked to Stephen. "He clearly loves books."

"You clearly love *him*," Stephen returned. "Don't let his labor of love fool you, Nora. The business of books is still very much a business."

It's true that Michael's sense of ambition is palpable. His imprint will probably be purchased by a top publisher one day; if anyone could find a way to make poetry profitable, it is Michael. June, by contrast, exudes ennui as she floats through Delancey's rooms, led by nothing more than her whims.

June dabbles in pet projects, keeping their social calendar filled with museum galas and black-tie benefits. She periodically sets out her watercolors and easel in her immaculate white office and then shrugs nonchalantly when friends coo, "June! My goodness. How do you find the time?" while gazing at her drippy abstractions.

Meanwhile, the groceries get delivered, the dry cleaning dropped off, the pillows plumped by strange hands. June hands out keys like she is the mayor. Nora wonders how many of them must be circulating through the city, in various pockets, dangling from key chains. Strangers handle the most intimate details at Delancey—

walking the dog, swapping hydrangeas for peonies in the thick, crystal globes. All June ever sees of them is their bill. Maybe that's the whole point of hiring someone. If you start wondering about the people fingering your underwear, arranging it in lacy rows, you might as well be doing it yourself.

"Girl, she be havin' a *closet organizer,*" Carol declared in her Trinidadian accent, the words lilting. Carol keeps her own key around her neck on a cord of silk. She and Nora had become fast friends when they discovered they had singing in common.

"A closet organizer!" Carol bellowed. "How can you be organizin' somethin'—" Carol paused, clutching her sides.

"—that doesn't exist!" Nora completed, and the two of them howled with laughter.

June had insisted on removing the house's closets, a notion she had learned about in one of her classes. "A lifestyle class," Stephen scoffed. "Taught by some pseudospiritual wonk for Rittenhouse wives. She tries to pass it off as an architecture seminar."

It wasn't merely that the closet doors had been removed. The framing had been pulled, whole walls blown open. "But where do you hide things?" Nora whispered to Stephen as they went from room to room. The pre-company ritual in her own house had been to stuff everything behind doors and then pray no one opened them. "The whole point is that you don't," he muttered.

Delancey had a feeling of openness that you couldn't quite place, like going to a city with no visible power lines. Nora delighted in pointing out the house's salient feature to guests. She watched as comprehension dawned on their faces. "A house without closets!" they exclaimed, shaking their heads.

Stephen and Leo must have detested it—two teenage boys, unable to be messy. Every item in Delancey has a place, exact and perfect. "When you put things out of sight, you invite disorder," June liked to say.

For Michael, his wife's vision of bright rooms thrown open to the light was perhaps a comfort after all those years in New York. Not just because he'd worked long hours in dark offices, but because he had stuffed away his passions. Perhaps he felt liberated, freed of the pressure to accomplish and earn, able to do what he loves. *No more skeletons!* Delancey trumpeted. Michael had dusted off his dreams and brought them out of hiding.

Leo had been glad to leave New York. "Wasn't it hard, being the new kid?" Nora asked him. She couldn't imagine starting school in a new place, walking the halls that first day. Leo shrugged his trademark shrug, one shoulder tossed up in the air, his jaw tilting to meet it. On balance, no big deal, his upper torso declared.

Leo's upbringing was so different from her own in New Jersey. The girls at Union High smacked their gum and did each other's nails in homeroom. The guys were smart alecks. She had been the freak for doing well, the honor roll a place of shame. What saved her from being an outcast was her voice. "Well, well," the music teacher had said, looking at her appraisingly. That was in the fifth grade, Mr. Granato. Everyone thought he was a pedophile, spreading the rumor even though they had no basis for it. And why? Why on earth had they done that? She later wondered if he had some inkling of it, poor Mr. Granato, the kids jeering behind his back.

She had been in every musical and concert from that point forward. It was a given that the lead would go to her. *Grease. Les Mis. West Side Story.* They were awful productions. The school never had the money for good costumes or sets. Nora used to raid her mom's closet for outfits from other decades. Meanwhile, she kept quiet at school about her training, never mentioning her voice lessons, her summer courses at the Met. Only at Yale did she feel she could finally embrace opera without being judged for it.

"So I gather you don't think she should be in the paper," Michael says to Stephen, jarring Nora from her thoughts. His question comes out as a statement, seeking confirmation, but it is empty of reproach.

Stephen shifts. "There wouldn't be an article about her if it weren't for your connections. She was hardly a cultural icon."

"She came to this country in 1939. A remarkable time to live through."

"And you think that warrants a feature in the paper?"

"I think *she* deserves a feature in the paper."

"But not a proper mourning."

Michael closes his eyes.

"That's enough," June says, snapping her clutch. Shaped like a clamshell, it reminds Nora of a set of jaws. Some company makes these bags, hard and jeweled, like glittering weapons. Nora has seen them toted around by June's friends. A collection of them sit on a shelf in her noncloset. "We've done the best we can. Nothing about death is convenient."

Stephen smiles sadly to himself.

How cold they can be. They never react with feeling, with heart. Even their dilemmas feel supercilious. Should Granny be in the Arts section? Should we cancel the gala? These are sort of grandiose problems, Nora wants to tell them. You guys get that, right?

But Nora isn't so sure they want a dash of perspective. She suspects that they enjoy their high-end issues, as though they themselves are a work of art. They would never want to be common, the Portmans. Even Leo—he is fascinated with the average life because it is novel to him. His blue-collar work ethic is a blue-blood experiment.

Nora wonders if they aren't so different from *Ulysses*. She had attempted to read it before her first Bloomsday party. "How do people get through this thing?" she asked Stephen. "They don't," he replied. "That's its claim to fame."

After all this time, she still feels held at arm's length by this family. And maybe that's how they wanted it. They didn't want to be relatable. Their life at Delancey was a spectacle, even their possessions out on display.

"It's good, you know?" Leo says, interrupting her thoughts.

They turn his way.

"It's good that the timing was terrible, even if it means we didn't have time to plan. Even if we don't get to mourn the right way. Because it means she didn't suffer."

Nora tucks her jacket around her, wishing she'd brought her heavier coat.

"Well, that's exactly right," June says.

Nora can feel them look studiously away from her. Look at the alternative, they would have said if she weren't there. Think of Nora's mom, all those years.

"We should go," Stephen observes. "We don't want to be late for the party."

June nods emphatically, oblivious to his tone.

She knows that Leo is trying to defend Michael from Stephen. "Think of the upside," she can hear him say. And it is true, that Grandma Portman didn't suffer. But to not suffer is its own form of suffering. Grandma Portman might have preferred illness if given the choice, if she'd been handed a form. "Sudden death?" Her pencil would have hovered next to the box. No, she would have thought, leaving it unchecked. Because then you don't get to say good-bye.

Leo doesn't see such dark choices. "Why on earth would someone choose illness?" he would ask, bewildered. But Nora imagines that her mom, in her own way, knew that those seven years had prepared Nora, had taken an edge off the shock. Neither of them had the heart to say it at the time, those last few weeks, her mom back in the hospital for good. But Nora had felt it, a strange, terrible gratitude that this wasn't her first time there. That they had rehearsed this moment before.

She and her mom, for better or worse, were pros.

The view from where Leo stands, high up, is of the big picture. Leo sees two roads: the helpful one that leads to the future; the other, meandering, that draws you away. Leo surveys, shrugs. How easy it must seem to him.

Death pulls you down into the dirt, she wants to tell him. Suddenly there is no road, no future. There is no magnanimous view, no such thing as a good death. There is only the current hunger, which does not go away. The hunger for something that will never be again.

Stephen, in the backseat, exudes dismay. "Sit with me," he urged before the others had joined them. She was happy to have at least convinced him to accept the ride.

"And leave Leo up front? Like a cabbie?"

"He's got his headset. You know he has work calls he's dying to make."

He'll make them anyway, she thought.

"We haven't talked in ages," Stephen continued.

"God, it's true." They looked at one another. How had it happened, this gap between them? Was it her fault?

You've been skipping brunch, she should have said, poking him. You and your hermit ways.

But that isn't fair. She, too, has gone underground. In sight, but absent. Present, but missing. There for all the brunches and dinners. By Leo's side when he drags her out to bars with friends. But she is elsewhere in her thoughts, barely registering the conversations. Certainly not taking the time to talk with her friend—to ask how he has been and then listen, the way a friend should. I don't know how it happened, she thinks as they depart the synagogue. This whole time? I don't really know where I've been.

Eight

*F*ishtown, *Fishtown.* Leo sniffs the air and gets a hit of dried salt. Plumes of smoke billow out from the yellow stacks along the river, a chemical miasma mixing with the breeze, the air reeking of smoked fish. It isn't unpleasant, exactly, but it's not for the faint of heart.

Leo parked two blocks from the warehouse. They made good time returning to the city, but the drive and the wooden pews had done a number on him, his glutes numb. He wishes someone could help him with one of those hamstring stretches they do in baseball, the trainer pushing the player's leg back, back, the knee coming to meet the nose. It is somehow this, of all things, that Leo most envies of athletes, that their bodies are not their own. He thinks of the number of ACL tears and sprains he has followed as a fan, tracking surgeries and injury reports. McNabb's broken ankle had been a heartbreaker. Could have won it that year, gotten a ring.

Still, now they have Owens, and that is something. "TO's a total drama queen," Dave told him, shaking his head. "Wide receivers always are," Leo said. But McNabb needs someone out there, *deserves* someone out there. "A quarterback is only as good as his receivers," he added.

City of brotherly love, maybe, but not of sympathetic fans.

"So you think we're going to take it this year?" Dave asked.

"I do," Leo affirmed.

The guys around the break room guffawed, and only then did Leo get the joke. Apparently they asked him this every year, his answer unchanging—a hopeful groundhog predicting nothing but spring. He grinned at them, cracking open a can of Coke, but felt a stir of annoyance. Maybe if they didn't heckle the guy, he'd have better luck.

Leo had managed to convince his dad to get season tickets this year, reminding him that they were a good networking tool. "I suppose that's true," his dad conceded. The Linc is brand spanking new, a jewel after the dumpy old Vet. Realistically, he'll probably only be able to coax his dad out for a couple of games, but maybe they can wrangle Stephen out, too, make a guys' night of it. Leo will chat them up, having perfected the art of carrying on a conversation with his eyes trained on the field. This isn't so bad, they'll think, settling into their seats beside him, the Sunday-afternoon air crisp. McNabb will connect with TO down the field and the crowd will roar. Stephen and his dad will stand, caught up in the moment, and Leo will try to hide his smug triumph.

He crosses Poplar down to the waterfront. The water bobs, murky and gray. It looks better from a distance, mysterious rather than dirty, the Ben Franklin Bridge arcing blue across it. The bridge is rusty, its paint flaking, but the views from the pedestrian path— where he's been trying, for some time now, to take Nora—are glorious. You just have to look past the cars, the green and white signs, past the visual noise to the view beyond. "Trust me," he needs to tell Nora, holding out his hand, because if he can get her out to the middle of that bridge, she will turn and see: the spectacular skyline, the puffed-up sailboats by Camden, the river curving with its great sweep.

He jogs up the steps to Helen's entrance. The sign for PinPoint Press has circles cut out over the *i*'s, holes instead of dots. Leo glimpses brick, trees, sky, the contents of the cutouts changing with the angle as he ascends. He has been to the warehouse a couple of times before, accompanying his dad to help him lug boxes home. The holes in the sign always come as a surprise.

They were a reference to some art school project, apparently, for which Helen had punctured hundreds of holes in paper. "The illusion of ink," she explained. "It's a play on perspective." His dad had fawned over the prints on the studio's back wall, but the whole thing confused Leo. Did it mean she didn't like ink? Would she rather be doing her art? "It's all *part* of her art," Nora told him, "the same way I do jazz and gospel." Yeah, but I don't really get that, either, he wanted to reply. If you train for the one thing, why change?

Artsy types never make sense to Leo. Lack of logic seems to be a prerequisite. A shadow crosses Nora's face when anyone asks her about opera. She'd been so good, a star. And though he is relieved to not have her touring, he wonders sometimes why she gave it up so abruptly.

An antique bell announces his arrival as he pushes open the front door. Helen's studio has the feel of a bungalow, the tall windows open, light flooding the room with its butter-yellow walls.

Helen's back is to him, in cargo shorts and a wifebeater, a blue apron tied around her neck. A delicate network of vines climbs up the back of one leg in an elaborate tattoo, the ink sharp against her skin. Leo watches the lines branch across the back of her thigh.

"Be right with you!" she calls over her shoulder in her Texan drawl.

"No problem," he shouts back.

She is operating a machine with a vise, safety goggles over her eyes, her hair tied up off her neck. She reminds him of Rosie the Riveter, her biceps taut. He wonders where the tattoo ends, how high it ventures up that expanse of tan, and is delighted by the image that comes to him, unbidden, of her shrugging out of her shorts so that he might see.

"Can I help you?" she asks, turning. She lifts the goggles so they perch on her head.

"Leopold," he reminds her, smiling to show that he doesn't mind.

"Oh! Right. Michael's son."

Her face brightens as she says this. Leo wonders if she has a crush on his dad. Most girls do. That mix of confidence and warmth pulls them in.

"Sorry," she adds, wiping the sweat from her face with her arm. "I saw the suit before I saw you. Some exec from Comcast is stopping by for a project. Is Michael here?"

She peers past Leo, as though his dad might spring out and surprise her. Leo wonders if she put on the shorts with his dad in mind. If she thought of him while shaving her legs in the shower that morning, the razor gliding smoothly over the tangle of vines, her foot perched on the tub's edge.

"He couldn't make it." Leo pauses, wondering if he should say more. May as well get her sympathy. "My grandmother died, actually. Funeral was this morning."

"Oh!" Helen's hand flies up to her mouth. "His side?"

Leo nods. "She was getting up there, though."

"I'm so sorry." She shakes her head.

His dad had taken him aside after the funeral. "I'm supposed to pick up the banner for the party. Any chance you could get it?" Leo liked the way his dad leaned in against the driver's-side window and added, "Don't tell Mom. She thinks I already have it." Leo relished the conspiratorial moment that passed between them.

"I've got your stuff in the back," Helen says, leading the way to the rear of the room.

His dad was probably wiped from the funeral. He'd probably gone upstairs to take a nap. But Leo appreciates that none of this was said, that there is no extraneous information between men. There was just the question, simple and straight: Can you go?

Guys never apologize for things that aren't their fault. They do not simper, elaborate, stew. Is that all right with you, Leo? Is that okay? Do you think me awful, horrible, do you secretly mind? If he couldn't make it to the printer, his dad wouldn't have given it a second thought. He wouldn't have stared at Leo resentfully and said, "Well, what is it that you have to do, *exactly*?"

"So what's the Comcast project?" Leo asks.

"Oh, that." Helen reaches for a cardboard tube, unflasking it. "Nothing big, just a gift for some VP who's retiring. Nice little handmade book with notes from colleagues. A bitch to compile with the deadline they gave me, but they're a good client."

Leo is impressed. This letterpress thing might be an art, but it is a business, too—managing customers, generating accounts. Deciding, for example, to not offer delivery, to make people come to her—a ridiculous practice, some would say, but the perk was that you got to see Helen bent over the letterpress. No wonder his dad loves it here.

She unfurls a long, white banner printed with green text. "Yes I said yes I will Yes," it says in bold lettering, **One hundred years of Joyce** centered beneath in smaller font, spaced evenly along the bottom edge.

"Michael said not to do too deep of an impression, so I kept it light. And the ink is an exact match to the sample y'all gave. The cocktail napkin? Took me ages to mix it, get it just right. Kind of a cool grass green, not too much yellow. Might make it a permanent addition."

"Hmn," Leo says, nodding, though he comprehends none of what she just said. She indicates a sign on the wall listing available ink colors. Leave it to his mom to insist on something custom. "Portman Green," he ventures.

She smiles. "I checked the proof about a dozen times. That last capitalization on the *yes* looked so strange! Anyway . . ." She takes a step back so that he can evaluate the thing, and Leo scratches his ear, at a loss for what to say. He should have asked his dad if there was anything he was supposed to do.

"Terrific," he says after a beat, pretending to examine it.

"Michael approved the proof, but I always like to do a final check." She rolls the banner back up.

Leo feels reluctant for their transaction to end. "So, you do a lot of corporate work?"

"Oh, you know. Invites, events. Companies like letterpress printing when they want to look classy. It's nice when they become repeat customers."

Leo nods, thinking that must be the trick, to become a company's go-to. "Stick in an extra card," he says suddenly. "I'll pass it along at work." He wonders whom they use for the holiday party. Someone in Admin handles events (Martha? Michelle?), a mousy type with stringy hair and a big nose. His dad will like that Leo helped Helen.

"Thanks," she says, surprised. "Appreciate that."

She is trying to remember what he does, and he lets her. He attempted a soft pitch on her once. "What kind of software do you use?" he had asked. "Software?" she repeated, laughing. "You mean like a website?"

No, not like a website, he had wanted to reply, but this is why he isn't in sales. "We offer business solutions to help companies grow," he explained. "Strategy, infrastructure, day-to-day operations. We streamline processes." He kept the jargon out of it, not wanting to scare her with techno-talk. She is a small fish at any rate, probably not worth the trouble, but he liked the idea of introducing her to a more efficient way of doing things, even if she managed, relying on word of mouth, men in bars mentioning the girl with the racy tattoo and the Southern drawl. You should check her out, they would say, cracking open peanuts and casting off the shells.

Helen had no team, no tangled organizational chart, probably just a freebie cell phone and a Mac, one of those clamshells in Blueberry or Tangerine from her days in art school, sure to crash any day now, taking her Excel spreadsheet (not backed up, naturally) with it. She didn't know that she could build a platform—not a website, Helen, but a platform—that would allow her to track projects, vendors. Allow her to showcase her work, manage information, anticipate needs. "I could connect you with every letterpress company in the country," he'd said. How much time might she save if she could send a quick message over the waves: "Anyone have a recipe for grass-green ink?"

All of her laborious tasks could be coded, performed at the touch of a button. Clients could see her portfolio from the comfort of their offices, no need to constantly venture to this crumbling old warehouse with its diluvial smell of river. No need for her to pause in her work, clearing off her counter to show them samples. Orders could sit in databases, linked to her phone, her email, her website, so that when she needed more of that custom ink, good Lord, you could press a button rather than reinvent the wheel.

"What we really do is help companies operate more smoothly," he explained, wanting to show her that her life could be easier, better. "Trust me," he should have said, holding out his hand, his card.

But of course he had done no such thing. He had let her nod, brow furrowed, squinting at the glimpse of the future he offered. "Maybe one day," she said wistfully. But someone else would beat her to it; another letterpress company was probably at it. A team, a man and a woman hunched over a computer. Helen would hear of them soon enough; they would be featured in a glossy magazine. "Must've gotten lucky, known the right folks," she would say to herself, admiring their website. But to know the right folks, Helen, you have to be able to reach them.

"Well, please tell Michael I'm thinking of y'all." She tucks her hair behind her ear. "I'll be seeing you soon."

Leo nods and thanks her. He catches another glimpse of the vines as she turns, a flash of thigh. He pictures her on the wide counter, the metal letters pressing into her back, upside-down *a*'s, backward *e*'s, crooked letters imprinting into her skin: *b d q z o o*, the list of inks above them trumpeting vermilion, cadmium, umber, sap.

He carries the long tube out the door. His phone blinks *1:39*. There is just enough time for him to grab a bite.

He had deposited Nora back at the loft so she could get ready in her painstaking way, wiping the canvas clean only to bring out her makeup brushes again. "You sure you don't want to get ready at Delancey?" he'd asked that morning. "Ugh, I'd have to pack everything," she replied, making a face, as though contemplating moving mountains. It was a classic Nora moment, the idea of slipping her dress into a garment bag too much for her. He had half a mind to pack everything for her. And at one time she would have appreciated it. "Wow," she would have said, surveying the black bag lying flat across the backseat. He would have remembered her makeup, even her hairpins, and she would have been touched by his thoughtfulness. They'd been happy. Happier then. Mainly because she had leaned on him more. If you push a guy out, where does that leave him?

Nora doesn't like the idea of help, and Leo suspects Helen is the same way. Modern women. No one talks about it, but they leave no room for men in their lives, so intent on being strong.

He feels the sign's eyes on his back as he descends the rickety stairs, as though Helen herself were watching him. He imagines her in art school cutting out what she did not want, proud of what she had excised. Was she content at the end of the day, happy with the life she had chosen? She'd given no indication of wrapping up, and he imagines her working late into the night, ignoring invitations to bars and parties. Being a one-woman show must get lonely.

Soon he will be back at Delancey, where some other errand awaits. But for now, there is just enough time. Primo's, he thinks hungrily, and his stomach rumbles its approval. There is one on this side of town, on East Susquehanna if he's remembering right. Hopefully they haven't yet sold out of bread. A Suprimo, the prosciutto salty, the mozzarella wet, the bread soft with its nutty seeds.

Being a good son has its perks. He can taste the first bite of his hoagie already, wrapped in its wax paper, some of those pepper shooters on the side. He can picture the moment, parked on the side of the road. His reward for doing the right thing.

Nine

Hot water cascades down Stephen's head, running in rivulets down the sides of his face. His scalp tingles, not unpleasantly, from some strange shampoo of June's. Organic argan oil, he read on the bottle. Tea tree oil. Eucalyptus extract. He can feel the layer of tissue just beneath his hair awakening, his cranial membrane aflame. Hello there, it pulses, singing, a thousand little birds chirping. He wonders if June uses the shampoo instead of coffee, her scalp jolting her awake for a different kind of cerebral buzz.

"Ooh, you *have* to use the new shower," she had enthused in the kitchen when he strolled in, covering the mouthpiece of the phone.

"Isn't Dad napping up there?"

"He's in his office." She rolled her eyes. "Go on, you'll love it."

Stephen perceived the strange demand in her enthusiasm, that abyss of need. He could tell that she wanted him to admire the new fixtures and delight in the showerhead, a bright round disk with a thousand holes like a decapitated sunflower.

He needed a shower after the train anyway. "Okay," he said, shrugging, and his mother emitted a thrilled little bleat.

The same dynamic followed whenever she gave him one of her gifts: the shaving set in December; the cashmere scarf at the start of the term. "Go on," she always urged. Her hands pushed forward boxes from Barneys, Bergdorf, Bloomingdale's. Then she sat back in anticipation, watching his face.

Truthfully, he didn't mind the gifts themselves. The scarf had come in handy all winter, impossibly soft and light and warm. June had exquisite taste. He never groaned, *"Mom,"* while holding a tacky reindeer sweater. He was always quite sure, accepting her be-ribboned parcels, that he would like whatever was inside.

But there was an undercurrent, too, some dynamic he could not name—as though by accepting these gifts, he was agreeing to a con-tract he didn't understand. Something passed between them, a mo-ment so subtle he would later think he had imagined it. A court stenographer would be unable to capture it, the transaction occur-ring outside of words:

JUNE PORTMAN: Darling, I saw these Brunello Cucinelli's at Nordstrom and thought of you.

STEPHEN PORTMAN: Oh. Thanks.

JUNE PORTMAN: They match your briefcase so well, don't you think? Cordovan, but not too much red in the undertone. More of a warm butterscotch.

COURT REPORTER: Could you spell *cordovan*?

JUNE PORTMAN: Are they supposed to interrupt?

STEPHEN PORTMAN: C-O-R-D-O-V-A-N.

COURT REPORTER: Thank you.

JUNE PORTMAN: *Anyway*, I find that particular shade incredibly difficult. But this will match exactly, and what could be more professorial than wing tips? You will be a vision!

Here, June would wrap one of her hands around his and give it a squeeze. Sometimes she clapped her hands together as though the two of them were in on a delicious secret. "I knew you'd love them, I just knew!" she would trill, and Stephen would look away, embarrassed, stuffing the box out of sight.

Maybe it's loneliness, Stephen reflects, soaping his arms. June has acquaintances. She has people to air-kiss at parties, elbows to hold floating up and down stairs. People speak of her, speak to her, but no one is a trusted confidant. There was no one to listen sympathetically as she went on about the renovation. "I went with the Carrara," she told him the day the demo started. It took him a minute to remember that this was a kind of marble, veined like cheese. "Your father has his Porsche. Now I have my bath."

He could tell she had rehearsed the line. She will try it out later on Sissy or Catherine. "You chose tile?" Sissy will say lazily, glancing around the gleaming bath. "I prefer slab." Sissy and Catherine aren't friends, after all, but more like competitors in an ongoing game of one-upmanship. June will smile thinly and prepare a zinger to deal Sissy later.

Stephen isn't sure he likes the renovation. The result feels more like a showroom than a bathroom. It isn't entirely comfortable under the shower's assault, the water falling straight from the ceiling. He can find no angle, no jet stream for his back. No pulse of water to lean into, turn, lean into again. His usual movements have been rendered useless, his shower waltz impossible with such a static and upright partner. A "rain head," his mother had called it, but who wants rain inside? There is no place to look but down.

The bathroom before had been perfectly fine. "Serviceable," June had conceded, "but not ideal." The renovation was supposed to be cosmetic. "Nothing major," she breezed. "Just a little accessorizing. What's the word they're using these days? *Zhuzhing?* I am zhuzhing!"

But the promised afternoon of construction had turned into ten days, sending Michael off to mope—and, it seemed, nap—in the far recesses of the house. "None of it could be anticipated," June said. The plastic sheeting came down the day Hannah Portman's sheet was pulled up.

Now that her jewel box of a bath is complete, she wanted her son to witness it. Like the proverbial tree falling in a forest, June requires a listening ear—someone to admire her taste and accept her offerings, as though without him, none of it would exist.

June's life is a revolving door of renovations and shopping sprees. Before the bathroom, her big project had been the formal living room. "What do you think, darling?" she had said, cornering him after dinner one night. She held the paint swatches out in a fan. Farrow & Ball, the logo read, which Stephen knew was the good stuff. ("Ninety dollars a gallon!" Michael exclaimed. "It's paint!")

Stephen considered her outstretched hand. She was asking for so little, yet it sometimes felt like so much. "Gray is gray, Mother."

God forbid she just come out and ask. Stephen holds out a leg to be rinsed, the hair matted down by the water. He sympathizes with his mother for wanting a friend. But at times her inquiries feel invasive. Tell me what you are, that outstretched hand seems to say.

June has surely noticed his lack of interest in dating. He imagines the puzzle of his situation troubles her. The last thing she wants, after all that renovating, is one last closet.

The gifts and paint swatches became litmus tests. He felt her scrutiny, as though his response to a scarf might tell her everything.

Then there are her comments, scattered here and there. "Of course, we'd love our sons no matter what," she might say offhandedly at a dinner party, her eyes lingering on him. Which, strictly speaking, is untrue. Leo risked losing their love whenever he cracked open a beer or tried discussing the war. Leo, in their house, is the equivalent of a gay son in a right-wing family. He is the black sheep, wanting nothing of their artsy show.

What bothers June isn't the prospect of Stephen's being gay; it's that she doesn't know whether he is or isn't. She would never ask. That would be far too vulgar. June lives in a perfumed cloud of associations and hints. She deals in allusions, pleasantries, subtly exchanged looks.

June's parents never talk openly either, shaking ice-cold martinis in the evening, chatting around each other from their club chairs, gazing out at the Rhode Island bay. Happiness for them entails a serene pleasantness, which in turn necessitates gin. Nothing in excess, just a chilled measure to lubricate them through, a piece of thread getting licked so that it might pass through the eye of the needle.

And so it goes with all the Whittakers. Stephen's uncle, Thaddeus William Whittaker, wears madras plaid and Lilly Pulitzer ties, shorts with embroidered lobsters and crabs scuttling across khaki seas. He stands tall, with his Ken-doll hair and too-white teeth, when June throws her arms around him for their annual embrace. "Thad!" she shrieks, kissing his cheek, and from the way they laugh with manufactured warmth, no one would know they only speak once a year.

So June never comes out and asks. She doesn't realize that her unasked questions accumulate in their own closet. And rather than do the mature thing and point this out to her, Stephen toys with her. Because on the days it isn't irritating, it can be amusing.

"It looks pewter," he might say, contemplating the paint swatch while touching his earring. June would nod encouragingly, hopeful for more.

Stephen's romantic life, or lack of it, has become one of those Great Unnamed Things in the Portman household, there but never to be examined. And how they accumulate! The GUTS, Stephen reflects, pleased by the acronym. Those distressing innards, pulsing with life.

The Portmans never allude to June's lack of purpose, what she does with all that free time. They pretend Stephen doesn't attend Saturday service. They leave Aunt Sharon's side of the family unacknowledged, too deep a source of embarrassment. And then there was Grandma Portman.

She was the bridge between the old and new. She came from cabbage and Yiddish, dressed like a peasant. June had tried buying her new cardigans, but Grandma Portman politely declined them.

She reminded them of Michael's true roots, how easily he might have turned out like his unremarkable sister in Delaware. Grandma Portman was troublesome, not in her behavior or because of anything she did, but because her presence served as a reminder of the past, one that Michael had worked so hard to escape. So they stuffed her away at Pine Grove.

His parents preached a life of liberal acceptance. They sought the life they read about in the *New Yorker* and the *Times*, where tolerance and higher education and art are virtues. But they wanted it on their terms. They never anticipated Leo, who had no interest in books or travel, who—unspeakably—had voted for Bush. They never envisioned a son like Stephen, who embraced the religion Michael wanted to forget. So they smiled and pretended such wrinkles didn't exist. Because if they attended enough galas and wrote enough checks and spoke with their elitist friends about their charmed life, they could believe they had achieved it. Michael could convince himself he'd engineered the life he always wanted—that those years spent working and not seeing his family hadn't come at a cost.

Michael and June didn't want to see the emptiness around them. They didn't want to hear the rumblings of those GUTS. They wanted—needed—to think that theirs was the great success story, the modern American family, gorgeously rendered: one son who had attended Yale, the other now engaged. Theirs was a lovely life, artfully lived.

June, meanwhile, lets out her fishing line into the bubbling pools, paint swatches and scarves bobbing like bait. She strings along her gifts, hoping Stephen will bite. Not only because she wishes to know—without wanting to ask—whether he is gay, but because some part of her probably hopes he is. Sitting there on her rock, watching the dark waters rush past, June hopes her fish will come in, wriggling and pink.

A gay son would be the perfect development for her. He could be the longed-for companion she secretly sought. In truth, he goes along with her act not merely because he wishes to toy with her but because it is a relief to be what she wants.

Also she has been on the hunt for a social cause. "The way Sissy goes on about autism!" she fumed. Sissy's nephew had been di-agnosed with it, and Sissy overflowed with statistics on mercury and vaccines. "We're fortunate that he's high functioning," she re-marked. "He's exceptionally gifted, actually."

Catherine was always walking for pink, donning T-shirts and hats. "Just a lumpectomy!" June complained. "She never even had cancer."

His mother wants her own cause. "We could have a coming-out party," she will say. "We'll trim the cocktail napkins in pink!"

"I am interested in neither cock nor tail, Mother," he should tell her. But where would that leave her?

His parents don't want the truth of who he is. A gay son would be more convenient. June could begin planning fund-raisers and benefits. "Well, you know, my son Stephen," she would say into the phone, eyeing her manicure, her hand held out at an angle. She would be so pleased to be dealt that card, a jack of spades. It would give her a full house, a royal flush. A way to trump her friends.

It isn't right of him. He lets the water from the shower berate him. Not only because it is disingenuous to encourage her, but also because he plays the fool. The mocker is never taken seriously when he is most serious.

People look where you tell them not to; they don't focus on what you think they should. He stays mute on the subject of romance, and that is where June circles back in her fluttering way, revisiting the subject with only the most delicate inquiries.

In the parking lot they hadn't bothered replying to his remarks. But he meant them, could only voice his thoughts through sarcasm, because how else was he supposed to say it? It's not like his parents have ever modeled healthy forms of communication.

It's the same with Nora, he realizes as he reaches to turn the water off. The lever is sleek, German—a work of art in his hand.

He hadn't known how to talk with her about Leo. He didn't understand what the two of them shared and was foolish enough to tell her so. That talk had gone disastrously.

It was winter break, soon after she and Leo had started dating. Snow was on the ground, slushy and gray, accumulating at intersections. Nora and Stephen had a few days together at Delancey before Leo came home from Boston and Nora headed to New Jersey for the holidays.

"So how far are you taking this Fred Flintstone fling?" he asked as they walked, arms linked.

"What makes you think it's a fling?" she returned, frowning.

They walked a few paces more, the broad sidewalk empty. They'd had a glorious day together: brunch, followed by a long walk through the city, followed by a bottle of red wine at a bar on Pine that didn't card. Stephen tried to keep his voice light, bringing the buzz back between them from the bar, but he recognized the change in his tone when he said, "Because it should be. He's beneath you, Nora."

She stopped abruptly. Their arms fell apart like a magician's rings.

"Is that how you picture us?" she said sweetly. "Or did you assume he likes to be on top?"

"Nora—"

"Don't," she warned.

So this is it, he thought, standing on the sidewalk. It was the moment they had skirted ever since Leo had entered the scene.

Stephen didn't feel jealous, exactly. It was more that he didn't understand how the two of them clicked. They were two circles on a Venn diagram that were never supposed to overlap.

"You're awful to him," Nora said. "You treat him like he's the village idiot. He makes me *happy*. And isn't that what matters? More than your approval?"

They spent the next day avoiding each other. Nora left the house early to go to the museum. Nora hated museums. Stephen dejectedly headed to the library to do some research on *Hamlet* for a paper. When Leo got home from Boston that night, bounding through the front door, stopping to pet the dog and kiss Nora and slap Stephen on the shoulder, Stephen felt relieved for the circus of activity. He was glad to have the tension break. The three of them went to dinner without a word about it.

It'll pass, Stephen told himself. He figured Leo and Nora wouldn't make it to spring. But then Nora's mom was diagnosed with ovarian cancer. Stephen watched as she started to lean on Leo. And Stephen understood that he had grossly underestimated their relationship.

He tried making it up to her.

"Could one of you guys check on her?" Nora asked over the phone from Milan. It was the following fall. The phone line was filled with background noise—Stephen imagined her at a booth on the street—but the panic in her voice was clear. "I know it's a lot to ask, I just—I need to know that she's okay."

"Of course," Stephen told her. "Of course, Nora."

Leo could change a tire or plunge a toilet, but he blanched at the thought of seeing Nora's mom. "I wouldn't know what to say," he stammered. "I'll go," Stephen offered. He didn't seek points for it. He didn't say, "You owe me," the way Leo would have.

He drove out to New Jersey in his parents' sedan. It amazed him how a small state like that, a pinkie toe, could contain so much—the sprawling lawns of Princeton; the ghettos of Newark. There were lovely suburbs on the way to Nora's house, but the green soon gave way to gray. He passed strip malls, shopping centers. Union was a wasteland.

He knocked on the door with its white metal frame. A tear in the screen, and the top step was loose. Nora's mom yanked open the door and stood in her bathrobe, appraising him. "Not the one I expected," she said, turning so he could follow her.

They crept up the carpeted stairs. Nora's dad was watching golf on TV. "Other room," she said. He nodded and clicked off the set, heading past them down the hall. A minute later, Stephen heard the muted *Ahhh*s of the golf crowd, their strange stage whisper.

"So," she said. "Get you anything? Soda? Coffee?" She pronounced *coffee* as if it had a *w*. *Cawfee*.

"No, thank you, Mrs. Reed. I just—"

"Iris. Please." She gestured for him to sit on the couch while she took the recliner. "An easy visitor. My favorite kind." She tossed him a smile.

Stephen glanced around the room. The television set, an old model with wood paneling, sat beside a glass-tower stereo system with a record player, trinkets displayed on top: framed pictures, snow globes, souvenirs. If only June could see.

"So you're here to get the report, huh?" Iris nodded from the chair. Her robe was secured over flannel pajamas. She wore big, fluffy slippers in the shape of cats.

"Nora's worried about you. She can't help it. Leo says one day we'll be able to do phone calls with video feed—" Stephen stopped himself. He was babbling. Nora's mom seemed to be taking him in, watching how this Yale kid, this alleged best friend, was doing. He took a breath, steadied himself. "It's hard for her, being away. I think it makes her feel better to have a friend come see you."

"To make sure I'm not croaking and not telling her about it. Which, let's face it, I would do." Iris reached over to the side table and drew forth a glass filled with breadsticks. "It helps," she said, encouraging him.

With what? he thought, mystified, taking one. The nausea? Or did she mean that it helped in such moments to have a prop? Something to point with, something to munch on? Something to break the awful silence?

"What's there to say?" She shrugged and snapped her breadstick in half. "The radiation is like punching in at a job. You go, you sit, you leave. There's nothing to tell, really."

"They weren't supposed to do radiation," Nora had said on the phone. "I'm worried it means she's worse."

"Scars, sure. Different machines, different side effects. But otherwise it's the same. I tried telling Nora, it's just to shrink the tumor. Then they'll go back to the chemo again. I'll tell you, though, the change is refreshing. Just to be doing something different."

Iris munched on her breadstick and nodded as though discussing current events. "They're the generals, you know. The docs give you the plan. Your job is to show up. You try not to complain too much. If you complain, it affects things. They think you can't take it. The radiation is just a different weapon. Same war, different weapon."

Stephen had the sensation of having wandered into a stranger's house, of having to kill time until someone would fetch him. As though he were a boy, and at any minute the sound of his mother's heels would signal that he could leave.

He sat up straighter. He had to do better than this for Nora. "I imagine it does feel like battle. Your body's waging a war against an invader. How strange that when the doctors look at you, you're the patient but also the enemy."

Iris regarded him. She inclined the breadstick toward him, a pointer. "I see why she raves about you. And, you know, those damn doctors, they do exactly that."

He ended up staying for two hours. Some thin line of comfort established itself, then grew. Iris had things she wanted to say. Not so much for Nora's sake, but perhaps for her own. She was like a stand-up comic with months' worth of saved material. "There's this one nurse," she said, squinting, "with these damn fingernails. They curl! I'm not kidding. The nails curl on themselves! How can that be legal?"

It wasn't that she wanted a laugh. She just wanted someone who would listen without pitying her, without bringing the burden of their nerves into her living room. The breadsticks, he realized, had helped.

By the second hour, she let him get up to make coffee. "I think you mean *coffee*," he teased. "Oh ho, Mr. Classy over here," she said. When he poked his head out of the kitchen, she was smiling.

International Suisse Mocha, read the rectangular tin. The fragrance of cinnamon wafted up to his nose. Maybe she had bought it imagining Nora in Milan. Maybe that was as close to Europe as she could get.

Iris was the sort of woman who bought her pantyhose at the drugstore, the same place she probably picked up the coffee and the breadsticks. Her handbag, on the kitchen table, was old and faded, a patchwork of leather, and it probably held everything from an umbrella to Band-Aids, anything a person might need. Iris was grounded, no-nonsense. She was the opposite of his mother. She was, in short, a real mother.

When Stephen brought out the coffee, Iris had nodded off in her chair, her head turned to the side. He set the mugs down and walked over to the pictures on top of the stereo. There were no family shots of the three of them. No professional portraits in black and white that looked staged, even the dog regal.

Instead, there was Nora. Nora with her high school friends. Nora at prom. Nora onstage, a playbill from one of her shows.

You didn't marry for you, Stephen thought to himself. You didn't marry for money or romance. You married because it was what you were supposed to do. Then Nora came along and made it worthwhile.

When he leaned down to turn off the light by her chair before leaving, her hand flew up and trapped his wrist. He couldn't see her expression. It was evening by then, the room dim. "Tell her I looked good," she said. "Tell her I made the coffee."

"Of course," Stephen said uncertainly. "Of course, Iris. I will."

Stephen had done exactly that. He called Nora in Milan the next morning and assured her that her mom seemed well. "Two hours!" Nora mused. "She must have really liked you. Did she give you the fancy coffee?"

Stephen steps out of the shower onto the white bath mat, its velvety surface plush. He has often thought since then that maybe Nora was enamored not with Leo but with Delancey, the fairy tale of the place. There were no ripped screen doors or loose brick steps. "I can't believe you *live* here," she'd murmured when she first visited. When Leo came down the stairs that day, maybe he carried some of Delancey's glow with him. Maybe in the light from the skylight above, the frog appeared to be a prince.

Then there was Leo himself. Unassuming Leo, with his blueprints for a settled, suburban life, felt perhaps like a remedy to Nora. Maybe he answered her hope, her restless hope, for normalcy. Be careful what you wish for, he should tell her. It gets granted in middle age.

Nora didn't see the GUTS of the place. She didn't see all that got swept aside by the Portmans—all they ignored and avoided. But maybe she didn't need to. Maybe our choices are too complicated to dissect. We choose without knowing why. We choose because, we choose despite. The heart does not make it easy.

"I regret nothing," Grandma Portman had told him. "Not a thing! Because of you, *bubeleh*."

When he confronted Nora that day on the sidewalk, some part of him knew it was a losing battle. What was he expecting? He couldn't convince her to dump Leo. He couldn't sink his hooks into her and drag her back to their old friendship. Life didn't work that way. He could be the best friend in the world, driving out to New Jersey to sit with her sick mom, but it was Leo she would lean on. She made her choice.

And so Stephen receded. His grandmother became a substitute for his best friend. Because—and it strikes him now as so naïve—he had thought she was the one person who wasn't going anywhere.

After all this time—he'll be thirty soon, Grandma Portman had reminded him—life and death still come as a shock.

Nora doesn't want to know the truth about her fairy tale. And maybe she'll find happiness. Who is he to say? Maybe contentment will be waiting for her at the end. Stephen has been convinced that Leo is trying to trap her, but isn't he doing the same? Fantasizing about escaping with her to the city when she has plans of her own?

The lines of an old nursery rhyme come to him. *Peter, Peter pumpkin eater, / Had a wife and couldn't keep her.*

He tries to recall the rest of it. He pauses before the mirror, white with steam. "The chandelier makes all the difference," he will tell his mother. "The heated towels are superb."

He remembers the lines as he reaches for the door. *He put her in a pumpkin shell, / And there he kept her very well.*

Ten

N ora waits for the elevator, pressing the button with one hand while checking her phone with the other. She knows the phone will tell her nothing new when she flips it open. *W e l c o m e,* the Sony Ericsson starts to scroll. Nora shuts it when she sees no envelope blinking for new voice mail.

She once read something about the importance of control, even if it is an illusion. People waiting for an elevator need a button to push. There could be no voice mail—the phone would have sounded in her palm—but checking gives her something to do. She glances at the elevator button, a harvest moon, and remembers how her mother used to jab for extra morphine in her sleep, requiring comfort even in her dreams.

The elevator chimes a bright, shrill D. Nora wonders how people would react if it were suddenly switched for a lower octave, a butler with reproachful eyes. The steel doors part.

A man with side-swept hair holds open a copy of the *Times.* "Kerry Takes Lead in Ohio," the front page announces above the fold. John Kerry flashes his horsey smile beside an article about

E. coli outbreaks. He is trying to look casual in a denim button-down, the sky vast and blue behind him. A beer in his hand, still in the bottle. Bet he turned down the burgers, though.

"He's too soft," Leo had complained last Sunday at brunch. "Soft?" Michael had repeated pleasantly, his eyes narrowing. Leo shrugged, not wanting to pursue it. "This election has everyone's panties in a twist," he muttered that night, squeezing toothpaste onto his brush. He never bothered capping the tube, so a dried blob formed at its mouth. The toothpaste came out reluctantly, after a great exertion of pressure.

"People get too heated about politics," he continued. "All this talk of moving to Canada if Bush wins." He shook his head and turned to Nora. "You don't think Stephen's serious, do you?"

"I think you should've told your dad what you think." Leo had a point, after all; Kerry looked like a strong wind might knock him over. Michael, however, was too filled with policy to notice. "Kerry has to win," he said grimly, shaking his head at the television. "He *has* to." Nora smiled sadly at his conviction. "Why?" she wanted to ask. "Because you and your friends think he should?"

It's terrible, the first shrink had noted, his long academic fingers steepled, when the narrative doesn't unfold as we expect. This was his way of alluding to her mother's death, through language tidy and convenient. She had looked away angrily.

The doors open to the lobby. Miguel mans his post at the front desk and his face lights up upon seeing her. "You have the big party tonight," he says warmly. The side-swept *Times* reader hurries past, too important to say hi to the doorman.

"I do," she affirms, touched that he has remembered. Miguel attends night school at Drexel, an MBA program; his wife is studying to be a nurse. He sets down a picture of her and their newborn son at the start of his shift, clearing space for them on the cluttered desk.

"You want me to call a cab for you? Bad weather today."

"No, that's okay. It's a short walk." She holds up a foot to show him her practical shoe choice and thinks of the joke that Leo would make: "Flip-flops! Of course!" He was disappointed in Bush but could not abide Kerry.

"Take an umbrella, at least." Miguel gestures to the stand.

A gem, Miguel, not that anyone in the building would notice. The complex is filled with obnoxious twentysomethings, their laughter echoing through the hallways at 2:00 a.m. on weekends. The place had felt so grown-up when she and Leo moved in. Nora had been impressed by its industrial feel, the exposed pipes and soaring windows suggesting a life pulled from a magazine. But she has started to feel exhausted by the girls in elevators wearing too much perfume, the guys, behind them, scoping out their legs. No cute elderly couples loiter the halls; no families return from the store with groceries.

Nora thinks of Miguel's wife in her nursing scrubs in their apartment, the baby playing on a quilt. She thinks of Miguel hurrying to make it home before bedtime. She imagines him putting the key in the door, eager to see his family.

Leo, apparently, is in no such rush—Leo, who was supposed to call after his trip to the printer's and pick her up to avoid precisely the concerns Miguel has so gallantly mentioned. 2400 Locust to 2035 Delancey. It is nothing, a nondistance. Around the corner, really. Unless the skies are darkening and you're wearing a white dress. Unless you had hoped to arrive at the party looking perfect.

It's fine. Really, it's fine. This is what Nora will say to Leo in a breezy, high voice, because that will have more of an effect on him than a hundred angry voice mails ("Where are you? You were supposed to call!"), which he would find a way to dismiss.

Instead she will stroll through Delancey's double doors and switch into her heels, leaning against the wainscoting. "No big deal," she will say, an uncomplaining trouper like Miguel.

The building's automated doors swing open. The air outside is a strange, humid mix, cool but thick. Nora's nose reacts to the mugginess, her sinuses contracting.

Locust has a small hill, which Nora ascends toward Center City. She spots the bright blue mailbox on the corner and cringes, remembering the undeposited check sitting on the kitchen counter. The lawyer's accompanying letter informed her that it would be the last one.

She hasn't looked at the amounts closely or tabulated if the sum matches the number that had been read from the will. Surely, she should verify it. Her mom would be scandalized that she hasn't. But Nora can't bring herself to do it. The checks have appeared over the months in absurdly varying amounts: $12.87; $26,423.29. She imagines a group of lawyers standing guard, pulling a lever and letting the pennies pour forth. Life insurance, she thinks. An awful term, because what does it insure?

Death money. They should call a thing what it is. Nora turns right on to Twenty-third. She knows that even if the amounts don't match, she wouldn't do anything about it. It could be short by hundreds, even thousands, and she would let it go.

At the lawyer's office, her father had been cowed, for once. He cleared his throat, convinced an error had been made. "She listed me as her beneficiary," he said. "Didn't she?" Nora had almost felt sorry for him. But he wouldn't learn his lesson or think about his wife's final rebuke. The money only made him resent Nora more. The lawyer shifted and answered stiffly, a long-winded explanation to avoid having to say, "No. No, she didn't."

If she hadn't died, proceedings of a different nature might have occurred at that law office. "Based on what?" Leo would ask skeptically. *Divorce* is a dirty word to him. But he doesn't understand that miserable parents who stay together could be more toxic than parents who separate. "You only think that because yours never did," he would point out.

Leo idealizes her suburban upbringing. "Look at this place!" he whistled when she first brought him over, trudging down to the basement. He surveyed the old Ping-Pong table and shag carpeting, the beat-up couch and outdated decor. "Just so we're clear, you actually *like* all this?" she asked. "Like?" he repeated. "Nora, I love it! This is exactly how a house should be!"

He threw himself onto the couch, and a cloud of dust arose from its cushions, showering him like confetti at a parade. "We never had anything like this. Even when we moved." She pictured him at fifteen, excited to leave Manhattan, imagining a house (finally, a house!), only to be greeted with austere Delancey. "There was never a place where you could put your feet up and relax, you know?" "Yeah, but, Leo," she wanted to tell him. "That's just furniture." How nice to have problems that could be solved by an ottoman.

A pregnant woman approaches, pushing a stroller, her head tucked into her phone. A child born every minute somewhere. And how casually it is all treated! How nonchalant, the sci-fi act of pregnancy. The woman's belly balloons out from an orange maternity shirt, the fabric snug, the outline of her navel just visible, circular and deep as a hot tub. Leo would ogle the woman if he were here and nudge Nora unsubtly. *Look, look!* As though other people's babies might be theirs. As though they are already a family.

A blinking red hand alerts her to stop. Nora pauses at the corner of Twenty-second and Spruce, not wanting to rush through the intersection. June would never show up sweaty or be seen in flip-flops.

But then, June was one of those women whose feet seemed to have permanently adjusted to the shape of a heel. She traversed the city in them, strolling with Dedalus through Rittenhouse Square, his leather leash swinging jauntily. When someone stopped to admire how well trained he was on the leash, June didn't explain that he had just been jogged along Museum Mile by the dog-walker. Dedalus swayed his golden tail, too tired to even lift his leg.

"It's the quality of the heel," June would say, dubiously eyeing the Payless espadrilles Nora had purchased for the party. BOGO, the signs advertised. What's the difference? Nora thought, lifting one from the shelf while women swarmed around her with their shopping bags. Could anyone even tell?

June wears Manolos and Louboutins, Stuart Weitzmans and Jimmy Choos, rows of them in tasteful colors arranged on open shelves, an array of calfskin, crocodile, satin, suede. When June and Michael were away, Nora slipped them on. Teetering across the plush carpet, she felt the same pinches and aches.

The light flickers, a blinking man. Go go go.

There is no secret. Nora knows this now. For so long, she'd believed she simply had to master a set of rules. Invest in good footwear. Sit straight in chairs. Reapply lipstick throughout the day. But testing out those constricting slingbacks and riffling through June's vanity, Nora saw that no magic was behind it all, no sleight of hand or trick. June's perfumed deodorant didn't cause Nora to sweat any less. Slipping on a Chanel blouse, she didn't feel transformed. No, she thought, carefully putting the items back on their hangers and in their compartmentalized drawers. It wasn't like in the movies, where the downtrodden Jersey girl just needs access to wardrobe and makeup to become Cinderella. Princesses don't come from Paramus. They are born, not made.

She spots Audrey Claire with its chalky-green shutters ahead. Stephen's favorite restaurant. "Don't let her frighten you," he once counseled, looking at her from across the table. "You probably intimidate *her*." Nora smiles at the thought of her friend's words. But she suspects this is the consolation of the rich to the poor, the beautiful to the ugly. Such advice only goes in one direction.

The jazz café on Manning sits down the street and to the left. She is glad she took Spruce, unconsciously avoiding it. Her palms grow clammy at the thought of her gig tomorrow, a tickle creeping into her throat. "You can't possibly be nervous!" Leopold would tease, holding up her hand as evidence. "You perform there every week!"

But that's just it. The regularity of the gig unnerves her. She worries that one of her students will show up and then see her as a two-bit performer. She has a small following now, regulars who come on Saturdays to hear her, mostly retired couples. They ask in encouraging tones if she's ever thought about putting out a CD, not realizing that their questions depress rather than flatter her.

Choir is different. Everyone at the church knows her through Carol, a longtime member, and from her first rehearsal, Nora was treated like family. They know better than to pry, to ask if she misses opera. Other performers understand that such questions aren't simple.

If she's found solidarity at choir, losing herself to the group, she's found tranquillity in jazz and its wandering riffs. Opera had required her to transform, each performance a metamorphosis. Jazz isn't like that. She doesn't have to commandeer the stage, taking the reins of an aria to drive it home, translating the language through her gestures. Jazz is cruise control, singing with her eyes closed. No need to act. *The very thought of you / And I forget to do / The little ordinary things / That everyone ought to do.*

"Of course you want to do it in B-flat," the drummer will groan at rehearsal tomorrow. He keeps hoping for a solo, something peppy. But the upright-bass player, who is older, will smile to reassure her. "B-flat it is," he'll say, tuning his strings.

Nora turns right and passes a group of men on a stoop. Beautiful town houses line Spruce, but Philly is Philly, and she prays the men don't call out to her. There are three of them, old black men, one holding a brown paper bag, and they erupt into laughter, a flash of gold teeth. One spits a jet of juice that arcs from his mouth. She resists the urge to touch her hair, check her pins.

She turns the corner unnoticed, relieved. She wonders about the brown bag, why they bother. It's more of a tell than a disguise.

Carol would scowl at the men if she were with Nora. "Old men *drinkin'* in de afternoon!" she would say, loud enough for them to hear. "People be walking by with dey *chil*dren! People be walking by on dey way to *church!*" The accent in Carol's schoolmarm voice of island reproach would heighten with her disdain. "In Trinidad," she would continue, yanking her garments around her with a huff, "men did not sit around *drin*kin'."

Approaching Delancey, Nora wonders if June has ever heard her housekeeper on one of her tirades. Carol slips into a nearly unintelligible stream of gossip when on the phone with her aunts and sisters, punctuated by spurts of laughter. Around June, Carol switches into perfect English, suddenly accentless.

"Yes, of course," she says, polite, agreeable.

But then, this street might just do that to you. Nora knows she has an irrational love of this block, but she feels it every time she turns the corner: Delancey Place, with its brick and cobblestones, its town houses erect and tall, the arched entrances like horseshoes. Those men wouldn't have sat on any of these stoops, pristine and maroon. Delancey is a block away from bums sprawled on benches, but that block makes all the difference.

Above her there are gabled windows. Her favorite, across the street, has an expanse of gridded panes set at an angle—windows that can be propped open to let in the air. She imagines a space with exposed beams and knotted-pine floors, the sort of place where she can picture Stephen clacking away at his beloved typewriter. *16 June 2004*, he would type, the machine dinging brightly at the end of the line.

Nora comes to a stop at the familiar black double doors and hops up the stairs. She roots in her bag for the key.

The foyer is quiet. Nora pauses before the hall mirror, tilting her head to check that the pins are in place. The study, where the party will be, fills with light in the evening. Leo's eyes will dart toward her hair uneasily and then look away. Daylight is always the worst.

She sets her bag down and reaches to switch her shoes, but no one is there to express concern. No one to exclaim, "You walked? I thought Leo was picking you up!"

She gazes around the empty foyer.

"Stay busy," the cognitive therapist had advised. She was a perky redhead with an assured mouth, her office walls lined with modern prints. Two Eames chairs sat across from her glass desk. "If you know the behavior tends to occur when you're alone, then don't give it the opportunity."

Nora liked the personification of her disorder. She imagined a greedy banker who couldn't be sated, wanting more and more. She imagined a villain with a top hat, tying her to the railroad tracks.

"Identify your stressors," the woman continued. "Identifying them is half the battle." She talked about cognitive techniques they might employ, thought records and habit-reversal training. Nora watched her as she spoke, impressed by her authoritative voice and confident demeanor.

"Have you ever treated someone with trichotillomania before?" she asked.

The woman shifted in her chair. "I've treated many compulsive behavioral issues. We treat them all essentially the same way."

Cognitively, Nora had thought, tasting the word in her mouth like a bright penny.

Nora suspects that she has become a broken record to Leo and his family, stalled and skipping. They ignore her. As long as she shows up when she is supposed to and follows the general script (Sunday brunch, the occasional dinner), they don't mind that she is distracted. *You'll never know / How slow the moments go.*

The Portman meals, predictable and polite, she can handle. Any breaks from routine are harder. She can't stare out windows with strangers or depend on them to make small talk. Strangers don't know the placement of the mines. "Engaged!" they will exclaim. "Your parents must be thrilled."

Upstairs, June is likely assembling battle teams. She'd probably roped Leo into some task before he could call Nora. "Help me with this one thing," June would have simpered, and Leo would have set down his phone and wallet obligingly.

No. It is better that no one had been in the foyer. She won't give Leo a hard time for forgetting to call, nor will she play the martyr. It was a simple lapse, and poor Leo didn't mean to forget. "There you are!" June will say sharply when she spots Nora, as though she is late. "Hey," Leo will say, nodding and wiping sweat from his brow, a cardboard box filled with flowers heavy in his thick arms.

Today isn't about her. She needs to remember this, to relegate her anxiety to a compartment in her mind. Today she must play the future daughter-in-law, unruffled and at ease. "How are you holding up?" Stephen had asked in the parking lot, and it had come as a relief. Because even if you don't know the answer, Nora thinks, leaving the foyer, it is nice to be asked.

Eleven

Everything good down here?" Leo ducks into the kitchen, where the warm air hits him like a wall. The staff look up like startled penguins in their bow ties and vests. They regard him uncertainly, but Leo knows his next move. "Any chance," he ventures, "of a pre-event beer?"

The guy directly across from him, in the midst of filling clear shot glasses with soup, relaxes. "Yeah, man. Bottles just got unloaded." He gestures with his chin.

Leo ambles over to the tub filled with ice and selects a Flying Fish IPA. He holds the red-labeled bottle an inch above the counter, judges the angle, and then brings his other fist slamming down.

"Jesus," a girl to his left cries, jumping.

Leo smiles as the metal cap spins across the white marble.

"That doesn't hurt the counter?" She stares at the spot where the bottle made contact.

"Not if you do it right."

Condensation drips from the bottle, but he knows better than to ask for a towel. Stephen would ask for a towel. Stephen would ask for a glass, pouring it daintily while the staff looked on and smirked. "Leo," he says to the girl, nodding at the others.

College was good for exactly two things. One was that being an RA had taught him how to do this, how to enter a room and put everyone at ease.

"Sam," she offers. "Well, you know. *Samantha.*" She says this with a grimace, as though nothing could be worse than the feminine name foisted on her by her parents. Try Leopold, he thinks.

Boston University's other gift was that in such moments, he remembers he is a Pike. Once a Pike, always a Pike. "A brotherhood of gentlemen," Stephen had read from the brochure. "Does that pertain to the bikini contest?" But Leo carries it with him like a security blanket, that feeling of belonging. Brotherhood, he wants to tell his brother, is the best feeling in the world.

"Clay," the guy across from him says, doling out the soup. It pours out of a metal dispenser, the opening controlled by a lever under his thumb. From where Leo stands, the shot glasses look uncannily even.

Samantha is around nineteen or twenty. Still in school by the look of her, in that world of summer jobs and evolving majors. She has a silver rod shooting through her eyebrow and a black hoop between her nostrils that gives her the appearance of a bull.

Clay looks a little older, twenty-three maybe, a sleeve of tattoos on his left arm. He wears the tortoiseshell glasses that have been popping up everywhere. A guy at the far end of the kitchen assiduously chops herbs, looking up from his work only when the back door smacks open.

"Whew!" The caterer bustles in, heaving a crate of glassware onto the island and wiping her forehead with her sleeve. "You get the rest," she says to the herb chopper. "Truck's open."

Her eyes adjust to the inside light and come to rest on Leo. "Man of the house," she remarks with a smile. She remembers. It is his recurring duty, sent to the bowels of the kitchen on this day every year to check on the troops.

"Good to see you." Leo holds up his beer in salute.

"You're allowed, I suppose," she teases, her eyes twinkling at the sight of the bottle. She has a long, thick braid draped over one shoulder and wears chef's whites. Her eye makeup is smudged from the heat, but it lends her a sultry look, tendrils of brown hair framing her face. A nice smile in those turquoise eyes. Leo takes a pull from his beer. The icy cold of it runs down his throat.

The caterer turns to check on the progress in the kitchen, surveying the platters and trays. "Don't forget the garnish, now," she reminds Clay, and Leo can tell from his nod that he is not bothered by this, that they have a smooth rapport. Her hips sway as she traverses the length of the kitchen, patting Sam's shoulder, counting in midair, her fingers ticking pots, pans, glassware, platters. Her eyes skim past Leo as she turns, but not without shooting him a quick wink.

This is what you should see, he wants to tell Nora. The woman has a thick waist, her white, buttoned top an undulating hill of curves, but her easy confidence gets him, moves him. "It's not about being skinny," he always insists to Nora. "It's not about wearing the right outfit." "Then what's it about?" she asks, confused. But he can never bring himself to say it. Because what could be worse than telling an insecure girl she needs confidence?

They say older women have more of it. Leo remembers feeling the same spark last year, watching the caterer command the kitchen. She was playing music, and "One Love" drifted through the room. "Let's get together and feel all right," she crooned, her hands in the air, and Leo thought, That! That's it! That delicious moment when a woman loses self-awareness, sheds it like a second skin, and you are left with the tender heart of her.

The first time he had seen Nora perform was at that snooty Yale thing, Stephen sitting with his long legs crossed like a girl's. When Nora took the stage, Leo felt a swell of nerves, his heart pounding for her. But something happened when she opened her mouth, a sort of alchemy. She became a vessel, the sound pouring out of her. She was extraordinary at that moment, radiant, the audience in her palm. Her voice was a winged creature, fluttering, exotic. It soared, a bird, and held its flight.

"Bravo!" There were roars at curtain call, all for her, her green eyes blazing. "Bravo, bravo!" People actually called this out, even the undergrads. Nora stood onstage, the flowers raining at her feet.

After, in the lobby, Stephen was filled with his pretentious chatter, *legato*, *vibrato*, bouncing with excitement as if he were her manager. But it was Leo's eyes she sought, a question in her gaze. You saw?

He smiled, surprised that she needed to hear it. "You were amazing," he told her.

"How're we doing on the liver?" the caterer asks, peering over Clay's elbow.

"I was about to check it," he replies, wiping the edge of the platter.

"How I'm supposed to make liver 'less gamy, more modern.'" The caterer's index fingers carve out air quotes. "If you don't want liver, then don't serve liver!"

Leo recognizes his mother's words in this, can hear her orders, prim and directive. His mom was accustomed to getting her way, the world bending to her whims. But really, he wants to tell the caterer, it's about the feeling you give her—the sense that you are on her side. Every year, he assures her he will check on the staff, but all he ever does is sneak a beer.

In truth, his mom will forget what she said once the party begins. The lists, the menus, the precise instructions—they will all go out the window. All she wants is for the party to be a hit. She doesn't understand that she could best ensure this by letting go, relaxing her grip on the reins. She forgot that the point was to attend to her guests rather than stoke her own need for compliments. Each year she wanted more, a junkie needing a hit.

"If you think the liver doesn't work, nix it," Leo suggests. "Seriously. She'll only notice if it's bad."

The caterer considers this. "Stick around and taste a couple of things," she instructs. Her clear eyes meet his. She turns to the stove and Leo can feel her awareness of him, knowing that his eyes will linger on her. Men are idiots, he thinks, a vague stirring in his groin. He remembers Helen and her climbing vines. We are fools.

"You're whipped," Dave has told him at work. "You get that, right?"

Dave's remarks started when he caught Leo looking at rings online. "No," Dave groaned. "No, no, no." In the world according to Dave, men settled down in their late thirties at the earliest. Anything sooner was a crime. "You watch," Dave told him. "You give her that ring, you'll be getting less action than ever."

"Better than none, *dude*," Leo retorted, and guys in neighboring cubicles laughed. Leo isn't bothered by his friend. He feels sorry for him. Because one day, at Nora and Leo's wedding, Dave will feel a shadow of doubt pass over his convictions. He will wonder about the stream of girls making him feel more lonely, not less.

Dave doesn't know what it's like. Neither does Stephen. They are islands of loneliness, adrift at sea. And it isn't about sex. It's about that feeling of being with someone, joined. When he and Nora are talking about nothing at all—small things, inconsequential things—Leo feels a happiness that pierces through to his core.

The caterer hands him a Chinese soup spoon, a white porcelain boat filled with a heap of greens and cheese. "Gorgonzola salad," she says as Leo stuffs it in his mouth. It hits him like a punch: peppery greens and bracing cheese with something wet and pungent in his nose. "Mustard vinaigrette," she adds as a sheen of sweat breaks across his forehead. A bite of pear waits at the bottom, sweet and clean, and Leo clings to it like a raft, feeling a wash of gratitude for its presence.

He chews, swallows, the mix of flavors lingering on his tongue: spicy, cool, sweet. "A revelation," he says, conjuring the word, surprising himself. The caterer beams. "Really, that pear—" But she has already turned, satisfied, moving on to the herb chopper.

Leo looks into the bowl of the empty white spoon.

"That's awesome," Dave acknowledged when Leo recounted the story of the proposal. Dave said it grudgingly but with a show of goodwill, slapping Leo's shoulder and doing the half embrace of men.

Leo had adjusted the story slightly for his audience, the group of guys at work. He cut to the moment of collapsing down on his knee, skipping the part about how Nora had been so moody that morning that he'd nearly aborted the plan. He had taken her to the corner of Seventeenth and Walnut, not knowing if she would remember. It was the place where she had turned to him during that first summer together and said, "Don't you think this is how things should always be?" He had stopped and gazed at her because she had echoed his sentiments exactly. "Remember this corner," he had murmured into her ear, thinking that one day he would propose.

Pedestrians pointed. It was an early-springtime scene, and Leo knew the guys would get this, the pressure of a crowd. He knew that they would appreciate that, for a moment, he had made the city pause.

"She stood there forever," he said, shaking his head, and the guys chuckled. "I mean, seriously. *Forever.*" And they laughed appreciatively. But then she nodded and smiled, he told them, and he slipped the ring onto her finger, and she was hugging him, the crowd clapping. "And what'd you do after?" Nick, a programmer, asked. "Well, we were *supposed* to go to dinner," Leo replied with a grin.

It was mostly true, especially the part about her standing there, taking her sweet time. The sidewalk was cold and hard, and Leo had resisted the urge to shift his weight.

She had not smiled.

He held the velvet box up to her, and the speech he'd rehearsed sailed right out of his brain. "I know it's been a rough year," he started, trying to keep the box from shaking. Nora waited politely. He felt the pebbles of the sidewalk in the joint of his knee. "A rough year," he repeated, his mouth dry, a cardboard cave. "But, Nora, will you marry me?"

A look of incredulity passed across her features. He saw her call it back, the decision to not be exasperated. Her features reassembled, and then she gulped, swallowing something. Doubts? Grief? Annoyance? What emotion had Nora choked down? She finally nodded, more to herself than to him. Okay, she seemed to say to herself. Okay.

"I should be getting back," he calls out to the caterer.

"Oh, one more." Her voice is playful. Samantha glances at him from where she is arranging piles of cocktail napkins in fanned stacks.

"Do you want to call anyone?" he asked when they got back to the apartment, adrenaline still pumping through his system. He wanted to call his parents right away, his brother, his friends. He wanted to broadcast the news to the world. "I mean, we have dinner reservations at the Striped Bass, but it's okay if we're late."

"Oh." She pulled off her scarf. She regarded the phone on the counter between them. "Oh, I don't know."

He ended up making calls from the bedroom while she lay on the couch, staring up at the ceiling. He tried coaxing her out to dinner, convinced that a glass of champagne would make her pliant, relaxed. "I was so nervous," he would confess, the Striped Bass quiet and hushed, and she would finally smile. "I had a whole speech prepared and everything." They would laugh about it, and he would be able to tell her what he meant to say. He would remind her about that corner. Her eyes would mist over, remembering. And just like that they would be returned to that place between them where everything felt okay.

But Nora seemed so tired. She ended up falling asleep on the couch. He tucked a blanket around her and watched her face. "I got the ring when your mom was alive," he wanted to tell her. "But then she took that turn, and I just—I didn't know what to do." The velvet box sat stuffed away in his basketball sneaker in the hall closet, burning a hole there. How long were you supposed to wait after your girlfriend's mom died? It wasn't a question the "Four C's of Diamonds" had answered.

"This one's the toughie," the caterer says, sidling up to him. She holds out a slice of toasted baguette on a napkin. *Re-Joyce!* the napkin says in bright green. Portman Green. Leo's fingers graze hers as he accepts it.

"Fried liver with caramelized onions," she announces. "With panko and smoked bacon."

Leo crunches into the baguette. The liver's bitterness hits him, heavy and thick.

"I was so worried you'd find it," he'd wanted to tell Nora. How many times had he imagined her cleaning out the hall closet, the velvet box tumbling out of his sneaker? He imagined her opening it, leaning back against the wall, gazing at the diamond he had picked out just for her.

But he was fantasizing, he knows now. Nora hadn't cleaned the apartment for months. She wouldn't have been going through the hall closet. He could have kept a monkey in there without her noticing. Leo had finally hired a cleaning lady. When he mentioned it at the hospital, hoping it would be one less thing for her to worry about, it barely registered. No questions about where he'd found the service. No "How do we know she won't use the same rag to clean the toilets as the kitchen?" Just a nod, as though she had barely heard him. Leo felt as if he were trying to talk to her underwater.

The bacon and liver comingle on his tongue. He should have known then. Right then. Should have known that, no, the ring hadn't been discovered. That, no, when he walked with her on Walnut that day, took her to what was to him their street, their corner, their spot, she wasn't secretly hoping he was about to propose. That, no, he couldn't make her forget.

He is aware of the caterer's eyes on him, Sam's and Clay's, too. Aware that even the herb chopper has paused in his steady chopping of herbs. He chews, the liver and onions and bacon a greasy tangle, and suddenly he feels queasy, the heat of the room pressing on him.

The turquoise eyes regard his face. "It needs something," he finally manages. "It needs—"

"Balance," she says. "Yes. It's too one-note, too heavy." And watching her nod to herself, Leo thinks that sometimes you need someone to say out loud what you already know.

The air is instantly cooler outside the kitchen, the temperature noticeably different in the living room.

He sits on the tufted ottoman, breathes. There was no magic thing he could have said. He knows this now. That part about it being a tough year—it had come out all wrong. But his words, even if they'd been perfect, could not have fixed things.

He had looked up her disorder online after she showed him the spot. He stayed up half the night researching it. For the next few days he went to websites looking for something, anything, that might help: treatment options, what to say, what tone to take. But after his dozenth chat-room visit masquerading as a sufferer *(pullerinphilly)*, where he read about women who pulled out their eyelashes, pulled out their armpit hair, pulled it out and *ate it*, he understood that he was out of his depth. He was on the outside of something, in the dark. And just as he was to not mention her mother, he was not to mention this.

He proposed anyway.

He doesn't know if the spot is bigger, smaller. Whenever he tries discreetly to look, it is hidden, carefully concealed. Nora's eyes dart up, catching him in the act. He feels strangely guilty in such moments, as though trying to catch sight of a naked girl, and Nora looks away, dismayed.

He squeezes her hand, not knowing if he should say anything. "I can't even see it!" he sometimes wants to bellow. The monster that has consumed Nora, causing her to spend so much time intricately arranging her hair and checking her reflection in mirrors—it isn't even perceptible. Would she believe him if he told her? Would it offend her to know her spot loomed large only in her mind?

He isn't sure. So he squeezes her hand and says nothing, swallowing his words out of love.

Twelve

I was just sitting down for the first time all day," Stephen protests. "I mean, here I am, about to get some quality time with my
brother—"

Leo snorts beside him.

"—and now I'm supposed to get up and perform manual labor?"

"It'll take five minutes," June says coolly.

Stephen sighs. "The very first time *all day.*" He gazes up at his
mother and gives her his most delicate look. I am your fine-boned
son, his eyes say.

"I already tried getting the caterer to do it," June admits. "But
apparently they can't, for liability reasons. Like hanging a banner is
so much to ask!"

"They have their hands full down there," Leo interjects. "Relax,
Mom. We'll take care of it."

"Just be sure not to crease it," she sings on her way out of the
room. A manicured hand rests on the doorjamb. "And put the ladder back in its place when you're done."

The banner lays across the sectional, held down at its corners
with books.

"I'm the one who brought it home," Leo mutters beside him. "I haven't creased it yet."

"You went and got it?"

They are in the den just off the study. The media room, June likes to say, because it has a soundproof door and blackout shades and a giant plasma sitting on a console table. In their mother's eye, the room is used to screen French films. In truth, Leo watches endless hours of *SportsCenter* there.

"Dad asked me to," Leo says with a shrug. Stephen sees his barely concealed pride, as though the king had asked him for a dance. Normally Stephen would say something chiding, but he resists.

"Nice of you to go," he offers instead, and Leo frowns.

Stephen doesn't mind him as much today. Strangely, it is the one day they are brought together. "Our parents," Stephen can say at any moment, "are *nuts*," and Leo will nod sagely, remembering all the Bloomsdays they have been subjected to in the past: the year their parents insisted on a costume party, forcing everyone to dress in period pieces; the year they attempted the all-day reading and guests nodded off in their chairs, making hasty excuses to leave. June tried to intercept them, offering coffee and dessert, while Leo high-fived Stephen in the corner.

Leo stands, stretches. "'Yes I said yes I will Yes,'" he reads. "This is like a famous line from the book, right?"

Stephen smiles. He likes Leo's lack of self-consciousness. Likes that he doesn't get flustered or make fumbling attempts to sound smart. Leo—you had to hand it to him—never fakes it. "Its very last line," Stephen affirms. "Spoken by Molly. And, yes, the most famous one, arguably."

"Huh." Leo considers this as he studies the words. "Well, it's no wonder. I mean, who wouldn't like the thought of a woman moaning yes? Sounds like a giant orgasm if you ask me."

"Leo!" June chastises from the hall.

"Jesus, Mom. It does."

She pauses in the doorway, holding a clipboard. "It's not about *sex*. It's nothing like that. The 'yes' is to love and marriage, to everything beautiful. It's a lovely soliloquy." She pronounces this last word with great care, as though handling a delicate piece of china.

"My, my. Someone's been practicing," Stephen murmurs.

June throws him a look. "There's nothing *vulgar* there. Surely you agree, Stephen."

"'I put my arms around him yes,'" he recites, "'and drew him down to me so he could feel my breasts all perfume yes and his heart was going like mad and yes I said yes I will Yes.'"

"Whoa," Leo says. "Maybe I should read the thing after all."

June waves a hand dismissively. "Well, of course it's there if you look for it. Let's get that banner up already!"

Leo grins at Stephen after she saunters away. "Cool that you have it memorized."

"One sees it enough that it sticks."

"I've never memorized anything."

"You know more sports stats than anyone I know." Leo used to spend hours when they were kids poring over baseball cards, a Yankees hat loyally on his head. Michael would get tickets to games and the nanny would take them on the subway. Stephen, bored, would bring a book for the long ride while his brother bounced in his seat. Other passengers smiled at the adorable boy eagerly clutching his mitt.

"Yeah. Because I'm the *only* sports fan you know."

"Good point."

Leo reaches for the banner.

"Careful," Stephen warns. "Mom will flay us if her precious broadside creases."

"Mom's a giant pain in the broadside crease," Leo mutters.

They hold the banner between them and do an ungainly shuffle down the hall. The study has already been set up, light reflecting off the champagne flutes at the bar. The liquor bottles stand in rows like a group of men waiting for their portrait to be snapped. An empty table on the far side of the room will be filled later with hors d'oeuvres. Oysters will recline on ice; fruit and cheese will cascade out in tiers.

"I think Mom wants it up there," Stephen says, indicating the bay windows. It is his favorite spot in the house, the French casement windows opening onto the street.

They rest the banner across the seat cushions. "I'll get the ladder," Leo says. "You get the tape."

Stephen glances around the room. His dad's massive desk has been removed for the party. He heads for the alcove with its antique secretary, a diminutive desk with thin legs.

A financial magazine sits open on the writing surface. Michael still follows the markets faithfully, unable to fully pull out of the game. Stephen glances at the article and sees that it involves insurance. *Look into policy trades,* reads a sticky note. *The mortgagee can't recover on the policy.*

Just underneath, he catches sight of a familiar logo, an oval inlaid with trees. *Pine Grove,* the crest reads in Copperplate font, and for a moment Stephen sees the trees spreading before him, the meandering gravel path.

He sits. The page has spilled out from a manila folder, and *HP* is scrawled on its tab. He feels a pinprick of anger. Not her full name. Not *Mom.* He imagines his dad creating the file, leaning forward in his leather chair. He must have known that one day the folder would hold her death certificate. He must have known it would be a repository of her last days. But anyone looking at it would think Hewlett Packard, Harper Perennial. *HP* they would see, flicking past.

Stephen opens the folder.

There are a couple of pages of notes in Michael's hand. *11/22/03.*

Assurances were given that the matter would be attended to. What matter? Stephen thinks wildly. He tries to recall that November, right before Thanksgiving. Grandma Portman had seemed fine.

He flips through the paperwork, pausing when he sees an itemized list of doctor's visits. Stephen recalls the specialists she had seen that spring. "Weak heart sounds," the cardiologist had said. "Maybe he has weak ears," Grandma Portman grumbled. Stephen had smiled. "No lack of heart here," he affirmed. "I can attest to that."

But when he scans the list, he sees that it predates the embolism. *Psych consult,* the first line reads next to an October date. *Psych follow-up,* says the next. His eyes travel down the page: *psych, psych, psych.*

He shuts the folder, shuts his eyes.

Hamakom y'nachem etkhem b'tokh sha'ar avelei tziyon viyrusha-layim.

"I'm sorry," he hears behind him.

He is aware of Leo standing there, breathing heavily from having carried the ladder.

"For what?" Stephen asks the space behind him.

He hears the bracket of the ladder creak. He hears footsteps above them, footsteps below.

"We all know, okay? I'm sorry, but we do."

Stephen turns in the chair to face Leo.

"Dad got her appointment book when he collected her things. He saw that you'd been going out there. And that director chick—"

"Miriam," Stephen supplies it automatically. "Miriam Maxwell."

"Yeah, well, she said something. About how much they'd miss you. She assumed Dad knew."

Stephen feels the weight of the folder in his hands. His blood seems to be in his arms, not in his head, and he is glad for the chair beneath him.

Leo plays with the bracket, a silver bridge that arcs and flattens.

"I don't think you should hide something like that from us. Especially today."

Stephen laughs. He knows his brother means well, Leo, whose heart is as big as a lion's. "I shouldn't hide it? But that's what we do in this family. We sweep everything under the rug. Just in time for the guests."

"What's that supposed to mean?"

"Mom and Dad wouldn't have wanted me going out there. You know that."

"They never said anything about not visiting her."

"That's because they didn't think we would. *They* certainly didn't. How many times do you think they visited?"

"No idea. Not that it matters."

"Take a guess."

"Look, they didn't know she was going to die." The bracket has become a tool in Leo's hand. "It's not like she was sick."

"That makes it worse, you realize, that they stuck her in a nursing home preemptively. How many times?"

"I don't know."

"Guess."

"I don't know!"

"Quit playing with the fucking ladder."

Leo looks down at his hand. A red welt has formed on his thumb. He pulls it up to his mouth absentmindedly, and he looks briefly like a boy.

"Twice." But the heat of the moment is gone and Stephen finds that he does not relish saying it. "Once in, once out."

"That's not—" Leo starts. *That's not true.* Stephen can see the thought as it forms, the look of protest. But then something else, as Leo struggles to remember their ever mentioning having visited her.

"Dad called her pretty often. They spoke by phone. But they never went to see her. It was the last place they wanted to be."

Leo is silent, still nursing his thumb.

"They stuck her out there like she was garbage."

"You don't think you're being a little dramatic? It was a nice place. *You* sure seemed to like it enough."

"Leo, it was a nursing home. Despite what Mom and Dad said, it was not camp. They sold her house, you know. All her possessions. Decades' worth of stuff, suddenly gone."

"Then why'd she agree to it?" Leo's voice hits on this as though scoring a point.

Stephen sets down the folder. "Dad was worried about her being alone. That she'd take a fall on the stairs, slip on ice. Liability reasons, to use the caterer's words."

"He told you this?"

"*She* told me this. She didn't want to burden him. When they brought it up with her—" Stephen clears his throat. To his horror, a lump has lodged there. He forces the words around it. "When they brought it up, they talked about it like it was their problem. She wasn't complaining—she just explained it that way. 'They were relieved,' she said. 'It would be such a hassle for them if anything ever happened to me.'"

His brother looks away. Wanting to refute him, but also recognizing the truth of these words, so exactly what their grandmother would have said. "So, what? You decided to start visiting her to get revenge?"

"If I wanted revenge, why would I have kept it a secret?"

"I don't know. You tell me."

It's so typical, Stephen reflects, so utterly typical of his brother. "Because anything that doesn't involve you is unacceptable, right?"

"What's that supposed to mean?"

"You hate secrets, Leo. Everyone knows that. Mine's just the one that came out."

Leo opens his mouth to speak, but stops.

"I liked her, okay? I went out there because I *liked* her. I didn't expect to, but I did. And, yes, I even liked being out there. I know it's weird, and I know how it sounds." Stephen pauses. Was he really having this conversation? With Leo of all people?

He regroups. "When her mom got bad at the end, Nora got sucked into a hole. You must have felt it, too, like she suddenly wasn't there anymore. She was my best friend, and she was gone. Or maybe it's different with you two. Maybe you're closer than ever." A bitter laugh tumbles out of Stephen's mouth.

"It wasn't some big plan on my part. I never thought I'd go as much as I did. I went because I felt bad for her. And then—I don't know. We became close. She was a good listener. Everyone out there—" How to say it? How to tell Leo? "Everyone out there was *kind*. There wasn't this competitive thing of having to prove yourself."

It was the opposite of *this*, he wants to say. It was the opposite of this party, this day, this family. His grandmother didn't ask if his briefcase was calfskin. She didn't ask if Stephen's classmates had already turned in their proposals. She never sized him up, assessing him, comparing him. When Stephen was with her, he didn't feel Michael's stick prodding him or June's carrots luring him in different directions. He felt only her concern, unfaltering and pure.

"I still don't get the secrecy. I still don't get the cover-up."

"Because our family is so easy to talk to. They listen so attentively when you talk about your job, for example."

"They were looking out for her," Leo insists. "They didn't want her falling on the ice or whatever. That's not a bad thing."

"She hated it there. Did you know that?" Stephen stands and

crosses the room to look out the bay windows. The second floor is at tree level, and he sees sprays of branches, a tangle of arms.

He and Nora had gotten high here once, that summer she stayed with them. The two of them had leaned out the windows one night, passing a joint back and forth, the rest of the house asleep. Nearly a decade ago, he realizes. Everything felt possible then, as though nothing between them would ever change.

"She lost her sense of purpose out there. She'd lie in bed not wanting to get up. All that stuff they had—the classes, the field trips—that wasn't her." He is glad his back is to his brother, that he can speak the words to the glass.

"I used to get her to take a walk with me when the weather was nice. Miriam said it was good for her. And she always put on a smile, acted like she was fine. But I could tell—" Stephen finds that he knows what he is about to say, that he has known it all along. A hint of sunlight filters through the clouds, touches the leaves.

"I could tell she was sad. When I left, there was nothing for her. I tried to get people to visit her, some of the other residents. I asked if they could check on her."

They would agree, touched by his request. But he could tell they were unsure what to say to the withdrawn woman who kept to herself. The woman who ate her meals alone. Who never took pottery classes or attended events. Who never went to museums. He sensed this but ignored it, relieved when they assured him that, yes, of course, they would knock on her door. Even though he knew, he knew, it was not those faces she craved.

"If Mom and Dad were so concerned about her, why not have her live here? God knows there's enough space. Mom could've hired someone to keep an eye on her. They raved about Pine Grove. But they never asked if it was what she wanted.

"She was a lot like you, Leo. She loved family. That was the most important thing in the world to her. I think some part of her assumed when they put her out there that she'd see us more. That we'd visit." Those years in New York were hard, she had admitted. Not because Michael was busy, but because he was unavailable.

"I don't think Dad likes to think about where he came from. Maybe you make a giant leap like that and you can't look back. But she definitely got the message. He wanted to forget about being Jewish, his past."

"Maybe he never was so Jewish to begin with," Leo counters. "Maybe that wasn't his scene."

I did it, too, Stephen reflects. I let her sit on that couch like an outcast. Because I worried what everyone would think. Stephen closes his eyes. His vanity. His stupid sense of vanity had kept him from being kind.

"Or maybe," Leo continues, "it was to make Mom feel more comfortable. It's hard when someone feels left out."

Stephen turns, wondering if Leo can hear himself. "The way they make you feel, you mean?" Stephen shakes his head. "Do you remember that time I tried to host Passover? Back in New York?"

He was in middle school. June had acquiesced, and he'd excitedly called his grandparents in Brookline to invite them to the city. He picked up a copy of the blue-and-white Maxwell House Haggadah from Gristedes. "Maxwell House, as in the coffee?" June asked, bewildered. "Does Zabar's have something nicer?"

Stephen set the table, carefully placing pillows on chairs, adjusting their angle. He set out the parsley, the dish of salt water. Tears, he had learned. A bowl of tears to remind us.

But when his grandparents arrived, Michael and June stood back like they were strangers. It was Stephen who had rushed forward to take their hands, eager to show them the dining table. "Perfect!" Grandma Portman declared. "Everything is perfect, *bubeleh*."

June winced at the term of endearment. She frowned at the strange rituals of the seder. The dirty Jews, he felt her thinking.

He had imagined a warm reunion, wisdom and tradition encircling them at the table. But when he looked at the salt water, he felt his own loss.

"Mom was awful to them. Dad didn't really join in. He pretended not to know about the seder, like it was all new to him." Normally expansive Michael was reluctant to speak that day, like a boy with a stutter.

The Haggadah was supposed to be an act of telling. "Tell your son," it said. But how could that happen if his father refused to speak? If he went silent at any mention of the past?

They never attempted it again. Stephen didn't have the heart to subject his grandparents to the humiliation. Passover became a modernized meal with matzah and merlot, cleansed of religion. "Persecution," Stephen says. "All the history of the world is full of it. You just don't expect it to happen in your own home."

"Please. You're being ridiculous."

"Leo, who fits in? When it comes to our family, who actually fits? You? Grandma Portman? Nora? Mom and Dad set the rules. The trouble is that they come at everyone else's expense."

"You!" Leo suddenly bellows.

Stephen takes a step back, startled.

"You're the one who fits in! It's *you*! Don't try to play the victim. You're—" Leo casts about for words. "You're the golden boy!"

Stephen regards him for a minute and then bursts out laughing. "Me? *Me?* You can't be serious. I'm the one who took refuge in a nursing home."

"You're the smart one, the artsy one. You're tall—" Leo pauses. "You know what I mean."

"Listen, do you know how hard I fought them to go to Hebrew school? Do you know how much they hated having me convert?"

"Oh, please. That's just a religious thing."

Just a religious thing, Stephen thinks. Because God is no big deal. "You know the other place I go once a week that we don't talk about? The synagogue. Why do you think we have brunch on Sunday? They know I go there, and they gloss right over it. It never dawned on me to tell them about visiting Grandma Portman because they've made it abundantly clear they don't want to know."

Leo shifts uncomfortably.

"When you think about what you want, your future home, your family, is this what you picture?" Stephen gestures around the room. The crystal gleams, silent.

"Don't you picture a family that's close? A family that actually talks about stuff?"

"But you're blaming them! You're blaming them for your secret."

"No. I'm blaming them for not wanting to hear it. They never made space for her in this family, even after Grandpa died. If they were so concerned for her, why not have her be a part of our lives?"

Leo does not answer.

"I think—I think for a long time she saw the choices they were making and went along with them. Wanting to be supportive, not wanting to meddle." No Haggadah, she would have thought sadly. Okay. Okay. "But when they put her out there, she saw how they felt about her. She saw that they wanted to live their lives without her."

"But she had a say in the matter!" Leo interjects. "She could have refused."

Stephen looks across the room at the folder on the desk. She was depressed, he wants to tell him. I didn't want to see it, but she so obviously was. She was probably on antidepressants to rouse her and sedatives to help her sleep, a circle of drugs to bring her up and down. "Let's try the meds," Michael would have said briskly, the folder spread before him. "Maybe she'll perk up."

She didn't feel as if she had a choice. Because what was she supposed to do? Refuse their help? Turn them down when they were all she had left? And so she made the best of it, figuring she might as well.

Stephen turns. "Let's get this up," he says, indicating the banner.

"What? She did speak up and they ignored it?"

"We probably don't have much time."

"Why are you changing the subject?"

"I'm not." Stephen turns and is surprised by how close Leo is. A foot away, right before him. Leo's brown eyes are hurt, confused.

"She was no doormat, Grandma Portman," Leo says.

"I know."

"She could have left that place, if it was so awful. No one forced her into anything."

Stephen hesitates. "It's complicated."

"What's that supposed to mean?"

"People don't always do what makes them happy. Sometimes people go along with things because they think they should. They go along because they don't think they have a choice. They go along because happiness feels impossible."

"Oh, Christ. Christ, Stephen. Is this about *Nora*?"

"I didn't say that." Stephen looks down at the banner.

"You're seriously linking this to Nora?"

"You're the one who brought her up."

Leo shakes his head. "Right. I brought it up. But you think it, right?"

Stephen eyes him, unsure of what to say.

Leo laughs into the silence, and this time it's his laugh that sounds bitter. "You've never approved. I get that, okay? But let's not go there. You had your shot with her."

Stephen's heart sinks. "No, Leo. It's nothing like that. I was never . . ."

"No?" Leo says harshly. "Then what is it? You think I make her unhappy? You think I'm like the nursing home, trapping her?"

Yes I said yes, the banner's bright ink cries.

Leo crosses his arms across his chest and Stephen looks at the familiar pose. Leo, five, dejected he can't play Little League. Leo, eight, waiting up late in his Phil Simms jersey for their dad to get home. Leo, fifteen, watching Stephen fill out college-application forms.

"I don't think any of those things. I just think—" Stephen knows that whatever he says, things will never be the same between them. "I just think that I've known her for a long time. I was friends with her before you two started dating."

"I get it! You were BFFs."

"Let me finish, okay? I don't think you're bad for her. You're my brother. And I was never interested in her that way. It's just—I *know* her. And I'm not saying I know her better than you or anything like that," Stephen adds hastily, seeing that Leo is about to interrupt. "But I knew her before her mom got sick. I knew her before everything got crazy. And she's *changed*." Stephen looks at his brother, who is grudging, guarded.

"Our grandmother—I think she felt like everything was out of her hands. She felt like it was all decided, like she had no choice. She faded out there. I saw it but didn't want to see it." The institution of marriage, he thinks. To you, it's camp. "I just think—when someone is suffering, when someone is ill—and Nora *is* ill, Leo, she saw her shrink this morning—then it's not the right time to be making decisions about the future."

"This morning?" Leo repeats.

They hear a noise behind them and turn. Nora is in the doorway, clutching two floral arrangements, a strange sound having escaped her.

"Nora," Leo says, starting toward her.

But Nora takes a step back. She gestures with the arrangements, each one moving in her hand, as if to say, No, please, continue.

Stephen watches the vases nervously. "I'm sorry—"

"We weren't—" Leo starts.

"Talking about me?" she says, finally finding her voice. "But you were."

The three of them stand looking at each other.

"We were," Stephen finally acknowledges. "I don't know how much you heard. But you're right, we were. Only because we care."

"Because I'm *ill*? I heard plenty."

Leo draws a breath and takes a step toward her. His movements are so cautious that Nora laughs. "What do you think I'm going to do?" she asks shrilly. She looks down at the vases in her hands, her grip on them too tight. "You think I'm going to throw these? You think I'm going to—?" Then Leo is there, relieving her of them. He takes them from her and places them on the empty table.

"Are there more of those?" he asks quietly.

Nora is silent for a moment, looking at her empty hands. "Downstairs," she says finally. "A whole bunch. June asked me to bring them up."

"I'll get them," Leo offers. "You take a load off, okay?"

As if he could fix everything, Stephen reflects. As if her world were broken in some way he could repair. "I should go," he says. "I need to get ready for the party."

He brushes past their convergence at the door. Nora has changed into an ivory dress with green embroidery, and he wonders if Leo knows, if he had even noticed her black dress earlier. It was the same dress she had worn to her mother's funeral. Nora had sat on the couch that day staring at the box of ashes, the empty rocking chair a few feet away.

Stephen pauses on the landing and watches Leo jog down the stairs. Nowhere to go but up, he thinks, and begins the climb.

Thirteen

The summer evening had begun to fold the world in its mysterious embrace. Dusk, that magic hour, the day bleeding into its own end. Nora catches sight of the setting sun through the small laundry-room window. The air in the room smells of starch and ironing. Carol's housekeeping supplies line the shelves, scouring powder and cleaning agents in canvas bins. An ironing board is next to a more elaborate machine, where, seated, Carol can feed linens through a press, her foot operating a pedal. Nora rests her chin on her knees and leans back against the washing machine.

Strands of hair litter the ground beside her. Just one, she had told herself. Her hairpins lay scattered across the sink, an explosion of metallic lines like fireworks across the porcelain. She had placed them so carefully earlier, thinking, this way I won't, this way I won't. She was pleased with her reflection at the loft, enjoying a boost of confidence before leaving the apartment. But how long had that lasted? An hour?

"Darling, do me a favor and bring these up," June had said, pressing two vases into her hands. There was no question in her voice. It was an order, as though Nora were one of the staff. The arrangements were green and white, a broad leaf encircling the vase's interior to conceal the water and the stems. "The boys will do the rest," June added. Only while Nora was ascending the stairs, hearing Stephen's and Leo's voices, did it dawn on her that June was referring to her sons.

Nora had stopped in her tracks when she heard them arguing. They talked about her as if she were a child. "And she is ill, Leo," Stephen said. As if he were an expert! As if he knew anything at all.

She hadn't heard much before that—only a few words about their grandmother. Leo must have confronted Stephen about the visits.

"You shouldn't presume to know what's best for me," she should have interrupted in a dignified voice. Instead, a squawk came out, a sound before the words could form. They turned, startled. Stephen's face showed concern. Leo's face crumpled.

After they left, Nora gazed around the room. She could feel their argument linger in the air. She felt Stephen's discomfort, his sadness. She felt Leo's determination to pretend everything was fine.

"There," Leo said, returning with the last of the flowers. He set the vases down and hopped up the ladder to hang the banner. Watching him work, she wondered if the scene had really happened. Leo seemed so calm and unfazed. "What?" he asked, when he caught her staring, and she shook her head.

They stepped back to examine the banner. "Do you think it'll hold?" she asked, looking dubiously at Leo's roll of masking tape. She imagined the banner floating down during the party and landing on June's head.

"It only needs to last a couple of hours."

A couple of hours! It seemed so obvious when he said it. "And you're sure it's straight?"

Leo shrugged. "People will think it's straight because it's supposed to be." With that, he sauntered out of the room.

"Whoa!" Nora trotted after him. "Where are you going?"

"I figured I'd see if my mom needs anything else. You know how she gets." Leo regarded her. "You okay?"

"I was worried—" But Nora stopped, unsure how to continue. She was worried about the fight she'd overheard. Worried about her friendship with Stephen. Worried that one day Leo will turn to someone and say, "I need to check on Nora. You know how she gets." Nora had a thousand worries she did not know how to name.

Leo reached out and put his hands on her shoulders. "Relax, love. Go get a drink. Everything will be fine."

The bar wasn't fully set up, and Nora felt too self-conscious to reach for the vodka. So she headed to Carol's nook under the stairs, the ironing room, June called it. But Nora thinks of it as Carol's room, a secret space in the house that is nearly tropical, the sultry warmth from the dryer mixing with lingering steam from the irons. How many hours had she and Carol spent there, laughing about something from choir, gossiping about June? Nora always sits on the washing machine, watching Carol feed bedsheets through the rotating press. It's the one place in the house where Nora doesn't have to worry about her posture or manners, where she can relax.

She half hoped Carol would be there, called in to do some last-minute chores. There she would be, pressing hemstitched napkins into perfect squares, looking up with her liquid eyes when Nora turned the knob. But the room was empty. And Nora knew when she found it vacant how this would end.

Was she ashamed that she couldn't hold out? She was, but the relief exceeded the shame. Her fingers were exquisitely attuned to her scalp, and when they raked over its surface, some process commenced of its own accord, her mind going blank, focused only on the precise millimeter of space she touched, her mouth filling with saliva just before she pulled. One, two, three, the hairs came out. The first three were duds, but the fourth had the prized white bulb on its end, glistening, a scepter. Holding it, she felt triumphant. Just a few more, she thought.

This is how it goes. There is always a reason, a special set of circumstances. She doesn't pull out of habit, the way Leo seems to think. "You pulling?" he sometimes asks. As if she would do it without realizing.

He had left his browser window open one time. The website came as a shock. She clicked past the medical pictures with a shudder, whole scalps plucked bare, and looked at the lists of clinical terms. *Trichophagia*, she read, flinching. As if she would ever eat her hair.

She didn't feel a rush of recognition. She never pulls from other parts of her body. It doesn't interfere with her functioning. Besides, isn't it arbitrary, what gets deemed a disorder?

People do worse. Those men on the stoop, drinking to get through the day. And then Jon and Mike, smoking. Sharon, too. Aren't those behaviors more harmful? Wouldn't a doctor prefer that she pull her hair rather than ruin her lungs and liver? The outside of the body is a surface. People tattoo it, pierce it. Yale probably has anthropological courses on how such behavior is relative. Probably somewhere in the Amazon women from indigenous tribes sit in circles, grooming one another, plucking hairs and swallowing them.

But no one wants to hear her speculate along such lines. Even the academic shrink had paused, eyeing her. Worse than I thought, Nora could see him thinking.

Leo had told his family about it without asking her permission. She thought she'd been imagining their little looks, June's eyes drifting to her hair. "Of course I told them," Leo said blankly when she asked. "They don't judge you, Nora." She looked at him and laughed. "Your mother invented judging. Do you really not see that?"

"What do you think his motives were?" the academic shrink asked, gazing at her. "He cares about me," she was supposed to reply. "He loves me. I guess he just wants to help."

Her habit was supposed to become the demon. Her tick, the trich. It was the bad boyfriend she was supposed to dump, choosing virtuous Leo instead. Love would conquer all. She simply had to make the choice, to marry rather than be ill.

But what if they were wrong in how they classified problems? What if the men on the stoop and her dad needed shrinks more than she did? When she rejoins Leo upstairs, he'll be pleased to see her relaxed. All she needed was some downtime, he will muse, thinking that his advice worked.

This was what she tried to explain to the cognitive therapist. How do you stop doing something when it feels like it *helps*? What do you do when the solution to the problem is the problem?

Ultimately, she doesn't fault Leo for his efforts. He thought he could erase her problems as if they were stains. Leo the Fixer. Leo the Problem Solver. She imagines a white can in one of Carol's bins with a sketch of his profile, assuring and calm. "Two shakes gets the problem out!"

That has been their dynamic all along. It was he who convinced her to stay at Delancey that summer, after her mom was diagnosed. "Oh, I couldn't," Nora said with a nervous laugh when he suggested it. She loved the idea of spending the summer with him, but there was just no way. "No way?" he repeated, raising a brow. This was not a phrase in the Leopold lexicon. "Why's that?" "Oh, about a hundred reasons," Nora replied as he wrapped his arms around her, thinking of money, her mother, logistics. "I don't want to spend the whole summer apart," he murmured. "What would I tell my parents?" Nora asked. "We'll make shit up," he told her.

That was exactly what they had done, fabricating a story about a musicologist at Penn. "It's an amazing opportunity," she explained to her parents over the phone while Leo looked on, coaxing her with his hands. "And it's free?" her dad asked. "Yeah. I mean, this guy's a friend of my program director's. At Yale? And Stephen's parents offered to put me up. They have this whole attic—it's got a bed-room and everything. On its own floor? You know, separate." Leo was waving at her frantically to stop talking. A pause on the phone ensued. Free, she could hear her dad thinking. But she felt the word in its other register.

"Of course you should do it," her mom said. "Sounds too good to pass up."

Did her mom know? Did she suspect Nora of lying? "He's a mad-man," her mom would say after a fight, picking up the things Nora's dad had thrown. Then why? Nora could never bring herself to ask. Why do you stay?

Maybe her mom understood that Nora couldn't abide by her choices. Maybe her mom was glad one of them was getting away.

Nora had never liked being at home, but at least she and her mom used to hang out. When she came home on break, they would spend a day at the mall, catching a matinee, then visiting the pet store to see the kittens, touching them through their cages. Later they would go out for ice cream and trade stories. It was a silly ritual, but it was theirs.

After the diagnosis, Nora felt their dynamic shift. Her mom wanted to ignore being sick, but it couldn't be ignored. So it sat in the house like a bad smell. "Do you want to go see a movie?" Nora asked when she came home that spring. "Maybe tomorrow," her mom replied, too stubborn to admit that she was tired. Nora was left in limbo, not knowing what to do. If she went out with a girlfriend, her father would berate her. "You're supposed to be here to help!" he'd yell.

He, on the other hand, had no trouble ignoring his wife's ill-ness. He went right on expecting his meals cooked, his laundry done. "Let him do some of this stuff," Nora hissed when she saw her mother unloading the dishwasher days after her surgery. "He doesn't know how," she said with a smile, letting Nora take over.

She sat down in her chair. "Marry one that cooks," she advised. "Apparently they exist now."

The two families had gone out to lunch once at the end of that summer. Nora finally told her parents about Leo, and an awkward meal at Devon Seafood ensued. Nora cringed at the collision of her different worlds. "Jeez," her dad said, looking at the prices on the menu, "does the ocean come with the fish?" Michael smiled pleasantly across the table while Nora wanted to sink beneath it.

They stumbled their way through the meal, Leo cracking jokes to put her parents at ease. Her mother tried to engage with June, nodding thoughtfully at her airy remarks and stories of her time in Manhattan. "I grew up in Brooklyn, you know," Iris said. "Ah, Brooklyn," June replied.

In a polite battle at the end of the meal, Michael tried to slip his AmEx to the waitress. "We insist," Nora's mom said with a polite smile. "On splitting," Nora's dad clarified. "Oh, Frank." Nora's mom shook her head.

"Well," her father said, stuffing his credit card back in his wallet and nodding to Leo. "You've got your work cut out for you with this one. I give you credit for even trying." Everyone froze as if a current of electricity had shot through the table. "She's not so tough to take," Leo replied after a beat. Nora's father made a face of incredulity as though Leo had said something absurd.

Michael, at the head of the table, cleared his throat. "We adore having Nora stay with us, Frank." Michael hesitated, as though about to say more, but then Leo changed the subject in his smooth way, steering them into a different conversational lane.

Delancey had been her shelter that summer, the architectural equivalent of Leo's arms. Nora often had the place to herself. Leo worked during the day and Stephen studied at the library. Michael and June were usually out until the evening. Nora listened to CDs on their expensive sound system. She studied scores in the sunny kitchen and made herself tea. She imagined she was in Paris, put up in a fancy hotel. She imagined crowds gathering to see her. Each morning she woke up and, seeing the attic's eaves, remembered with a smile that she had escaped.

Leo came up to her room most nights, the queen bed pitched under the roof's peak. Nora would be listening to Chopin or Debussy. Maybe this is how it can always be, she would think. They made love loudly, having tested for sound once during the day, Leo jumping on the bed and yelling while Nora, one floor below, heard nothing but her own laugh.

After he had fallen asleep, she would study his face, illuminated by the bedside lamp. He's a good guy, she would reflect, watching his chest rise and fall. He even cooks.

Vacations can't last, she would tell herself in the morning, walking to work. She was waitressing at Manning, and it was an easy walk. She started with breakfast and lunch service, but soon picked up night shifts, the time slot of glorious tips. She was saving up for airfare to Milan, hopeful that she could put enough aside to buy her mom a ticket to visit her.

At first, she ignored the live jazz at the restaurant. Her head was filled with Maria Callas. There was agony in that voice, suffering laid bare. Maria Callas made you forget the technical skill, the hours of practice. All Nora heard, busing the tables, was the fight of feelings, their delicate war. She carried trays of drinks but rode the current of that voice, entranced by how it lulled you and raised you at will.

On Saturday nights, a singer with a fuchsia mouth held the microphone too close and compensated for lack of range by being breathy. Nora began to grow impatient, listening to her wavering pitch. She went back to Delancey and listened to *Tosca*. But she wondered if she could do better than that lipsticked fraud.

She didn't stop to think about what it would mean, taking a job as a lounge singer. What mattered was the dreamy feel of that summer, as though it could be preserved. As though the logistics might change—a loft swapped for the attic; real jobs in place of summer ones—but the feeling would remain.

What Nora hadn't anticipated was that disaster could occur on vacation. That you could be shipwrecked, even though the water looked so clear. Here was what she had so often dreamed of, an oasis from the fights and turmoil. Abundance rather than lack.

Her mom's chemo was deemed a success, and Nora grew excited for Milan. Her vocal scholarship wasn't supposed to include a semester abroad, but the program director had applied for special funding. "We'd be remiss in your training to not send you," he told her. "You'll see opera as it's meant to be done."

A week before Nora left, her mother's scan came back showing abnormalities. "But they said they got it all," Nora protested. "Apparently this happens," her mother said. "We'll do another round of chemo. No big deal. Don't for a second think of canceling your trip." "Do what you want," her father said tersely. Nora couldn't choose right either way.

She winds the hairs around her finger, then drops them into the trash.

"Have you pulled before?" the cognitive therapist once asked.

"Sort of." Nora remembered pulling when she was eleven. She had tried it as an experiment late at night, pulling a patch of scalp clean over a few weeks. Who knew where the impulse came from? Her parents never discovered what she was up to, and she reveled in her secret. It had stopped on its own, fleeing like a foreshadow, showing itself in a glimpse, promising to return.

In Milan, opera began to lose its heart. Nora felt glum recognition when her voice coach yelled, "Listen! Hear the anger, the hostility! Then the sorrow, the loss, oh—the bitterly held last note." Opera had been abstract before, but Nora now understood those emotions better than any junior in college should. She felt herself turn away from them.

"You don't want to do opera anymore?" her program director repeated when she returned to New Haven.

She shook her head.

He considered this. "I always encourage students to explore different facets of music. But, Nora—you are gifted. Dazzlingly gifted. Your place with a major house—one hesitates to say it is assured . . ."

Nora stopped listening. One hesitates to say, she thought. Yes, one hesitates. One should hesitate. What is the point of singing in French, in Italian, in strange tongues? She took history-of-music courses the next semester, courses with textbooks that she could read on the train. She decided not to audition for the Paris program. She decided to stay close to home.

Her senior year, she struggled to pass. She didn't tell her program director about her mother, even though he kept trying to pry information from her. Her scholarship was in jeopardy, and she knew the logical thing would be to explain her circumstances, as Leo urged. But she didn't want to be looked at with pity, passing through the narrow halls of the music department. By April of her senior year, her mom was in a second remission. Nora turned in her midterm papers late and begged for leniency. "I'll pass you," the director said finally. "But only if you stay on for a year as a voice coach." "Me?" Nora repeated. "Those who can't do, teach," he said lightly.

He had hoped she would see how much better she was than the freshmen, that she would fall in love with opera again. Marilyn Horne and Renata Scotto were the master-class teachers that year, and they both advised that she continue with her training. "You are meant for La Scala," Renata Scotto told her in her lovely, lilting English. "This is not a compliment! This is the calling. You must answer."

Instead, Nora discovered that she loved teaching. She was good at it. "That's great," Leo said. "You can give lessons when we move to Philly."

"Do you see what's happening?" Stephen groaned. "Already you're regressing because of him."

Maybe, but being in New Haven that year had worked out well. Leo was finishing up school in Boston, and her mother seemed to be in the clear. Soon, she and Leo would be in Philly once more. She would give lessons. Maybe she would even try her hand at jazz. The feeling of that summer would return.

No one could have known what the next few years would hold. No one would have thought the end was so near. Their glorious summer retreated into the distance, and over time the memory of it confused her. What had once been her escape had become a prison. How does one escape the escape?

Nora scoops the bobby pins from the sink. She faces her reflection to ready herself once more. The creak of the ceiling tells her it is time.

Fourteen
———

Leo imagines it was the grief talking. He watches the bartender assemble his gin and tonic, tiny bubbles racing past the ice. A wedge of lime bobs at the surface like a bloated corpse.

Stephen didn't mean it, Leo will assure Nora later, assuming she decides to join him at the party. Who knows where she had run off to?

The bartender plucks a cocktail napkin from a stack. Leo recognizes it from the kitchen, the bright green edges fanning out to the world like steps in miniature. The bartender places the drink upon the napkin with great ceremony and then bows. "Er, cheers," Leo says, taken aback by the man's solemnity.

People are weird. It is Leo's only way of making sense of the world, the patronizing Stephens and strangely formal bartenders. But at least the bartender has respect for his trade. "Whatever one does, one should take it seriously," Michael often remarked, and Leo looks for it at work. Guys like Dave wear slouchy khakis and play video games, too cool to care.

Leo spears the lime with a thin, red straw. "People don't always do what makes them happy," Stephen had lectured. Leo takes it out on the lime, the wedge turning pulpy.

Across the room, Stephen chats with a tall woman in a silver cocktail dress. Leo recognizes her as one of their mother's friends. She smiles as she speaks, toying with an earring, regarding Stephen through a fringe of lashes.

Leo has long been resigned to his brother's being the handsome one—there is no fighting it. But he also suspects that women can somehow detect Stephen's aloofness in the way that mosquitoes are drawn to certain blood types. They sniff out the sweet challenge of him from across the room.

Not gay. Then what? Stephen looked crestfallen when Leo suggested he was jealous. "It's not like that," he protested. "I was never . . ." Stephen had let the sentence trail off, but that blank contained everything. Never attracted? Never bold enough?

Regardless, Stephen was trying to meddle. That much is clear. Their grandmother's misery was supposed to serve as a grand lesson for Leo. Stephen had dangled the comparison before him, waiting for his doofus brother to get it. Like he was an undergrad, and Stephen the professor.

But maybe that's *you*, Leo wishes he'd replied. Maybe that's what *you* think, what *you* see. The parallel between their grandmother and Nora is absurd, visible only to Stephen's abstract eye. "People aren't books," Leo should have told him coolly.

Of the two women most important to Stephen, one was getting hitched and the other was interred. Of course they seemed similar. They were both unavailable.

But Leo had said nothing, letting Stephen spin his theories. "She's changed," Stephen had remarked, like he was offering some great insight. No shit, Sherlock. But what were they supposed to do about it?

Wait, apparently. "It's not the right time to be making decisions," Stephen had argued. But there was never a right time. There hadn't been a right time in years—since Leo and Nora had met, really. According to Stephen's logic, Leo shouldn't have dated Nora when her mom got sick, shouldn't have invited her to Philly for that first summer. And who could argue with that summer?

The truth is that he and Nora always planned around her mother's illness. Nora needed to be close to Union if something happened; after Milan, she refused to go on vacation or travel. Nora was like an undertaker, needing to be perpetually available for death. They had lived with Iris's ghost before she died.

And even if Nora is struggling, doesn't that mean she needs Leo more than ever? Nora needs an anchor, but Stephen treats him like he's causing her to sink.

Stephen likes to speak with great authority. "She saw her shrink this morning," he had said. "I *live* with her," Leo wanted to retort. "But suddenly you know her best?"

A few guests wander into the room. It is that first trickle, the droplets before the downpour. The early birds are always the same, nervous types with damp armpits who arrive precisely at the stated time on the invite, standing on Delancey's stoop at the stroke of seven. They jam their hands out before you fully open the door, so eager to please.

Nora was like that once. She'd set out to read *Ulysses* for her first party, treating it like homework. "Don't bother," Stephen told her dismissively. But Leo found it sweet, his girl trying to please his folks. She got a little awkward with it ("I'm still trying to make sense of that Oxen of the Sun episode, where the language gets so strange," she had said to a startled June, not realizing that this was the last thing his mom wanted to discuss), but it was touching that she wanted to fit in. It was touching that she *cared*.

He shakes the ice in his drink. What happened to that Nora? He looks around the room, at the polite circles of small talk. What happened to the Nora who would never have been late to the party? Who would have been right by his side? The ice clinks softly, echoing his questions.

Grief is a bitch. It is its own strange animal. If only Nora stayed up late crying or wanting to be held, if only she had quit her job or yelled at him or decided to camp out and watch TV, stuffing her face with potato chips—if only she had *done* something, lashed out, thrown a fit. Then he would have known that this was the time to see her through. How easily he could have stepped into that role, reassuring and solid, comforting her. Instead there has been nothing for him. She resumed giving lessons after a week, not wanting to let her students down. She attended rehearsals and performed. She was there in every way, except that she wasn't.

How do you get someone back if you don't know where she's gone? How long do you stand on that bridge, your hand outstretched, waiting?

Stephen would leave you on that bridge forever. Grief gave Stephen another reason to put off engaging with the world—Stephen, who knows nothing of responsibilities. He still accepts an allowance from their parents, the money getting wordlessly deposited into his checking account each month. He's never worked a day in his life, but it's all okay in the name of the obscure academic drivel he cooks up in that apartment. "I made my own way up the ladder," their dad always said firmly. "No one handed me a thing." It is what Leo has done, too, going from intern to developer to manager.

Not that anyone seemed to notice. They deferred to Stephen, fawning over him. "What do you think, Stephen?" "Did you read that article in the *Times*, Stephen?" "We should go check out that new play, Stephen." Even this latest scandal of moonlighting at the nursing home—it briefly put Leo in the warm circle of their father's confidence, but how quickly he will be on the outside again. Leo can feel it coming. No matter what Stephen does, he will always be the favored son. "It's sweet, Stephen, that you befriended her," they will croon. Meanwhile, no one noticed that Leo had hung the banner. Certainly, no one thanked him for it.

Leo gulps down the rest of his cocktail. He feels the current of gin reach him and gives in to it. *Laid-back,* they used to mouth at frat parties, aping their arms in the air. *With my mind on my money and my money on my mind.*

He nods at a familiar woman in a yellow dress approaching him. There are responsibilities, he reflects. Not to the dead, but to the living.

"Hey there," she says a little nervously. Her hair is loose, cascading past her shoulders, and only when her brown eyes meet his does he make the connection.

"Hey," he returns, surprised. The image of the tattoo comes to him before her name, the indelible vines climbing her leg. "Glad you could make it." He leans in to kiss her cheek, smells the perfume in her hair. Helen, he thinks, retrieving it. Her hair is longer than he imagined, luxurious as it spills past her shoulders, and she looks softer, more feminine.

Her dress, however, is unfortunate. It is mustard yellow and frayed, and even he, practical Leo, recognizes it as a misfire. The cheap fabric clings to his suit with staticky fingers, and Helen, embarrassed, beats it back.

"No dress code on the invite." Her eyes dart around the room. "I wasn't sure how fancy y'all would be."

The dress must have been a thrift-store find. Leo imagines her rummaging through a bin at the Salvation Army, not liking the color but liking the price. Helen was so confident at her studio, in her element. His dark suit there had made him feel like a stiff.

"You're perfect," he assures her. "Let's get you a drink."

He guides her to the bar, pleased to be in host mode. Leo often complained about his Manhattan upbringing, but it had trained him well for this. All of those Upper East Side parties and benefits his parents had dragged them to, the teenage boys sulking in their ties—what a bore those nights had been. But Leo knows how to mingle without having to think about it. He knows how to maneuver through a room to the bar and how to chat amicably with guests along the way.

"I'll have what he's having," Helen giggles, trying out a line from a movie.

To his credit, the bartender remembers and nods. "Another for you, sir?"

"Please," Leo says crisply. He turns to Helen. "I didn't realize you were coming tonight."

"Your dad invited me. I figured he was just being polite, but he insisted. No one's ever done that before. I mean, I *do* the invites, but I never *get* the invite." She pauses, her eye on the bartender. "Cool guy, your dad."

Leo smiles. His mom might not be thrilled to have the help mingling with the guests, but Helen is right: it is cool. How many events a year did Helen handle, printing invites and reply cards, while her own Fridays were spent in that warehouse with the whir of machines?

"It's terrible, about the funeral," she continues, lowering her voice after they've accepted their drinks. "What awful timing. I know y'all have been planning this for months."

"These things happen. If anything, it'll help my dad to be surrounded by friends. Here, we should go say hi."

He leads her over to the middle of the room where his dad is with two of his golf buddies.

"Helen!" he booms. "I'm delighted you could make it." Michael kisses her cheek, turns to his friends. "This is Helen Schafer. She owns the printing press we use. She's an extraordinarily talented artist." He gestures to the banner hanging above them. "Her work, in all its glory!"

"Hey." She nods, blushing charmingly.

"And you remember my son."

"Leopold," he says, thrusting his hand out, ready for their shakes.

"Am I remembering right that you're in finance?" Paul, the taller one, has receding gray hair and a matching silvery beard. His handshake comes on like a vise.

"IT consulting, actually."

"A dot-commer! I bet all that stuff is second nature to you. It's good that we're settling out after the bust, coming into a plateau."

Jake, the other guy, whose hand was clammy and cold, smirks.

Leo frowns. "Economically, you mean?"

"Well, and technologically, too. There were a couple of years there with Y2K . . ." Paul shakes his head. "There was talk of having to restructure your whole organization. Turns out it was all overblown."

"Well—" Leo begins.

"And look at where half those companies are now. Belly-up!"

"There was a lot of overspending," Leo concedes. "But—"

"My daughter," Paul interrupts. "She was trying to get me to join—what's it called? MyFriend?"

"Friendster. There's also MySpace."

"Right! What am I supposed to do with that? Why would I want to have a *profile*?" Paul shoots his friends a grin.

"I'm techno-averse, too," Helen pipes in, and the men turn to her. Jake's eyes dip down to her cleavage, for Helen, in her nervousness, has made the unfortunate move of hugging her arms across her chest. Jake catches Leo's eye and winks.

Slime, Leo thinks, downing his second cocktail. The men are off, asking Helen about her business, condescending questions about how *hard* it must be, running the company all by her lonesome little self, but Helen plays along. It is wise of her. Maybe she could even drum up some business.

Leo regards Paul and Jake, so comfortable and assured. They are middle-aged men who think they know it all, and they look to Helen in her slinky dress to confirm this. To them, Helen is a school-girl selling lemonade. They are pleased by how she defers to them. As it should be, they think, watching her cleavage balloon.

An evolution is happening as we speak, Leo wants to tell them. Sanjay, the company CEO, was always saying it. Adapt or perish. It was that simple, a Darwinian precept, except instead of jungle vines and predators, the new challenge for survival was virtual—a different kind of web.

"Our task is to convince people that IT doesn't mean having a website," Sanjay explained at the annual conference, to knowing chuckles. "IT doesn't mean email."

But Leo encounters it all the time in people like Paul and Jake, executives who believe that technology, like a stork, has delivered its bundled gift. Any developments from this point on will be in-cremental, they reason. Email will get faster; computers will get smaller. "No," Leo has told his dad. "Email is going away. Personal computers are going away." "Not in my lifetime," his dad replied. "Try ten years," Leo countered.

Systems are integrating. Bluetooth, microprocessors. Soon you'll be able to set your thermostat from your phone. Your refrigerator will send you an alert when you're low on eggs. Maybe you could even pull up a picture of its interior when at the store. Friend-ster, Napster, chat rooms—it is just a matter of time before they converge and the technology streamlines. Our watches will tell us where to go.

Technology is creating a new creature, a new species, and Paul and Jake are going the way of dinosaurs. Sanjay had told his employees at their off-site retreat about a friend of his in biotech. "We're talking about prosthetic limbs that interface with the brain," he said fervently. "We're talking about sensors that interface *with human thought*. Not years from now. Now! These guys just got FDA approval for patient testing. This stuff is happening."

Paul and Jake don't realize it, but the future doesn't look like them, silvery and pale. The future is guys like Sanjay, fast talking and dark skinned, sons of first-generation anesthesiologists and engineers who got into Ivy League schools because they ripped the SATs, not because their dads once wrestled at Harvard.

Ten years from now, Paul will be scratching his head. He will sit at a meeting, bewildered by the strange terms getting traded by younger faces regarding that creature, Technology. Paul will feel his own irrelevance, not even comprehending the verbs and nouns they use, for even language changes. Paul will not understand how it happened. The end comes suddenly like that.

"That plateau you mentioned, Paul?" Leo wants to say sweetly. "It turns out that's just the start of the graph." But Paul will never realize that he should have accepted his daughter's Friendster request. That he should have embraced every new twist and turn technology had to offer, even when he was uncertain of its utility. Because the point is not to understand technology or even to enjoy it. The point is to adapt.

But denial can be a funny thing. Pregnant women don't want to think about labor. Parents don't want to imagine their perfect newborns one day having sex. Who wants to contemplate what is coming at you like a train? It's easier to shut your eyes and take comfort in what you've already done.

Last week, Dave had sent Leo one of those email chains at work. *Copy this message and fill in your answers,* it said. *Then forward this to your friends, including the person who sent it to you.* Filling it out,

Leo felt a wave of nostalgia, like when they used to trade yearbooks in high school, even the guys writing *KIT!* for "Keep in touch" and *Have a good summer, man.*

1. NAME: Leo Portman.
2. AGE: 27.
3. LOCATION: Philly.
4. HEIGHT: 5'9".
5. WHAT WILL YOU REMEMBER MOST ABOUT THIS YEAR? The Knicks getting swept in the first round.
6. GIRLS, WITH OR WITHOUT NAIL POLISH? Yes.
7. FAVORITE DRINK: Newcastle.
8. BEST FEELING IN THE WORLD: Duh.
9. WORST FEELING IN THE WORLD: Boredom.
10. WHERE DO YOU SEE YOURSELF IN 10 YEARS? A dad mowing the lawn. With a Newcastle. Not getting enough of #8.
11. WHAT'S THE FIRST THING YOU THOUGHT WHEN YOU WOKE UP TODAY? How much time can I waste on email?
12. WHAT SONG BEST DESCRIBES YOU? The opening of *SportsCenter.*
13. FAVORITE MOVIES: *Star Wars. The Breakfast Club.*

He filled out all forty-two questions, cheerfully clacking away, quite enjoying the exercise, realizing with a laugh that his kids wouldn't do this—that this was the Internet equivalent of getting up to change the TV channel. And so he'd hit print after he was done, slipping his stapled answers into a folder marked *Misc,* imagining one day finding it and being delighted by it all over again. He and Nora will laugh at the old relic of it. She will tease him mercilessly about his answers, but he'll remember that exact moment in his office, anticipating their future, and will feel pleased that he has come full circle.

"And what do you think, Leo?" Helen turns to him.

"About which part?" he asks smoothly. It was an old trick from school for when he zones out.

"You worry about eating out these days? Fast food, I mean?"

"There is absolutely no chance," his dad chimes in, "of my son becoming a vegetarian."

"I'm not talking vegetarianism," Helen clarifies with a laugh. "I'm a Texan, please. But I won't set foot in a Taco Bell. Did you see that awful footage from the slaughterhouse?"

The *E. coli* outbreaks, Leo remembers. A kid in the ICU at the Children's Hospital had just died. Tainted meat had been recalled, diseased cows reported. But the elderly and kids were more vulnerable, right?

"I haven't changed my eating any," he says with a shrug. "Don't get me wrong. I feel bad for that kid at CHOP, the people who got sick. But you can't live your life that way. It'd be like staying home because someone got hit crossing the street."

Helen's lips purse. She probably had her liberal theories about the importance of organic and free-range food. She was a Texan, yes, but probably from Austin, a granola hippie who grew up playing the guitar.

If Nora were here, she would smile. She liked his pragmatism in these situations. "Organic cows live in factories, too," he would point out if she were beside him. People get too freaked-out, he always tells her. People watch the local news and then think they're going to die from a sandwich. "You're better than Xanax," she once whispered to him.

He scans the room, but there is still no sign of her. Was she off in a corner of the house somewhere, pulling? But he's being paranoid. He shouldn't assume the worst. She's probably redoing her makeup or checking her dress for the umpteenth time, turning before the full-length mirror upstairs to examine her backside, whether it was magnified or made small. He cannot comprehend such behavior. Because once the dress is on, the party about to start, isn't it more sensible *not* to look and to simply tell yourself you look great?

But girls—women—don't think that way. When he reflects back, every girl he ever dated had some sort of issue. Eating disorders were practically fashionable in New York. Abby Stern used to giggle with Marni Siegler over who could eat the least at lunch, bragging about how they subsisted on carrots and pickles, while Leo smiled tolerantly. Because the thing was, even if they were both too skinny, in need of a solid cheeseburger, they were hot. "I can't believe you're dating Abby Stern" got muttered to him repeatedly throughout the eighth grade.

It was ridiculous how women tortured themselves when they should be revered. "You can make a *person*," he sometimes wants to tell Nora when he sees her frowning before the mirror. "Multiple people! You could make an army!"

Paul and Jake, talking down to Helen, do not realize they would feel like pansies if they ever saw her in her workshop operating the machinery. They don't think about how she might be more talented, more driven, more capable than they are. She is more diplomatic, that's for sure. There is never any acknowledgment that women hold a power men lack, the greatest power for happiness on earth, their insides magically rearranging themselves to incubate a human. How fantastic.

But no one sees it that way, and Leo fears that it might not be possible to raise a confident girl. From what he can tell, it all goes fine during childhood (the girls playing by the Giant Frog statue at Rittenhouse Square are spirited, bossy), and there is hope for adulthood (behold the languid caterer!), but everything in between is a mess. Maybe girls part with their confidence in childhood but then reclaim it later, like a scarf from the lost and found.

If we ever have a girl, he wants to tell Nora, we need to do something. "Do what?" she will ask, amused. Well that's just it. He doesn't know. Give her brothers? Forbid beauty magazines? Even his mother fell victim to that constant self-assault, and she had grown up with everything. If money couldn't guarantee security, what could?

Nora, listening to him, would roll her eyes. "It's not about money, Leo," she would say, exasperated. But then her eyes would trail off and he would know not to ask, to let this particular mystery rest.

It could be that the Web will help girls gain confidence. The Internet is blind to its users. When you saw an elegant piece of code, you didn't know who'd written it. You saw the work before you saw the person. The tech world is filling with people like Sanjay, wallflowers and introverts. Maybe awkward girls are teaching themselves HTML and Java, ready to rise in the ranks.

Leo spots her then, across the room. Nora. Her dress is white with bits of green, and he realizes that it matches the decor, the invites and napkins. Still trying, in her way. She is talking to some old fuddy-duddy, a guy in a tweed coat and bow tie Leo does not recognize. She is talking in that lovely way of hers, with her self-effacing laugh, the brilliant girl who does not see herself as such. Thoughtful Nora knows how to put the old man at ease, delighting him, impressing him, charming him without realizing she has.

Stephen stands a few feet over, a circle of women around him drinking in his words. The women laugh gaily, tall Stephen so good at making the women laugh. For a second, his eyes shift and meet Leo's. For a second, the room stills.

Leo looks quickly away and focuses on Nora. Beautiful. He will tell her tonight, will sidle up to her with a glass of champagne. I saw you from across the room and you looked so beautiful. Her hair is different, pulled up into some sort of complicated twist.

I don't make her unhappy, he thinks to himself. Yes, it's a rough time, and, no, I don't know how to fix it. But we're trying, and that's what matters. If you fall, you don't wait to get up.

He remembers a space of lawn one soft May evening. He was

visiting her at Yale, her senior year. "It looks like it's all going to be okay," she had said happily into his chest. They were in that grove of lilacs, purple and white, fragrant, slender spectators around them leaning in to listen. "Of course it'll be okay," he murmured, the heady smell of the flowers overwhelming the air.

He kissed her shoulder, kissed her neck. He reached his hands under her thin sweater. They made love right there, the world parting for them. Somehow they had known that they wouldn't get caught, wouldn't be seen, as though that garden on that day existed just for them. Later they walked back to her dorm hand in hand. I'm yours now, he thought as they climbed the steps. Sometimes you know a moment when you're in it, and that was it for Leo: that day, the lilac garden, the dark wooden stairs. I'm yours.

Fifteen

A bsinthe!" Stuart cries rapturously. "Your mother has thought of everything!"

Silver trays of martini glasses come forward like a fleet of ships, the glasses glowing green. "First the leg of duck, now this! What's next? Caramelized kidney? Joyce's food is brought to life!"

"You'll have to tell her," Stephen replies drily, knowing his mother will frown in confusion. "She'll be delighted."

"The green-eyed monster," Stuart muses as a tray nears. To Stephen's surprise, his white-haired adviser lifts two glasses. "Shall we? Hopefully this will not end in joint hallucinations."

They gently clink glasses. Stephen has never seen his adviser like this. He had worried Stuart would pooh-pooh it all, finding the party amateurish. But Stuart, typically elegant in his demeanor, is like a kid at a carnival, nearly vibrating with excitement over every detail. "'Re-Joyce!' Oh, very good, very good," he was exclaiming to Nora when Stephen joined them, holding up his cocktail napkin and waving it merrily. "Thank you," Nora mouthed to Stephen, looking slightly harried as she excused herself to get a drink.

Stuart lapped up Stephen's stories about past Bloomsdays, lapped them up like champagne. "An all-day reading," he said with a sigh, like a teenage girl hearing about a celebrity.

"If only I'd thought of it before," Stephen says, watching Stuart smack absinthe from his lips, "I would have invited you sooner."

"At least one of us would have enjoyed ourselves. To think that you have been complaining of this!"

Stephen smiles thinly. "It's all lost on me, I know."

"You are a Woolfian through and through, standing off to the side and scowling. Though I suppose such are the small rebellions of good sons, refusing to follow their parents' loves."

"You think my parents love Joyce?"

"You think they don't?"

"I think they want to. Which is different."

Stuart pauses, considers. "Well. That is admirable, too. It shows humility."

Stephen nearly chokes on his drink. "Humility! My mother probably thinks that's a brand of perfume."

Stuart chuckles. Stephen doesn't have the heart to tell him that his parents' knowledge of *Ulysses* is questionable at best. June has probably never read the thing. She pretends to love it, following Michael's lead, but also because in her museum- and play-going circles, bonus points are awarded for obscurity. It doesn't matter that no one understood why Damien Hirst's poor shark was frozen in formaldehyde, that yawns were stifled through Fritz Lang. What matters is that one could gloat, "We were at the screening of *Metropolis*, darling, and it was marvelous."

The funny part was that June genuinely loved museums and Broadway shows once. It was why they had lived in New York. But she soon learned that her taste in art was a source of mockery. "Monet!" her friends roared, wiping tears from their eyes. And so June gazed at *Water Lilies* in private while pretending to swoon over more in-vogue works. She kept *When Harry Met Sally* hidden behind the Godard and Truffaut DVDs until she forgot it was there.

As for Michael, he liked to talk about how he had read *Ulysses* at Harvard. "I was lucky enough to study with Richard Ellmann, the great Joyce scholar, you know." Stephen winced at his father's tone, the suggestion of modesty. Every time, he hoped his father wouldn't drop the name, but every time he did, the belly of a plane opening so that "Harvard" and "Ellmann" could hit their targets. In all likelihood, Michael had skimmed the book, as arrogant undergrads tend to do.

In fact, Stephen is the one responsible for the menu. When June cornered him months ago and asked that he handle the hors d'oeuvres ("It's the centennial," she pleaded), he knew he was being tasked with something literary, not culinary. "Leo's the foodie," he had been tempted to reply. "Why don't you ask him?"

Putting down his drink, too strong for his taste, Stephen tells Stuart, "There's something calculated about what my parents do. It's not just the ostentatiousness that bothers me. I sometimes think they're more interested in what *Ulysses* says about them than what it actually says. Our truest relationship with books is private. I love *Gatsby*. I love *Mrs Dalloway*. But I would never throw a party for them. A party ends up celebrating not the book but its title."

"Hmn. So if your parents were to read it to themselves in whispers and with the shades drawn, you would feel better?"

"But that's the thing. Joyce fans can never keep it to themselves. People who tell you that they love *Ulysses*—they wear it like it's a badge."

"Flaming. We're flaming, the lot of us."

"Pardon?"

Stuart smiles. "The Joyce community sometimes reminds me of the gay community. Some of us go quietly about our business, making our choices in love without fanfare. Others insist on being on the float as it comes down Fifth Avenue. Wearing the leather shorts with the ass cutouts."

Stephen laughs, startled.

"Joyce meant for his work to be a challenge," Stuart continues. "He didn't want it to be the shy girl at the party. Who was your friend again, that lovely woman?"

"Nora. She's my brother's fiancée, actually."

"A singer betrothed to a Leopold!"

"I know, I know. The whole thing worked out better than my parents could have planned."

"Life imitating art! Oh, it's too good. But, you know, she told me that she never felt so inadequate as when she read *Ulysses*, that it intimidated her more than any crowd. I encounter that often. Just the sight of it causes apprehension.

"The books you describe, Stephen. One feels drawn into their world, nearly hypnotized by the spell they cast. But *Ulysses* was never meant to seduce us gently. Joyce wanted it to confound."

"Yes, there's always an audience for that," Stephen mutters. "Literary acrobatics. You see it in the contemporary novel."

"You think it stunt work?"

"I'm skeptical of writing that tries too hard. Why can't writers just come out and say what they mean? Has sincerity gone out of style? I wonder if we've become too clever for our own good." But Stephen pauses. Doesn't he do it, too? Doesn't he hide behind his wit, using his sarcasm as a sword? How can he expect sincerity from the world if he isn't genuine himself?

"Novelists should have ambition!" Stuart counters. "They should aim for the fences. This is what one must applaud with Joyce. His work is Everest. Do you see? No one climbs Everest and says nothing of it. It's an accomplishment! We discover something meaningful in the climb precisely because of how it pushes us. It is a feat to read

Ulysses, just as Joyce intended. There are challenges and wonders at every turn."

Stephen reaches for his abandoned drink. He recognizes some of this speech from Stuart's opening lecture to his undergrads. Back when he was a TA, Stephen used to sit in the back row and watch their faces, set at an angle toward the podium, the light falling on them in profile. Some listened intently, studiously taking notes; others were inscrutable with their baseball caps and slumped posture. But you could feel Stuart's passion radiate out to the very last seat.

The course Stuart taught was ambitious: four epic novels read closely, painstakingly, over a semester. Those who signed up for it were there for the challenge. But though a few might falter through Faulkner or Proust, nothing caused universal agony like Joyce. No other writer thumbed his nose so flagrantly at the reader.

Stephen glances around as Stuart warms to his subject. Leo, on the far end of the room, is talking with Michael and his buddies along with a woman in a garish dress. Stephen watches as his brother accepts a martini from a passing tray, depositing his empty cocktail on it. The waiter makes a face as Leo's glass teeters.

We skipped dinner, Stephen realizes. They had planned on grabbing food earlier, knowing that hosts never get to eat at their own parties. "We'll swing by the deli and pick up stuff for everyone," Leo said, and Stephen could picture him selecting a different sandwich for each family member, wanting everyone to be pleased.

Stephen feels filled with regret. All Leo ever seeks is to please them, as if the family's happiness guarantees his own. Leo plays to them so eagerly and affectionately. Why on earth had Stephen been so cruel? What impulse had made him behave that way? He had been judgmental, harsh. Worse, he had feigned innocence. "You're the one who mentioned Nora," he had said. It is the noble art of self-pretense, puffing himself up as though it were his right.

"It's a book in which one finds everything," Stuart continues sagely. "I cannot tell you the number of times I've opened its pages and found a line, some passing thought—the most mundane detail—speaking directly to my set of circumstances! One finds it magically relevant, as though Joyce anticipates all. It is the great repository of everything."

But that's not what a book is supposed to do, Stephen reflects. A book is a place to lose yourself and then find yourself once more. A book draws you into its world like a charming host. It should not make you regret accepting its invitation.

"Mother!" he says, seeing her pass. He looks apologetically at Stuart, realizing he has interrupted him. "Forgive me, but I know you've been wanting to say hello. Mother, this is my adviser, Stuart White. Stuart, meet June Portman."

"How do you do," she says, turning on her radiant smile. Her white teeth are dazzling against her burgundy lipstick. "Michael and I have heard so much about you. We're delighted you could make it."

"The pleasure is mine!" Stuart beams. Stephen can tell that he is struck by June's beauty. "That woman did not seriously give birth to you two," Nora had once whispered to him. "I actually wouldn't be surprised if she hired someone for that," Stephen had replied.

"As someone who has spent the majority of his career on Joyce," Stuart says affably, "it is a pleasure to be in the company of fellow devotees."

A ripple passes across his mother's features, and Stephen can tell this is news to her. She never listens when Stephen talks about his adviser, always nodding in her way, her thoughts elsewhere. "Yes, of course, darling," she murmurs.

"And how dashing you look for the occasion."

"'In an oatmeal sporting suit!'" Stuart quotes. "Though I couldn't find a sprig of woodbine for the lapel."

June smiles blankly.

"Too obscure a reference?" He looks crestfallen. "I've always loved the wardrobe allusions."

"There's no such a thing as an obscure reference here," Stephen assures him. Why burst his bubble? He and his adviser have different tastes, and they often debate Joyce heatedly. But Stephen feels affection for him now, seeing how happy he is to feel included. "This is your parade," Stephen wants to tell him. He eyes his mother's satin shirt, her dangling earrings. "And here's your float."

Stephen makes as if he has spotted someone. "If you'll excuse me, I'll be back in a minute." He shoots his mom a glance in parting, imploring her to be kind. But he has deposited Stuart in excellent hands, a Miss America who might not always know the answers but has enough panache to hide it.

Stephen heads for the buffet table. The second one today, he thinks sullenly.

The smart move would be to stay by Stuart's side rather than dump him off like an unwanted drink. For now that Stuart is buoyant and buzzed, it would be the perfect moment to mention the idea of travel. Stephen could make a case for research, for wanting to see Woolf's papers. Stuart, in the sway of the party, would feel the romantic tug of a journey. "We must make sure you go," he would say, nodding, and just like that a plan would be set in motion, the ripples of a dropped stone circling out and sending Stephen across the pond.

A travel grant. After that, it would be easy to settle in New York.

Instead, Stephen finds himself staring at piles of food, the very items he had listed in a Word document for the caterer. He begins loading two plates with spiced-beef sandwiches and Gorgonzola salad, toasts with fried liver, and Stuart's beloved leg of duck. Stephen piles on oysters and slices of seedcake.

Will anything be different a year from now? Or will he still be procrastinating on his proposal and avoiding Nora and Leo? The next buffet might be theirs, he realizes with a start, Nora in a more elaborate white dress. Maybe this will be Stephen's fate, to wander from one buffet to the next, feeling only more alone.

He takes a deep breath and crosses the room. "I come bearing food," he tries.

Leo stands off on his own, absinthe cocktail in hand. "Thanks." Leo surveys the plates. "But fuck you."

"Look, you don't have to talk to me, but you should eat."

"Why? So you can feel better about yourself?" Leo's words slur just slightly, and Stephen wonders how many drinks he's had.

"We didn't eat before. You've been running around all day."

"Whatever, *Mom*. I stopped at Primo's, FYI."

Stephen pauses, momentarily amused by the image of their having a nagging mother. When, he wants to ask, has our mom ever pestered us to eat?

"Now you're laughing at me?"

"What? No, I—"

"Quit it, okay? Just stop. Whatever it is you're trying to do here, I think you've done enough."

"When were you at Primo's? That was probably closer to lunch. FYI."

"You don't know me." Leo steps closer, suddenly in Stephen's face, his breath a medicinal cloud of absinthe and lime. "You don't know Nora. Stick with books. Quit putting your nose where it doesn't belong."

Stephen is aware of a shift of bodies as Leo stalks away. He looks down at the plates in his hands. He is surprised by the sight of so much food, surprised to find himself holding all this.

He sits down on the window seat, setting the other plate across from him. It'll look like someone's with me, he thinks.

The party is reflected in the glass of the bay windows. He can't see out into the street, can only see the dresses and the bodies, the wash of warm light. His thoughts drift to his grandmother. This is where they would have put her—by the window, so that she would be out of the way. She would have watched the whole scene, and then Stephen would have talked with her about it on Tuesday.

He bites miserably into a piece of dry bread. Dinner with a ghost, he thinks, feeling the cool air through the window's glass. For just a moment, closing his eyes, he can feel her there beside him, keeping him quiet company.

Sixteen

N ora stands beside her friend, not wanting to disrupt his moment. He had closed his eyes just as she approached. She wonders if he might be trying to atone for the party, muttering a mourning prayer under his breath, but then his eyes blink open.

"That didn't go so great, I see." She gestures toward the second plate.

"I thought the surest way to his heart would be his stomach."

Nora smiles and sits beside Stephen. "That way might be blocked by a few martinis."

"I'm just glad someone's willing to sit next to me."

"Oh, I'm not the only one." Nora had watched the women turn their heads when Stephen passed. She picks up a piece of cake, flecked with poppy seeds. "Give him time. He'll come around."

"I'm not so sure he should."

"What's that supposed to mean?"

Stephen sighs. "I don't blame him for being mad. I need to learn how to shut my mouth."

"Oh, Stephen." Nora looks at him, hanging his head. "Don't be so hard on yourself. I didn't hear you say anything too bad."

"How much did you hear, exactly?"

"Enough to know you were just being a friend."

Stephen takes this in and reaches for a sandwich. "I hope Stuart didn't talk your ear off. It looked like you were cornered there."

"I didn't mind." She had been happy to listen to him, especially because he seemed so eager for company. The real issue had been her shoes.

Stuart had started talking to her smack in the middle of the room. There was nothing to lean against, no table or pillar, and she stood listening to him with a smile plastered on her face, wishing desperately for a chair. She shifted her weight back and forth, left to right, right to left, in silent counts of ten.

She remembered the magazine article suggesting that the trick at parties is to circulate. *Talk to each guest for ten minutes and then move on,* it advised. This struck her as so obvious at the time, in the purgatorial calm of the dentist's waiting room, that she made an impatient noise. Why did magazines specialize in the obvious? Later, in the dentist's chair, under the comforting weight of the lead apron, Nora imagined herself finally nailing the party this year and proving herself to be a worthy future in-law. This year, she would show them.

In practice, though, it felt impossible. How was she supposed to turn Stuart away when he was chattering on so happily? If she excused herself, where was she supposed to go? She didn't recognize anyone in her vicinity. This was not the conversational do-si-do she had imagined, gliding from one partner to the next. She was about to mumble that she needed to use the bathroom when Stephen appeared, saving her. And what did it mean that she felt more at ease at a dentist's office than at a cocktail party?

"I saw you talking to June and Friends," Stephen notes. "How'd that go?"

Nora makes a face in response and takes a huge bite of cake. Stephen bursts out laughing.

"That bad?"

It started so innocently. Nora relays to Stephen how June had gestured for her to come join her circle, introducing her to Catherine and Sissy. "You're the singer!" Catherine exclaimed. Catherine was tall and willowy, in a shimmery dress that accentuated her tan. She looked like the type who played tennis. Nora could picture her with a visor on, a white tennis skirt accentuating her long legs. "I've always wished I could sing. Do you perform?"

"Um, there's a café where I sing. Jazz? On Manning?" Nora's statements became questions as though she were fifteen. "And I just started singing with a gospel choir."

"Gospel?" Sissy stirred. Sissy was petite, her hair the color of autumn, wearing a navy dress.

"Nora studied opera at Yale," June interrupted.

"Gospel is wonderful," Catherine said, waving June off. "I've always loved it."

"Really?" Nora asked.

"We tried to get the Harlem Boys Choir for the last Komen event, actually." Behind Catherine, June rolled her eyes. "What an amazing thing that would be, don't you think? Pink ribbons on their black robes. They were booked, but we've got our eye on them for next year."

"Have you done gospel before?" Sissy wanted to know.

"Me? Oh, no. I mean, I didn't grow up going to church or anything like that."

"So what prompted you to join?" Catherine was so tall, but she had a gentleness about her, a permanent mildness in her expression. Nora decided to answer earnestly.

"I've always loved different forms of music, the challenge of trying something new. After being trained classically, it tests you to break those rules."

"That's wonderful," Catherine said warmly. "I'd love to come see you perform sometime."

"Oh! That would be great," Nora said, feeling pleased.

"We've been meaning to come hear the choir," June remarked. "Especially with Carol participating all these years."

"Carol?" Sissy asked.

"The maid," June said. "Though I should say *housekeeper*, which is the term we prefer. She and Nora are quite chummy, giggling down in the laundry room like a couple of sisters."

June smiled at her, and Nora felt the heat rise to her face.

"Ugh! Leave it to June," Stephen says, shaking his head. "That's awful."

It *was* awful. Nora had stood there, her cheeks advertising her shame while June sipped her wine. Nora felt like an exhibit at the zoo, the three of them white-coated scientists making notes on their clipboards. *Hangs out with black people. Flusters easily.*

"I, for one, have no talent in the arts," Catherine observed. "Though Bruce and I are thinking about dance lessons." June and Sissy cooed over this, but Nora's thoughts were still behind as, dazed, she felt the sting of June's words. What a fool she was, expounding on jazz and gospel, mentioning the club as though they would care.

"I should have been prepared for it," Nora says glumly. "I hate that feeling, you know? Being caught off guard is the worst."

"That's how my mom works, though. The minute there's a threat, she goes in for one of her jabs."

Nora gazes at her across the room, her chandelier earrings catching the light. June is wearing an emerald blouse with iridescent threads and long, cuffed sleeves. Surely that kind of sleeve has a name. The blouse is tucked into a satin skirt that falls to the floor. The collar, turned up, frames her face aristocratically.

It is a display Nora cannot keep up with, like the ever-changing windows at Saks. And it isn't just June's beauty, her perfectly assembled wardrobe. She also has a sort of polish, a refinement that Nora knows she will never achieve. When Nora complimented her on her shoes, satin peep-toes that sent her soaring into another stratosphere, June smiled indulgently. "D'Orsay heels," she said, and Nora felt the stab of her ignorance. This was the constant reminder, that Nora inhabits a world with objects whose names she does not know, blouses and shoes and furniture, a vocabulary she never learned.

"I don't feel like much of a threat," she confesses.

The women had continued on, mercifully ignoring her, talking about the latest gossip: alleged misconduct by a certain professional golfer, as reported to Sissy by the friend of a *very* good friend. "People just want to take him down because he's the very best," Catherine said dismissively. "I don't know about that," Sissy replied. "Men like that are never loyal."

"Who do you mean?" Nora wanted to ask loudly. "And if you prefer the term *housekeeper*, June, then why not use it?"

What a relief it would be to talk back! To voice her thoughts and be the uncultured loudmouth. Maybe it's how her dad feels, proud of his obnoxiousness. Maybe there is pride in the absence of manners.

"It's the worst feeling," she remarks to Stephen.

He raises a brow.

"Those comments. You're right that they're jabs. It would be better if she just came out and said something. But instead it's always in this sneaky way that makes you think you've imagined it."

Stephen nods. "People can put up with being bitten by a wolf. What riles them is a bite from a sheep."

Nora looks down at her plate of food. She probably has poppy seeds stuck in her teeth. The cocktail napkin in her hand is stuffed into the shape of a ball, and without thinking about it, she's slumped into her usual terrible posture, the shape of a C.

"I'm an impostor," she says.

"Nora! What do you mean?"

"I'm always trying so hard to fit in, to play the part. Every year I tell myself that the party will finally feel normal, that this will come naturally to me. But it's not who I am. All of this—it's never going to be second nature."

Each year, the party looms on the calendar. The hunt begins in spring for the perfect dress. She had overdressed her first year, trying too hard in red, then overcompensated the next in a casual floral wrap ("How very bohemian," June had murmured, surveying her). Every year since she has recalibrated, trying to get the look just right. The ivory dress on the hanger struck her as the perfect balance, slightly understated in the fabric and length, making up for it in the details. "It looks great on you," the salesgirl confirmed in the fitting room.

But June still managed to make her feel like a peasant, like someone who had wandered in from the shore, dirty and in rags, trailing seaweed.

"But don't you see? That's the point."

"What do you mean?"

"My mom doesn't want you to feel comfortable. That's how *you* would want someone to feel. She has none of that concern. She can only feel secure by putting others down."

"You really think that?"

"She doesn't just do it to you. Surely you've seen it in action."

Nora considers this. At one moment June had suddenly nudged Catherine and Sissy. "Look at Anne!" she hissed when a stunning woman entered the room. "Wearing a mink stole as if it's fall!" Sissy smirked, but Catherine shrugged. "Well, it was a chilly day," she pointed out, and Nora thought to herself that perhaps Catherine wasn't so bad.

No dress will ever cut it. This is what Stephen has been trying to tell her. June's game was predicated on undermining people. She came up behind you and settled her spectacular shoe on your end of the seesaw. She never wanted you to feel as if you'd gotten the balance right.

"Maybe," Nora admits. "But what am I supposed to do about it?"

"You could stop trying to please her. You could think about how you bring something else to the table."

"Which would be what? My charming Jersey roots? My heart-warming friendship with the help?"

Stephen regards her, his face thoughtful. "Think of all the people in our family as cocktails," he says finally. "Like what sort of drink would you say my dad is?"

"Oh, I don't know." Nora thinks it over. "Something high-powered. Scotch, I guess?"

"Scotch it is. Leo?"

"Leo's more of a beer."

"He's such a beer. And June?"

Nora looks at her, tall and elegant. "A glass of white wine."

"Chilly and tart."

Nora laughs. "I like this. And you?"

"Pick something good."

"A glass of red. Smooth and elegant."

"A pinot," Stephen says with dignity. "One day the masses will wake up from their love affair with merlot."

"And Carol would be like a rum and Coke."

"Carol?"

"You know, kind of spicy but sweet. Though maybe I'm just thinking of island drinks." Nora frowns, wondering if it's a racist choice.

"No, I was surprised you mentioned her. I thought the next candidate would be you."

"Oh." Nora bites her lip. "I'll bite, I guess." Her pulse quickens as she watches Stephen's face.

He leans forward. "Water."

"Water? Stephen, that's awful!"

"No, no! You're virtue instead of vice. A source of clarity in our corrupt household. That's the whole point!"

"Ugh! I can't believe you think I'm water. Municipal tap, right?"

"Nope. Fresh from a mountain spring."

"Uh-huh. Speaking of which"—she dangles her empty glass—"shall we?"

"Sure."

"No one ever asks for water, you'll notice."

Stephen smiles and picks up the plates. "I'll get rid of these and meet you. Something tells me our cold chardonnay wouldn't be pleased to see these at the front of the room."

"Okay." Nora feels lighter when she stands. It felt good to sit, and probably the champagne was kicking in. Being tipsy usually helps with heels.

But it's more than that. Stephen always has the ability to make her feel better. Leo would have batted her concerns away. "Nah, she didn't mean anything by it," he would have said if she told him about June. "She's probably been wanting to hear Carol sing." Nora, exasperated, would regret having brought it up.

Stephen was right. Nora is suddenly glad she hadn't shrugged off Stuart, making up some excuse the way that silly magazine suggested. She didn't have it in her to act that way, even when her feet have grown numb beneath her. She may not always know what to say, what to wear, how to handle guests—but at least she knows how to listen.

She makes her way to the bar, glancing around for Leo. He is talking to a group of people with yet another drink in hand. He catches her eye and winks, then makes a lewd gesture with his tongue. "Leo!" she almost chastises aloud, horrified. She shakes her head at him. He grins.

Drunk. Normally he can hold his liquor, but she's seen him down several of those horrible green martinis.

"Two glasses of champagne, please," she says to the bartender, who nods.

"I didn't really mind" was what she had meant to say to Stephen, seeing his failed attempt at reconciliation with Leo. Watching as he'd bravely offered that plate of food and been spurned.

The bartender passes her the two glasses of bubbly. "I didn't mind hearing you say what you did," she wanted to say. "Because it was a relief, in a certain way, to hear it."

But instead of relaying any of this to him, she had ended up talking about the ridiculous incident with June—as though Stephen didn't have more important things on his mind. She has yet to even talk with him about his grandmother. What kind of a friend is she?

A clinking of glass alerts her to the front of the room. The annual toast, she remembers, seeing Michael stand before them. Stephen is several yards away and makes eye contact with her, but there are too many people for him to squeeze through. He looks at her apologetically. Nora glances down at her two glasses, wondering what to do with the extra, then turns to the guest next to her. "Would you mind passing this down?" she asks. She points to Stephen. Somehow, the drink makes its way into Stephen's hand, and accepting it, he looks delightedly at her, as though receiving a surprise award. "Cheers," she mouths.

Michael, at the front of the room, clears his throat. "Thank you very much for coming." His voice is pleasant, an alto-baritone of amiability, its warmth carrying across the room.

"As you know, June and I always look forward to this day. Today marks an especially memorable Bloomsday because it is, of course, the centennial." Here he nods up toward the banner above him, and a ripple of appreciation passes through the room.

"If you'll forgive the shameless plug, I should also mention that there's a wonderful biography of Joyce coming out in honor of the occasion, published by a charming local press." A chuckle from the crowd, and Nora remembers the postcards downstairs on the entry table advertising the book.

"Today is also a memorable day for very different reasons." He pauses, shifting his weight. "For those of you who don't know, this morning we buried my mother."

Nora's breath catches. She looks around the room. June has the smile from the book plug still frozen on her face. People glance her way, surprised.

Michael clears his throat. "How strange it must seem, to hold a party the same day as her funeral. To drink champagne and chat in lieu of traditional mourning rites." Nora's heart gallops. What was Michael doing? She tries to catch Stephen's eye, but he is watching with a detached expression. Leo doesn't look concerned, but then again, he isn't entirely sober. The silence in the room is absolute.

"It might strike some as inappropriate. The rabbi who performed the services this morning would certainly frown on all this." Michael attempts a half smile, but the room gives him nothing in return.

"Many people would wonder why a book, of all things, deserves attention on a day like today. Or why we should have a party, for that matter. But to me"—he hesitates, perhaps sensing the vulnerable mood of the room—"to me, never before has this book or this party mattered more.

"Part of me thinks my mother would have wanted us to mourn in the traditional Jewish way." His eyes don't meet Stephen's, but Nora can feel these words directed at him. "Tradition meant something to her. Religion meant a great deal to her. But another part of me thinks—knows—that she would have wanted death to steal off with as little as possible. She always wanted what was best for me and my sister, and I think that was her real gift. She wanted what we wanted."

Nora hears the strain of his voice. From the belly, she thinks, imaging the air burdening his windpipe. It is what she always tells her students.

"As you know, *Ulysses* opens with a young Stephen Dedalus reflecting on his mother's death. He, too, wonders about the mourning he has denied her. 'You could have knelt down, damn it, Kinch, when your dying mother asked you,' Buck Mulligan tells him." This Michael reads from an index card that has materialized in his palm.

"Mulligan has little regard for his friend. His rebuke is meant to goad him, to get a rise out of him. He later offers a gruff apology, saying that he meant no offense to the memory of his mother. 'I am not thinking of the offense to my mother,' Stephen replies. 'I am thinking of the offense to *me*.'

"And this"—Michael tucks the card into his jacket pocket—"this is what struck me today when I went looking for answers. When I wondered why I was choosing to go forward with this party— when I was up in my office, feeling the weight of the day. Part of me was unsure. Part of me wondered if we shouldn't just cancel. If that would be the more appropriate thing." Here, his eyes finally do meet Stephen's, and Nora understands that children can challenge their fathers as much as fathers can destroy their kids.

"I don't know that I would've noticed these lines a year ago. Certainly, I wouldn't have looked at that passage the same way. At different times I've been struck by different things. By Stephen's intellect. By Bloom's humanity. By that scene where he shits in the outhouse, the shock of that, and how it is rendered into something beautiful.

"But today I saw those lines and they were a reminder. More, an invitation. That I think not of the offense to her. That I think instead of me.

"And so I find myself thinking two things on this day, the six-teenth of June, which, like the one before it a hundred years ago, begins with a funeral but ends with something all too lovely. I find myself thinking that with death, we must remember who is left behind. We think automatically of the departed, but we must also think of who is left standing."

Nora feels the wisp of a breeze touch her shoulder. Even at a party, she thinks. Even at a party about a goddamn book.

"Second, I am reminded that literature provides a comfort. We find solace in its pages. No one can say the right thing to me today; it is a day where words feel insufficient. But this book still speaks to me, after all this time. It always manages to reach me. And that is something worthy of being honored." Michael pauses and picks up his champagne flute from the windowsill. The room is still silent, but in a different way.

"And so today we celebrate Bloomsday. We celebrate a book's ability to move us. We celebrate all that makes life worthy, all that makes us rise out of bed when rain and a funeral await. We affirm Molly's glorious 'Yes I said yes I will Yes.' We celebrate this together, and in that I take great comfort. Because when all else has passed, this book will remain."

He holds his glass aloft. "On behalf of June and my sons, Stephen and Leopold, thank you for coming. Cheers."

And the crowd murmurs a quiet "Cheers" that is respectful but also a little uncertain, still heavy with the sobriety of the moment. June is gazing at Michael with a glow about her face, a well of feel-ing for her husband. Leo and Stephen are also looking at their fa-ther, Leo's expression sympathetic, nearly teary. The three of them as they look at Michael are like magnets, the ties drawing each one to him nearly visible.

That is what family means, Nora thinks. Around her, the crowd is milling, whispering. "A funeral?" she hears. "His mother?"

It is true they hadn't included her. Would it have been so hard for Michael to mention her name? Did June know that she'd been cruel? They could be aloof, selfish, without realizing it. But at times Nora catches a glimpse of beauty there. Not just beauty. Love.

Theirs was their own love. It wasn't like her mother's, protective and obvious. Maybe it was a selfish kind of love because it had trouble letting go of its own desires, but it was there. Sometimes you saw it when you least expected—not in an embrace, but in a speech. It came out before a crowd because that was their only way of expressing it. They couldn't access their sense of family at the kitchen table or in a hug before going to bed. They didn't go to the mall or to matinees. Theirs is not an everyday family. But it is a family nonetheless.

Nora's father had stood like a buffoon in the corner after the funeral. He smiled in his awkward way, nodding at guests, receiving their sympathy as if he had earned it. There was no speech.

He had started a fight with her that very afternoon. She wanted to kick herself for not having seen it coming. The dishes. She'd let the dishes go. "Your mother's funeral, and you can't even do this much?" His voice was thick with disgust. There was no thought as to what she might be going through. Was it so much to ask? To have a dad who cared?

Leo thought she was embarrassed by her parents' lack of money. He didn't see that his family's wealth is in its flaws. *That* is their luxury. Oh, they have their issues, issues that could be stretched into years of therapy should any of them seek it. But the absence of yelling, the absence of fear. To not know what it's like to have your father scream. To not tiptoe around that sleeping giant of anger, fearful of what might rouse it. To have this family's set of problems would be a laugh.

A hand snakes around her waist. "Hi," Leo breathes into her neck. She smells the alcohol on his breath. His arm around her is heavy. "So beautiful," he mumbles, though she isn't sure if he means the toast or her.

"I'll let you two have some time together," Leo had said that day. Thinking she and her dad would want time alone, the way a normal father and daughter would. "Okay," she replied, smiling weakly. "Sure." She watched him walk down the block to the park.

Some part of her hoped her dad might be a little different when she came back inside. That he might, in his awkward way, make an effort. "So it's just us now, huh?" Or "I know this has been hard for you, Nora." And it is this part of herself that she hates the most, the part that had hoped despite knowing better.

"You left dishes," he said in the kitchen. "You knew everyone was coming today."

"Here," she whispers to Leo, slipping her arm around him. "Lean on me."

"What kind of daughter are you?" The plate he was gesturing with fractured as he brought it down. Maybe he didn't mean to do it so forcefully. An edge sliced his finger and he looked at her accusingly, the red gash echoing his angry face. Tears sprang in her eyes.

Some air, Nora thinks, shuffling to the door. But when they reach the cool air of the hall, it is Nora who feels dizzy.

"I'll be right back," Leo says, lumbering to the bathroom.

When she called her dad a few days later to check on him, he was irate that she hadn't called sooner. "The food's running out!" he complained, and for the first time since her mom died, Nora wanted to laugh. He wasn't trying to be intimidating or frightening. In a strange way, he was a child. Of course he didn't know how to be father. "There's this place," Nora told him calmly, "called a *store*." She felt strangely peaceful hanging up, as if she had dodged a bullet.

Nora knows exactly what Michael meant about those left behind, the choices you make. Her father didn't make it hard. Michael opted for a party over grief. Why couldn't she do the same?

People always have choices. It is just a matter of seeing them. She doesn't have to be her father's keeper or come running when he calls. It occurs to her that maybe this is the one perk of her mother's absence. Maybe Nora no longer has to put up with him.

The Portmans had suggested what she might have instead. Not in terms of possessions or money. But their vision of what they might be, what they might still become, had perhaps shifted some part of her to feel she had a right to expect more. To love and be loved, to not know fear. To feel her choices and be brave enough to declare them to the world.

The hall around her is filled with chatter. Above the voices, she hears June's tinkling laugh. Enough with envy, she thinks. She stands up straighter. The wall, at her back, is solid, cool. The wall at her back tells her she is enough.

Seventeen

Leo stares at the toilet, the open bowl grinning, a white jack-o'-lantern taunting him. C'mon! it says. Leo, by the locked door, hesitates. To puke or not to puke?

That is the question.

He slides down to the cold slate floor. His dad had pulled a number on his mom with these tiles, switching the French slate she ordered for a cheaper option.

To Leo, it had seemed like a reasonable plan. When his dad held up the samples, they were indistinguishable: volcanic, rough to the touch. Leo shrugged. "Looks the same to me." "Good man," his dad said, cuffing him on the shoulder. When his mom spotted the cardboard box with the Oregon stamp down in the basement, she was livid. "But you didn't know when you saw the *floor*," his dad protested. "Only when you saw the box!"

Leo closes his eyes. His mom never took stuff like that lightly. On *The Cosby Show*, Clair Huxtable would have hollered, *"Cliff!"* And Cliff, in one of his geometric sweaters, would have pointed at her. "Gotcha!" he would have said, eyes bright. By the show's end, Clair would have decided to buy a new dress with the money saved from the tile—a perfect compromise, bringing the show full circle. Cliff would protest the cost of the dress ("You spent *how* much?" he'd say, holding the receipt), but then she would step out wearing it, pausing in the doorway, and he'd make his *Oh oh oh* face, his eyes rolling back while he did a little dance with his fists. Then he'd chase her around the bedroom. *The Cosby Show* almost always ended with the Huxtables about to have sex. It was no wonder they had five kids.

Leo loved that show growing up, watching it faithfully every Thursday. How they came together, those Huxtables! They had money but weren't obscene about it. And no matter what an episode started with—a joint found in Theo's textbook; Rudy stealing money off the counter—it always ended on the right note, balance restored.

There was probably a formula for it. Some sort of way to calibrate problems and bring everyone into harmony. "Fight with judgmental brother" could go into the Cosby calculator and it would spit out a script. "Bridal wedding jitters" could be handled, no problem.

At work, Leo makes his team put together a sheet of FAQs to go with every client proposal. *This sounds great. How much is it going to cost?* and *Why the on-site visits?* They customize it for each project, a chance to show that they've been listening. It works as a cheat sheet, too, a way for the client to get quick answers after zoning out in meetings. Look! Leo always wants to say when he passes it out. Look at us already anticipating your needs!

The thing has been a hit, and Sanjay had personally complimented Leo on the idea. FAQs have their own sort of golden ratio, information and brevity and tone all in balance, with little quips to keep everything peppy. Just like on a sitcom.

You could say things in FAQs that you couldn't say in meetings. The stuff you would never say aloud was suddenly right there on paper, complete with exclamation points. *Whoa! That price sounds*

steep. Where's the money going? In the polite, formal world of conference rooms, the chatty FAQs cut to the chase.

If only they could exist in real life, floating down from the ceiling
when you were faced with a dilemma.

**Q. If hammered, or well on your way, is it a good idea to
make yourself puke? Like if you think there's a fair chance
you're going to anyway? Or is that just kind of wrong?**

**A. Good question! We've definitely all been there. While not
a great strategy to turn to frequently, it is okay on occasion to
bow to the porcelain god. Chances are, if the idea occurs to
you, there's probably a reason why. Just remember to hit the
mouthwash!**

Leo has no desire to puke, feels none of that tickle of bile in his
throat. He isn't there yet. But he knows that if that last green martini
is permitted to reach his liver, he will be back here out of necessity.
And it won't be pretty.

Over to the bowl he goes. He gets down on his knees and thinks
of nasty things: the time in third grade Marty Goldman had chased
him around the room, snot running out of both nostrils, past his
chin, the horror of it stretched over his lips; that time Dedalus rolled
in shit, actual shit, and Leo had to bathe him in the maid's bathroom
because Mom didn't want the groomer to quit. Fecal clouds had risen
into the air—

Leo retches. He grips the sides of the toilet. The toilet is his
friend, sympathetic, waiting with open arms.

He doesn't mind being so close to it. It is impeccably clean, except for a single pubic hair caught on the rim, pitched like a flag. It
ushers in the second wave, his stomach emptying, and Leo thinks
he is in the home stretch.

He sits back on his heels. He feels a debt to the toilet. How se-
renely it accepted what it was given. We should all be so stoic.

No one ever sat there and felt grateful for the thing. No one ever thought, Well, damn, toilet, thank you.

One more. Leo feels the last of it come out. He reaches for toilet paper, wipes his mouth, then flushes.

In the mirror, his face is splotchy. He splashes it with cold water, rinses his mouth. Opens the medicine cabinet. No mouthwash, but he spots a toothbrush, his dad's, probably, and quickly brushes his teeth, the toothpaste bracing. The mint cuts into his gums and he wonders if they really put fiberglass in there or if that's a myth. Patting his face dry, he attempts to take stock of himself.

Q. Did that actually help?

A. Not really, no. Stephen was right, you haven't eaten enough. It's always a tough combo: drinks, empty stomach. Go get some food!

A tall order in view of his most recent activity. Just the thought of those oysters, that sweating mound of liver—

Leo feels the bile rise and grips the sink's edge. Steady, steady. The doorknob rattles as someone tests it. He remembers Nora waiting for him and does a last check of his reflection in the mirror. His face is flushed, but otherwise he looks good. He is wearing that shirt she likes, bright blue with thin stripes, the stripes perhaps making him look taller.

He feels grateful to Nora. She has gone easy on him today. He'd probably done fifty trips up and down the stairs that afternoon, fetching things for everyone else. But Nora mysteriously stayed off his list. She hadn't given him the wide eyes and said, "Oh, *shoot*. I totally forgot my coat back at the loft. And, well, I'd go get it, but . . ."

No one filled in that blank anymore for Leo. They didn't even let the sentence trail off convincingly. They sent him to do their bidding, not even trying to come up with a reason half the time.

Q. And why? Why do they think they act that way?

A. Because I let them.

It's true. Leo prides himself on being there for his family. He isn't especially good-looking or smart, but he's helpful. That's his role. He's so predictable in wanting to help that they no longer wait for him to offer.

Q. Does this mean that I'm a pushover?

A. Pretty sure you've answered that one for yourself, bud.

"Hey," Nora calls out. "You okay?"

Leopold crosses the bathroom, opens the door. "Me? I'm great." He turns to her. "Why wouldn't I be?"

She smiles. "Let's go get a drink."

"Um. Okay."

Leo does not bother with the Q and A's on this one.

"That toast was amazing," Nora enthuses. She is caught up in the party, animated, and she leads him through the crowd. He estimates forty or fifty people, a good number this year. "I mean, when he started out—I didn't know where he was going with it, you know? Did you expect him to say that?"

"Hmn? Which part, love?"

Nora throws Leo a look, not fooled by his trick. "The part about the *funeral*. That part. You seemed pretty moved yourself, there. Ooh, let's just grab these." She spots glasses of champagne ready for the taking.

"Did you eat?" he asks her casually. "Dinner, I mean?"

"I had a bite back at the loft."

"That's good," he says vaguely, steering her toward the food. He scans the table for something easy. Crackers, he sees happily, grabbing a handful.

"Anyway, I was so nervous for him. And you could tell no one had a clue—about, you know, today. It has to be strange, to hear it like that. To come to a party and then hear about a funeral."

You're so pretty in your dress, he stupidly wants to tell her. It has a V-neck. Deep enough that he can see where her freckles end and the creamy milk of her skin begins. He wonders what she has on underneath. Usually it was just boring beige, but sometimes for parties she puts on something special, black and lacy.

The crackers are crumbly, dry. He washes them down with some champagne. It's okay, he tells himself. You've eaten now.

"And then, the way he brought it all together at the end—it was so sincere. It was brave of him to go there."

Like the show, he wants to tell her. Just like *The Cosby Show*. "That's what a good speech does. A good anything. It goes somewhere weird but makes you feel like it turns out okay in the end."

She looks at him and laughs. "My, my."

"You look so good," he says, lowering his voice. "So beautiful."

"I do, huh?"

"I mean it. I couldn't stop talking to you when you were looking at—I mean, looking at you. When you were talking. To the old guy?"

Nora giggles. "Stuart? He was sweet."

"Who is he?"

"That's Stephen's adviser. Chair of the department." But she sees the look on Leo's face. "You're not still mad at him, are you?"

Leo looks away and drains his glass.

"You know he means well," she says softly.

Q. Am I the toilet of this family, accepting its shit?

He thinks of the white bowl with its leering grin. "Means well. Everyone means well."

"Come over here." Nora draws him to the alcove so that they can have some privacy. She stops in front of the desk where Leo found

Stephen earlier—a lifetime ago, it seems. She puts her hands on his shoulders and pushes him into the chair. He goes down easily.

"You never stay mad at people."

"Maybe." He feels strangely light in the chair, as if he might be floating.

"But you're mad at him. Over what?"

"He needs to mind his own business. He always has these opinions, like he's so high-and-mighty. He was talking about Grandma Portman one minute, and then suddenly he wasn't. He ambushed me!"

"Listen. I kept thinking about your dad today, that this was going to be an awful day for him. But I think the person hit the hardest by this was Stephen. It sounds like he was really close to her."

"'Sounds like' is right! None of us knew."

"But that's his business. He doesn't owe us any explanations."

Leo looks up at her and folds his arms across his chest.

"What?" she asks.

Q. What do family members owe one another?

A. The truth. Always, and nothing less.

"We don't know Stephen. We think we do, but he has these secrets. It's like he's a spy!"

"That's preposterous." Nora laughs. "Stephen's not like that at all."

"So you knew about his trips to the nursing home? And how much he loved it there?"

Leo watches her face falter. "We all have our secrets," she replies defiantly.

"Look, my dad—you liked that toast, and I know you like him, and there's a reason. It's because he's *open*. That toast—" Leo squints. He had seen a connection ahead of him like a mirage. It fades with his approach. "You liked that toast because . . ."

"Because he was open?" Nora tries.

"Yes! *Exactly*. Because he was open! Because he came out and said what he thinks! My dad doesn't *hide* anything. He doesn't suddenly tell you, 'Oh, P.S., I've actually been leading a double life this whole time.'"

"'Double life' is kind of strong."

But something bothers Leo, some pesky thing. "Like before, he was talking about life insurance," Leo says instead, ignoring the pesky thing. He pauses, slightly taken aback by his own words.

"Life insurance?" Nora repeats, puzzled.

"Yeah, with those guys. Paul. The other guy." Leo frowns, trying to remember the name. "Gary? Greg? Anyway, he was saying he thinks it's this new thing, financially." Leo can't make the words come out right. His dad had started in on his theory in his assured way. "Something I've been playing around with," he said casually, and the guys leaned in to listen.

"He talked about life insurance getting traded. People could sell their policies for money." Like if you knew you were going to die, Leo almost says, but he stops himself. Even when drunk, the traffic guard is on duty, red sign in hand. *No go.*

"Life is ours to gamble with," his dad had said. Leo had immediately seen the beauty of it. If you knew you were dying, why not cash out? You could pay the hospital bills or go on some grand adventure. Who knows? Maybe it even helped to have people bet against you. You could prove them wrong. Or you could go to the grave knowing you had paid your debt, brought a positive gain to others.

"God, that's awful. Is that really what we've come to?"

Nora doesn't get it. Insurance is like any other commodity. Why shouldn't you be able to sell it? His dad had phrased it so sensibly that you could tell his friends were impressed. Maybe even Helen, too. His dad had found the silver lining to the darkest cloud.

The minor is proved by the major, Leo wants to tell Nora. It was a small example, but it drove home a larger point. "He doesn't shy away from stuff," Leo says. "He's never reluctant to go there, to talk about things that other people won't."

"Hmn. So you weren't surprised that he brought up the funeral?"

Leo pauses. That, actually, had taken him aback. "Well," he says, hedging. He leans against the desk. The wheels of the chair suddenly give.

"Whoa!" Nora quickly stops the base of the chair with her foot and reaches out with her arms to grab him. "Easy there. You okay?"

"Yeah. Totally good. You were saying?"

Nora regards him. "I'm not drunk," he wants to say, but he knows this will only make him sound drunker.

"It's not always so easy," Nora says finally. "*You're* that way, and that's great. Maybe your dad's that way, too. But not everyone is."

That pesky feeling is back, and Leo frowns to himself. My dad's open, he had told Nora. But what Stephen said about the nursing home didn't exactly fit with that.

"I've struggled with that part of it," Nora says earnestly. "You know, it can be hard to talk about—about everything that's happened."

Leo makes his automatic noise of sympathy.

They put her out there preemptively, Stephen had said. The same way Leo had tried puking. It wasn't a great solution.

Q. Why isn't that strategy effective?

A. Because sometimes misery comes and bites you in the ass anyway. And there's nothing you can do to prevent it.

Grandma Portman had suffered the pulmonary embolism in February. When Leo looked it up online at the time, he read about the causes. Inactivity was first on the list. Bed rest, long flights. He vowed to get up from his desk more at work.

But what if being at the nursing home had contributed? Her house in Brookline was always immaculate. The few times they went up to visit in years past, it was obvious she took great pride in it, every surface gleaming, different pots bubbling on the stove. Leo thinks of his beloved old skillet. What if it got sold without his permission? What if it and his apartment and his job and his car—his car!—all got taken away?

Maybe that house had been her heart, sustaining her. Maybe it gave her a sense of purpose after her children had left and her husband had died. Maybe you took away the heart and the blood stopped pumping.

"This'll be easier," Dad had said in his reasonable voice. "And *nursing home* is a misnomer. It's a social living community for seniors."

"Makes sense," Leo had replied. He didn't doubt his dad for a second. Leo never stopped to think about whether it was what his grandmother wanted. He'd always assumed the embolism was inevitable, but what if that place had caused it? Maybe the clots were her accumulated misery, climbing the veins of her legs like the ink on Helen's skin.

"And it's the same with the wedding," Nora comments.

"With the wedding?" Leo repeats, jarred into the present.

"Leo, were you even listening?"

"Of course I was. You just kind of threw me for a loop there, at the end."

Nora regards him skeptically. She sighs. "Look, I just—I know this isn't what you want to hear right now. I know you're mad at Stephen. But, to be honest, it was sort of a relief to hear him say that stuff. It was nice to know that I haven't been forgotten. Because that's how it feels sometimes."

He feels his anger stir. Forgotten? She is in his every thought.

"There's this constant pressure with the wedding," she continues. "Stephen was right, in a way, that it's too much to think about right now."

"The thing is, love," he says, keeping his voice casual, "we don't actually think about it much anyway."

"You see!" Nora pounces. "That's just it! That's exactly what I mean. You're always alluding to it, referring to how we aren't planning, aren't doing enough."

"I wasn't complaining," he interrupts. "I was just saying—I fail to see how I'm putting 'constant pressure' on you." Leo thinks of his clients. He thinks about how he tries to echo their language back to them.

But Nora is shaking her head, and with alarm he sees tears of frustration in her eyes. Ugh, Leo thinks. He wants to throw his hands in the air. For the second time today he has been ambushed. But he isn't allowed to express his own anger in these moments. The traffic guard eyes him, whistle at the ready, redirecting him with a winding arm.

"What is it, love?" he asks.

"You don't pressure me. I get that. But I can feel you *not* pressuring me. Does that make sense? When you know someone really well, you can tell when they aren't saying things. And I can feel you not talking about the wedding. I know it drives you nuts to not have a date—"

"But I've never said that! I've never—"

"I'm not saying you have. I'm not saying you complain. I'm talking about the stuff you don't say."

Leo rests his head against the back of the desk. He presses against it, resisting the urge to bash his head into it. "Are we really having a fight about what I don't say?"

"Weren't you the one just talking about being open?"

"So what you're saying is that you want the wedding to go away?" She eyes him and then bites her lip.

"You can say it," he says tiredly.

"Yes," she answers in a small voice.

"Say more about why." He massages his temples.

"I don't want to feel like the delinquent, like I'm holding you back. I don't want the constant guilt of that. But I also don't think the planning should be filled with dread."

He tries not to wince. "Dread?"

"Every time I try and think about it—and I have, Leo, really. But all of that stuff—invites and dresses and guests. It's just too much for me right now."

"Okay." Leo nods. The way to the daughter is through the mother, he thinks. The way to mother through daughter. And suddenly he sees it.

Q. What if things aren't going as expected?

A. Change your expectations.

"And what if I were to make that all go away? The two things you just talked about, the guilt and the dread. What if I were to make them vanish?"

"How?" She glances down at her ring, as if he might perform a trick with it. He feels like a chess master who has seen three moves ahead.

"Let me plan the wedding."

"What?"

"Just hear me out a second. I think the issue here is that you're confusing the planning with the wedding."

"What do you mean?"

"Plenty of people dread wedding planning."

"But brides live for that stuff! They have binders! Magazines!"

"Not all brides. Wedding planners exist for a reason."

"For people who are busy," Nora says dismissively. "Those people still enjoy it."

"Says who? You're making assumptions." He watches her face. "I've been unfair. I see it now. I've been trying to get you on board. But you're right. That's a lot of pressure. And why? You don't want to be thinking about that stuff. Listen, Nora, all those excited brides? I bet most of them have reluctant grooms. We've just swapped roles!"

She smiles a little despite herself. He is suddenly excited by this version of events. "*This* is what we haven't been saying," he says eagerly. "You're absolutely right, Nora. There are things we haven't been saying. So let's just be open about all of it. You don't want to plan the wedding? Then don't! It makes total sense that you want nothing to do with it."

"It does?"

"You've had a rough year. I know how hard it's been. I know that better than anyone. So why add this to your plate?"

Leo is aware of himself seated while Nora stands. He gazes up at her. There should be a chair when guys propose, he thinks. "Let me do this for you. Let me take care of it. It's the least I can do."

She is quiet, looking off to the room beyond.

"You'll feel better knowing it's taken care of. I bet I could handle it in a weekend, make all the decisions. Then they'd be done. That way you know I'm not thinking about it. That way there's nothing between us." He wipes his hands together as though getting rid of crumbs.

"But doesn't it bother you?"

"What?"

"That I don't want to be involved? Don't you *want* me to be involved?"

If Leo had a ring, he would present it now. "But that's just it. I don't want you to be anything other than what you are." He knows it is a winning line, and Nora rewards him with softened eyes. She leans down and puts her arms around his neck.

"Is that a yes?" he says, smiling.

"Oh, Leo."

"I get it, I get it. No pressure." He thinks of the bartender and his ceremonious bow, tries to imagine some sort of gallant gesture. All he can think to do is to pat his lap.

She sits obediently but perches on his knee, looking distracted. He puts his hand on the small of her back to steady her and is aware, dimly, of his desire. If he plays his cards right, he might be able to close the alcove door. And why not? He thinks of the lilac garden. How long had it been since they'd felt passion like that? Christ, how long had it been at all? He imagines reaching across her body and sliding the pocket door shut. He imagines their bodies intertwined while the party continued, just feet away.

He touches Nora's leg, tracing circles across her knee.

At work, he feels vastly superior to Dave, takes pride in being more responsible, more on the ball. But some part of him cringes at the thought of Dave having diagnosed him so accurately. Whipped? Yes. Getting any? No.

Leo brings his hand up to Nora's face, touches her jaw. But his hand makes momentary contact with her hair and she freezes. She follows his gaze to the doorframe, to the crowd, as though she can sense his thoughts. There was a time when she would have been game.

"Maybe what you say is true," she concedes.

"Maybe?" he asks hopefully.

"I just don't want to feel rushed."

"Yeah, I get that." He tries to keep the bitterness out of his voice. "Just think about it, okay? Sometimes it's hard to see past the moment you're in. Sometimes you need someone to help you through it, to lead you to the other side."

"I know."

"Don't read into the wedding-planning stuff. You think about these things too much."

"I know." She smiles.

"We'll figure it all out." His hand returns to her knee and he hopes she will embrace him again. He starts to slide his hand up her thigh, but she abruptly stands.

"We should get back to the party." She nods at the room.

To have sealed the deal, he thinks regretfully, watching as she tugs at her dress. Oh, to have sealed the deal, with the whole party right outside. Then they would have rejoined the room, hand in hand, smiling at each other. They would have looked at each other, feeling assured. Because that is why sex matters, to give you the feeling of a secret you share with someone else.

Leo frowns, the word catching in his thoughts. But surely this is a different kind of secret, a *good* kind of secret. He picks up a champagne glass from the desk and drains it.

"We all have secrets," Nora had said. She had stated it in that voice of hers, obstinate and clear. Maybe she was right. Maybe being open was an illusion. His father, it turned out, hadn't been so forthright with them. Even if Stephen was exaggerating about their grandmother's unhappiness, in truth their dad had never said a word about what she wanted.

During the toast, Leo became aware of the loss of his grandmother for the first time. "She wanted what we wanted," his dad said, and Leo felt sudden moisture in his eyes. "She was a lot like you," Stephen had told him. Leo had never thought of Grandma Portman that way. He never imagined the two of them having anything in common. But what if she truly was like him? What if she had sacrificed everything for her kids, only to end up alone? The thought made Leo want to weep.

He wants to catch Nora's hand and ask her, "Do you think she was miserable? Did Stephen tell you that, too?" He suddenly wants to ask Nora a hundred questions. "That thing you said about secrets. What did you mean?"

He finds he wants to tell her things, too. "I wanted to do you in that chair, just like that time, your old apartment." Would she remember now? Would she look at him disgustedly? "I wanted to cry during my dad's toast because it all seems so sad." Would she understand? Maybe they were all seeking the same assurance but in different ways. Maybe they all wanted to close that alcove door and just do different things behind it.

He wishes he could ask Nora what it feels like when she pulls. "Is it like sex? Not orgasmic, but like that feeling after?" His mind searches for the description. That feeling like you can finally breathe. That you know something deep down, have been reminded of something primal. Is that how it feels? Like a release? And Stephen, with his trips to the home—could it be that he felt something like that, too?

Maybe they were all trying to escape, but in different ways. Maybe it was okay to escape if you returned to one another recharged.

But Nora is leading him out into the party, and he can't stop to ask her. She looks back at him, over her shoulder. She has her party face back on, ready to rejoin the crowd. "I'm going to talk to your dad. I haven't really had a chance yet."

"Okay," he mumbles. "Give what I said some thought."

"I will."

He watches her walk away, letting go of her hand, her petite frame in that white-and-green dress. Her body is compact in a certain way, athletic.

The game! He remembers it and glances at his watch. A few minutes after eleven. He might be able to catch the tail end. His heart skips.

He retreats from Nora, backing away from her as if he has hit a three-pointer. He slides the door to the den open, then closes it behind him. He reaches for the remote.

Detroit leads by twenty points, 99–79, with less than two minutes on the clock. Leopold feels tremendous. This is the moment he's been hoping for all day, convinced he would have to sacrifice it.

He settles onto the sectional. Detroit will win, he suddenly knows. Anything can happen in two minutes, but this game belongs to them. It has been theirs all along.

It feels so good to give in to this, to do what he wants. It is exhausting to accommodate others all the time. No one wants him to be in here, away from the party, which is why it feels so good to be doing it.

So maybe I do know, he thinks, turning up the volume. Maybe I do know about secrets after all.

Eighteen

Nora waits for Michael to finish chatting with his guests. He makes eye contact through the group to let her know he sees her there. Nora squirms. She tries to stop her thoughts from turning flirty with Michael, but it isn't always easy. His eyes do their twinkling best, making you feel as if there were no one else in the world. When the circle of guests finally breaks apart, Nora feels a slight flutter in her stomach.

"What a day." Michael shakes his head. "I've barely gotten to talk with you."

"You're in high demand." She wonders briefly if Michael has ever been on the other side of things, waiting to catch someone's eye. Had he ever stood outside June's dorm at Smith hoping to get a minute alone with her? It is difficult to picture. Michael seemed as if he never waited for others but merely smiled as everyone came to him. "I wanted to tell you—that toast was beautiful."

"Thank you, Nora. It's kind of you to say."

"Everyone was moved. I'm sure it wasn't easy."

"Yes, well. I wanted to say something without being superficial. I can't pretend this day has been a normal one."

"Of course. It's just—it's so tempting to let a moment like that get the better of you. To get up there and pretend, or worry about it being a party, or what everyone will think."

"We all have our different ways of coping. Who's to say that one way is better?" He nods at someone in passing. "Some people are more private than others. Stephen, for example." Michael's eyes return to hers. "Stephen would never air his grievances in a toast. He no doubt has opinions about the fact that I did. But that's fine. June and I always vowed to let our kids be their own way. With grief especially, all bets are off."

"You're already handling it more gracefully than me," Nora says with a self-conscious laugh. "It's been almost a year now. There's no way I could get up there and do what you did." She can still barely say the words to herself. As if shrinking away from what happened makes it hurt any less.

"But this is what I mean, Nora. Let's not forget that I'm twice your age. My mother led a long, full life. To lose your mom so young— that is a different thing entirely."

Nora looks away. Yes, it is a different thing. But this sort of pep talk ends up making her feel like the slow kid in class. Take your time, they tell her. What else can you say to someone who is lagging? If only she could find Michael's calm reserve. Two days later and he is in full control, philosophizing before a room. And how is it that, once again, a conversation intended for the one in mourning has become about her?

He seems to sense her thoughts. "You've been dealing with so much for so long, Nora. I remember my college roommate, when his mother passed—Have I told you this story already?"

She shakes her head.

"Our sophomore year. It was sudden, a car accident. One day

there was a knock on the door, the dean." Michael waves his hand. "The craziest part is that he was back on Monday. My roommate, I mean. He left for the weekend to attend his mother's funeral, and then he was back, going to classes, continuing as though nothing had happened."

Nora pictures Michael at Harvard, traipsing through the snow in a wool toggle coat, his head bent against the cold.

"Things were so different then. There was a timeline laid out for you that no one thought to question. I don't think it even occurred to him to take time off—a semester, a year. As if that would have put everything in jeopardy! Maybe how he reacted seems noble, at a glance. But in hindsight, it's absurd. Why should he have rushed back? Why should anyone so young feel so much pressure?"

Nora opens her mouth, about to reply, but has the sudden impression that Michael wasn't talking about his roommate at all.

"But here I am, rambling. No fool like an old fool." He smiles at her. "I should return to my hosting duties before I get into trouble." His eyes give a final twinkle. "If you'll excuse me, Nora."

She smiles in return, watching as he moves on, the hall crowded with bodies. The people in the house seem to have multiplied, no longer murmuring and contained but more expansive. People take up more room when they're drunk.

And he had done it, she realizes suddenly. She nearly laughs out loud. What was the line from the magazine? *Chat with each guest for ten minutes before excusing yourself.* It was textbook.

But you didn't detect it with Michael. You didn't feel your cheeks grow stiff with a fake smile while pitying him for trying to make conversation. You felt as if a warm light had been directed at you, and you felt bathed in its glow. They'd only spoken for a few minutes, but the conversation had been meaningful.

The story about the roommate—Nora pauses, mulling it over. It was as if he had known about Leo's conversation with her in the alcove. Were secret cameras recording them? Nora gives a little shudder. She imagines June watching the videotape of her trying on her shoes. She imagines Michael listening to her conversation with Leo and frowning.

But she is being ridiculous. Her emotions aren't that hard to read. Even to outsiders, it was probably abundantly clear that the wedding planning has been delayed, that circumstances aren't normal. Nora wonders for a moment if there really was a roommate. Had the story been dialed up for her benefit? She looks at Michael, talking and laughing with yet another guest, his hand gesturing in midair. A storyteller, she thinks, watching him. After all, Michael sold stories for a living.

"Tipsy and happy?" a voice asks.

She looks up and sees Stephen holding two glasses of champagne.

"Do I look tipsy?"

"You look happy."

How many glasses has she had now? Three? Four? "I feel immune to the effects of alcohol." Stephen laughs. Certainly, she is in better shape than Leo. "Maybe I'm a glass of champagne after all."

Stephen rolls his eyes. "That whole thing was designed as a compliment. If only you knew how to take one."

"I was just complimenting your dad on his toast."

Stephen makes a face.

"What? You didn't like it?"

"Don't get me started."

"Stephen! What on earth could you have found wrong with that toast? It was—"

"Compelling? Poignant? Did it touch you, Nora?"

"Oh, stop." She swats at him. "Seriously, what didn't you like about it?"

"Well, there was the whole life-imitating-art motif, for starters.

'Oh, look at us, a hundred years later, acting out *Ulysses*.' And then that line, written down on an index card, which suggests a kind of premeditation that's highly disturbing."

"Because his toast should've been spontaneous?"

"Because rather than thinking about his mother, or writing a eulogy, he was planning that speech. I can just picture him, rehearsing it upstairs, looking up lines."

Nora hadn't thought about this, but it is true. If Michael wanted to publicly acknowledge his mother, why not do it at the synagogue?

"You'll notice, by the way, that the line he cited came from the very beginning of the book."

I know, I know, Nora thinks. No one has actually read it. "I think part of that toast was aimed at you," she says instead. "I think he wanted to show you that he cares."

Stephen looks off, his jaw clenched. Biting his tongue again. She imagines how Michael's words would sound to him. "A full life," Michael had told her. She realizes that Stephen probably doesn't feel that way at all. To Stephen, Grandma Portman had surely gone too soon.

"Do you want to get out of here?" He gestures with his chin in the direction of the street. "Get some air?"

"Sure. It's warm in here, actually."

"Crowds will do that."

"Your mom lowers the thermostat for parties, did you know that?"

"She does?" He laughs. "June." He shakes his head.

"June," she concurs.

He touches her lightly at the elbow and leads the way down the hall. They have to walk single file down the stairs, passing a guest or two, then they push their way through the door. Nora is surprised by the cool that greets them. It isn't chilly out, but the air feels lighter, easier. She breathes. "What a lovely night."

"Do you remember," he says, "that night we got high?"

She smiles. "Up by the windows, you mean?"

"I was thinking about it earlier."

"God, I can't believe we did that. I probably killed a vocal cord. And right under your parents' noses!"

"Oh, they wouldn't have cared. You could shoot up in front of my parents and they'd be fine."

"As long as you cleaned up after."

Stephen smiles.

Nora remembers how they had leaned out the windows and muffled their laughter, the street and the trees suddenly hysterically funny. "Everything was so different back then. If you'd told me then that one day they'd be my in-laws . . ."

"What would you have said?"

"At the time? God, I probably would've had a heart attack just thinking about it. Here." She pats the stoop and they sit on the top stair, the party at their backs. Nora sets her champagne flute down and remembers the men on Spruce earlier. Who's drinking on the steps now?

"That feels like it was ages ago," Stephen remarks.

I miss it, she thinks. Not that everything was perfect, but nothing had happened yet.

She remembers crossing Rittenhouse Square with Stephen one afternoon, watching the light cast shadows through the park. They were on their way to Delancey—the house, in its splendor, still new to her. She remembers wanting so much to be a part of its world. How glamorous they had seemed. She senses him looking at her and turns, but his gaze drops.

"What?"

"Hmn?"

"You were looking at me."

"I wasn't." His long fingers touch the step beneath them. "June wants to redo this stoop, you know. Her next big project. Gold-plated concrete is probably all the rage." He looks up at the dark sky.

"You were, though," she insists. "You were going to say something."

He remains silent.

She sighs. "Let me guess. Leo is a moron. I'll waddle down the aisle in some lace monstrosity and will have to suffer bad music on what should be my day."

His face softens.

"I'll have kids and be swallowed into obscurity. As opposed to my current life of glamour."

"I was thinking no such thing. Do you really think I'm that judgmental?"

"I do."

He shoots her a look. "I've been thinking about taking a leave of absence," he says abruptly.

"A leave of absence?"

"London. Maybe New York. A change of scene. You know, it occurred to me—"

"Whoa, whoa, whoa. London?"

"Maybe New York."

"Where is this coming from? You've never said a word about this."

Stephen looks away. She feels it, then, how much he's been keeping from her. She wonders how long his jaw has been set like that, his words held back. "How long have you been thinking about this?"

"I don't know," he says absently. "A day? A year? I've been feeling a little bit stuck recently. Everyone is headed somewhere. And I've been in the same place for, what, seven years now?" Stephen pauses, shakes his head. "Seven years! I mix them up sometimes, thinking it's only my fifth or sixth, that it can't really be that long. They start to blur together."

"I know something about feeling stuck. I don't know that running to London is the answer."

"Maybe New York. And I wouldn't be running. It just dawned on me that I don't need to be in Philly to write my dissertation."

"But why? You'd be away from everything you know."

"That's sort of the point of travel, I think."

Nora looks at him, tasting panic. "Is this because of your grandmother? You—you feel like you need space?" She watches him as he collects his thoughts. "You can't leave," she wants to say. She tries to think of how to say it lightly, the way Stephen would, but she knows the worry will leak through her voice.

"My grandmother used to laugh at me for not seeing the choices I have. There she was, locked up in a nursing home, and I was the one complaining? She encouraged me to think about what I want. 'Whatever it is your heart craves, Stephen,' she said. 'That's what you should do.' But that's the tough part, right? Figuring out what you want? It's harder than it should be.

"And I have doubts. About everything. I don't know that the program is right for me, that I really want to be an academic. Don't ask me what else I would do." He throws her a warning look. "My thinking hasn't gotten that far. But I can't help but feel that I'm not going to figure it out here."

"But, Stephen—" she sputters.

He waits for her to say something.

"I just—I had no idea—" She feels herself floundering, and he looks away. She has made everything about her. All those times she fled to Union or ignored his voice mails, all the times when her needs trumped his. She had expected him to understand, even when she got engaged to Leo.

"I mean, it's great, if that's what you want." She tries to sound supportive. "If you think it will help." She can feel Stephen watching her. "Oh, who am I kidding? This sucks, Stephen."

He smiles and looks out across the street. A streetlamp illuminates his profile and he looks boyish, vulnerable. "I think I chose Penn, in part, because I figured you'd end up here. I mean, it's not like I was fighting off programs with a stick."

But you were, she remembers. Columbia, Hopkins, Stanford. "I've already done New York," he had said at the time. "And who wants to live in Palo Alto or Baltimore? Besides, the chair at Penn is Stuart White. He's brilliant."

"You and Leo were already pretty serious. I had this idea of it being like that summer—you know, where all of us were together. It sounds so silly now."

"But it isn't. It's what I wanted, too."

"It's dangerous, I think. Trying to replicate something from the past. Besides which, I can't plan my life around you two. What am I supposed to do, always live a couple of blocks from you guys? At some point I need to figure out my own life."

Nora looks at him. He seems to have already made up his mind, reached a conclusion without her.

"I lost you to him," he says quietly.

"To Leo? But you didn't! I'm right here."

"It's been different, Nora. We both know that. And once you guys get married . . ."

"I knew that's what this was about. Listen, you're still my best friend. You'll always be my best friend."

"But I think I want more."

Nora feels everything around her get still. "Goodness," she says, wanting to say something, but immediately feeling the idiocy of this choice, as though she were the school nurse. She tries to change course by going for humor, but her words get tangled. "I—well, that's . . . Stephen, are you . . . ?" She stops, not knowing how to complete the sentence.

"In love? Gay? Confused?" He laughs. "None of those, I think. Except maybe the last." His eyes quickly meet hers before he returns to probing a fissure in the cement.

"I don't know what I am, honestly. But I feel the future coming at us like a train. And I wish that I could make it stop."

He is staring off, focused only on his thoughts.

"I've tried keeping a distance. Not voicing my opinions. We all see how well that went today. When you feel something, it ends up coming out, I think.

"I know you love Leo. I don't doubt that. And I'm not trying to interfere, unlikely though it may sound. But I worry sometimes . . ." He looks at her quickly, searchingly. She sees his Adam's apple gulp. "I worry that you haven't thought past the wedding. And let's face it, you can barely even think about that."

"I can see what you mean. About the whole not-holding-back thing."

"I worry that the wedding terrifies you. I worry that you don't want any of it. That instead of feeling excited and like you're finally getting what you want, like you can't believe your luck—that instead, you feel like you're walking the plank.

"I said I wanted more," he continues gently. "I didn't mean romantically. Not due to any shortcomings on your part." He takes a breath. "I think if I were to be attracted to anyone, it would have been you. But I'm almost—I don't know—asexual. Is that even possible?" He pokes at the stoop for a few seconds before finally looking at her. "Is this the most fucked-up thing you've ever heard?"

She laughs. "No. Not by a long shot."

"I mean, my mom, with her constant insinuations. Obviously she thinks I'm gay. She doesn't seem to get that I would be, if I was. What closet would contain me?"

"I've never thought you were gay."

"Really?"

"You're just not the repressed type."

"Ah, but here I am." His hands unfold and stretch before them. "I think I've been pretending to be repressed, if you can believe it. It's easier, you know? Sometimes it's easier to go along with the story than to confront what's really there. Why not let them think it, if it saves me from having to explain? I wouldn't even know how to explain it anyway."

Stephen shakes his head. "Do you remember those LGBT groups back at school? I was always tempted to go to a meeting and declare myself. What would they do? No one ever talks about celibacy, especially in college. It's weird, you know, when you feel like none of the letters in the acronym apply. And that's part of why I liked my grandmother so much. I assume you know. About the visits, I mean."

Nora gives a small nod.

"She never pressured me to be a certain way. With my parents—Leo, too, for that matter, maybe Leo more than anyone—I always get the feeling that they're waiting, holding their breath. Maybe it's none of their business, what I do. Maybe I shouldn't have to explain. But I always feel like I do.

"And I guess I've wondered if that might be what's going on with you, too. If you've been going along with their version of events because you don't want to explain, either. If it's easier to ascribe it—I don't want to say *blame* it, so let's say *ascribe* it—to the grief. To let them think it's the grief. To let yourself think it's the grief. When maybe it isn't."

Nora stares at the empty street. It's as if the hand on a clock is stuck, beating in place, its thudding the sound of her heart.

"Are you mad at me?" he finally asks.

"Mad? Why would I be?"

"You look tortured over there. Please, tell me what you're think-ing, Nora."

God. What am I thinking? What am I thinking, doing, feeling? She cannot reply to what he has said. "So you've never been attracted?" she asks tentatively.

"To you, you mean?"

"To anyone? You've never felt anything?"

"I've had crushes here and there. Catherine was one, actually, in high school. It was sort of like *The Graduate*—the beautiful older woman." He waves his hand, brushing away the memory. "But that's just it. It's always been about the idea of love more than the feeling. The notion of love rather than love itself. And whenever I'm with someone, the physical stuff feels like a chore. I end up craving solitude."

She smiles at that.

"The only exception, in a prolonged way, has been you. You're the only person in the world who makes me not want to run from it, screaming. You're the only person I could see being a—a compan-ion." He regards her, and it seems it is her turn to dutifully study the step.

"If I could have anything," he continues, "to answer the question from before, I guess it would be a life with you. That's it, really. I don't know how it would work, what we would do. If we would live near each other, maybe even share an apartment. But I wonder sometimes if we've found something in our friendship, something rare. A sort of marriage all our own. I mean, couples who have been together forever end up sexless, right? Maybe we've just beaten them there."

Nora laughs a little. He has no idea how right he is.

"I feel the most sane with you, Nora. You never get in the way. I never toss and turn at night wondering how to get rid of you." He smiles. "That doesn't sound like much of a compliment, does it? But it is. It's the highest compliment. You never cause me to be anything but myself.

"We could—God, Nora, don't laugh, please—but we could go to New York. I mean, why not? We could go to New York and live together and just be. Do our thing. Write, audition. The inheritance will cover the bills." His words are tumbling out, poised to meet her objections. But she has said nothing.

"She left everything to me. They—they don't know yet. But it's her life savings. She told me a while ago, said there was nothing I could do to change her mind. That I shouldn't tell anyone about it. She just wanted me to know in case—in case it affected my plans."

Nora knows about inheritances. She knows all about them. Money that sits there, looking at you.

"And then when she died—" Stephen's voice catches. "When she died . . . ," he tries again. Nora wraps her arm around her friend.

"It all changed," she offers. Yes, she thinks. I know about that, too.

She watches as Stephen wipes his eyes. He is waiting for her to say something, for some sort of reply.

"I have an imaginary shrink." She stops, surprised by her own words. "I don't actually have a shrink."

He regards her.

She gulps. "It's just—I never liked any of them. I was supposed to see one. Made to see one."

His eyes dart up to her hair.

"For that, yes. And I hated them. I tried a bunch. It wasn't working. They all started becoming predictable, and I was sick of faking it with them. Playing a part, like you said. My weekly appointment, where I would go and say what I was supposed to. I knew it wasn't doing anything."

"So you're not seeing anyone? But you said before that you—"

"Saw one this morning? Yes." She clears her throat. "I don't know. I sort of talk to myself? I get Leo to leave the apartment. And I get on the couch. Literally, I mean. Sometimes I kind of whisper to myself. But then other times it comes out pretty loud. And I picture someone there, taking it in, asking me questions. He doesn't have a face or anything like that, but it feels like a dialogue.

"Leo doesn't know. He thinks I'm seeing someone. A real shrink, I mean. He doesn't know when exactly, just figures it's during the week, when he's at work. And on weekends I make him leave if I need it. He never asks why." She thinks to herself, listening to the babble of explanation, that it is amazing what they have been skirting around, she and Leo. The questions unasked, unanswered.

"I kind of close my eyes and it happens. And the next thing I know, I'm gesturing and saying all kinds of things. Things I need to get out. It felt weird the first time, kind of scary and crazy. It was supposed to be a little experiment, but then it took. And it helps. That's the weirdest part, but I feel like it helps." She risks a glance at Stephen, expecting him to be gazing at her in horror, but his face is composed. "This is the part where you tell me I'm crazy."

"You're not."

"And, you know, it hasn't exactly addressed the original issue." She thinks of her pins, of what they conceal.

"No wonder!" he says suddenly. "No wonder you said he doesn't say much."

She gazes at him, unable to believe that she has actually told him this. But there he is, her Stephen, taking it all in, his features as thoughtful as ever. "Frankly, it sort of makes sense to me, Nora."

"Oh, *God*."

"It does. No one was providing what you needed. And so you went ahead and provided it yourself."

Just like that, with those words, Nora feels something unlock. Before she can help it, before she even knows what's happening, her face is in Stephen's shoulder and she is crying. The tears come without warning, her nose streaming. His arms are around her and he is stroking her back. As if he knew, of his own accord, not to touch her hair, which even Leo still forgets.

She wants to laugh or make a joke of it, to say something silly to Stephen and shove him away, except that it feels good to lean against him like this. She sniffles and wipes her face, trying discreetly to dab at her nose. Oh, whatever, she thinks. She draws the back of her hand across her nose, an unceremonious wipe. What pretenses do they have between them now?

"I can't believe I told you that," she admits.

"I think that makes two of us."

"What, your whole solitary thing? Please." She rolls her eyes. "That's not as bad as an imaginary shrink."

"I'm asexual, Nora. I'm like an amoeba."

"The amoeba and the pretender. We're quite the pair."

She thinks of Michael, his tale of the roommate. Maybe it was fabricated, or maybe it was simply embellished, adjusted so that it applied to her. We all spin stories. That's what we do. We want people to see certain things about us and not others. What matters is whether you let others in to the truest story, the one that's the hardest to tell.

"I don't know," she finally says. "I honestly don't."

"About which part?"

"All of it." She cranes her neck to look at the town house behind them. It occurs to her, gazing at the brick façade, that nothing had really happened. Everything felt different, yet nothing had changed. She and Stephen had confessed the scariest parts of themselves to each other. Meanwhile the party continued, oblivious.

A flicker of blue light catches her eye to the right of the study.

She frowns at the dance of light, but then it clicks. "The TV," she says, pointing.

Stephen frowns, confused.

"Leo"—she wants to laugh—"he's playing hooky." He'd mentioned a basketball game earlier. Leo's world was rocked by such games, battles on shiny courts and grassy turf. She shakes her head. "I'm glad he got to watch his game. I used to think sacrifice was sweet—that love necessitated it. That it must be real love if a man gives up his life for her. But, I don't know. I've started to wonder. Catering to a woman, deferring to her. No woman wants to hold a man hostage."

"Except June, that is."

Nora smiles. She hugs her knees to her chest. She imagines Leo watching the game, his face tense. Perhaps he has been waiting for some fight in her to play out, as though she, too, is a game. As though he has bet on the outcome.

She darts a look at Stephen beside her and sighs. "I wish I could tell you . . ." Tell you what? That, yes, I will come with you to New York? That, yes, you are right, more right than you can know?

"I wish I could tell you that I *know*. How I feel. Or what I want. And that's just it—nothing feels right anymore. Most things don't feel one way or the other, honestly."

She pauses, knowing that this isn't what she is supposed to say. I like that you wanted to try it with me, she wants to tell him. I like that our friendship means that much to you. Because I can't imagine life without you, either.

"We both have so much to think about. It sounds obvious, but that's just it. I've been trying so hard not to think about it, to have life become normal again. But it's starting to dawn on me that this is what I've got."

She thinks of the night they sat by the windows, carefree and high. The street had been dark, lit only by streetlamps, their figures casting shadows onto the sidewalk below. Up by those windows they had laughed too loudly and leaned too far, with no thought of falling. They had seen none of this coming, and so they had leaned into each other and laughed.

We all get stuck, she thinks. Even if you travel the world. It isn't about being in one city or mired in a department. It's about tripping ourselves, ensnaring ourselves. It's as though we lay traps, except that they aren't for animals—they're for our own feet.

"I don't expect you to say anything," he says gently. "Seriously, Nora. I'm not looking to you for an answer. I don't even know what I'm asking. This is all new to me, too. The idea of leaving—I don't even know if it makes sense."

She nods. Her words are at the bottom of a pool, dark and deep. She can feel them, even if she is unable to say them. For the first time, she feels as if that's okay.

How lucky she is. How lucky to have this friend who sits beside her and accepts her silence. Nothing is expected of her, no answer or assurance. She needn't say a word. It's a relief to know that his decision is not on her shoulders. That she owes him nothing other than her honesty. That she needn't be anything more than what she already is.

If she had felt trapped, in an impossible place where everything felt inevitable, and the inevitable felt doomed, what does it mean that she has someone who understands? Who seems to have sensed it quietly beside her? What does it mean that they both feel stuck?

Maybe, she thinks, maybe I'm not so alone.

She recalls being in the loft that morning, on the couch, speaking into the air. She wonders if some part of her has been speaking to him all this time, wanting to tell him these things and confide in him. She wonders if her imagination had built a shrink that was, in part, Stephen.

She cannot say yes to Stephen. With Stephen, she never says things unless she means them. It's unthinkable to say something to him that isn't true. He never asks her to comply, to go along with something because it is already in motion. What was it he had said of his grandmother? "She never pressured me to be a certain way."

I can't say yes, she reflects. But how lucky I am that you don't need my yes. That you don't want my yes for the sake of a yes. You wouldn't believe it right now anyway. You'd roll your eyes if I said, "Yes! Let's do it. Let's go to New York and get the apartment." You'd say no. I could say yes, and you would say no. Because you know me. Because you've been with me this whole time.

It's just like that night we leaned out the windows, except now we're on the ground. After everything that has happened, in the violet dark of night, I still lean into you beside me. And I know that you are there.

Afterword

I t is different from what she imagined.

Milan is the same. Beautiful, refined. A shock how much it is the same. She had been prepared for it to not be the place she remembered. You cannot go back, she told herself.

But Milan was like that. Cobbled streets, the women elegant, the men pressed and ironed. Everything felt elevated, gilded, even the doorways and window frames. The Juliet balcony of her flat is a thing of beauty.

There is no anger. This is what surprises her most. The world had not come crashing down.

The envelope sits on the table in the foyer where she keeps her keys and change. She had not known what to do with it.

The ink this year is tangerine. The stock is a soft blue-gray. It was a bold choice. She's still got it, Nora thought wistfully when she opened it.

The invitation was a surprise, yet utterly predictable. She laughed when she received it (how she could picture June composing the guest list!), laughed, but then felt her eyes mist over. She placed it

on the table, shaking her head. How life continues! How life continues, spinning like a top.

It had been anticlimactic with Leo. "Okay," he had said, less
sullen, less shocked, less argumentative than she would have predicted. He nodded to himself in confirmation. "Okay."

"You aren't mad?" she asked uncertainly.

He looked at her, his eyes sad. "Nora, it's okay."

In some way, she thinks he must have known all along. Those
constant efforts to pin her down, to finalize the wedding. Maybe, in
a strange way, he was relieved to have her just come out and say it.
Listening to her plan, her decision, he had merely gulped, nodded.

Stephen had not taken it well. "But what am I supposed to do?"
he asked baldly.

"Stephen!" She laughed, exasperated.

"I know, I know. Go to Milan, then. I will have to fend for myself.
God only knows what I will do with you an ocean away."

It wouldn't have been right, she wanted to tell him. It wouldn't
have been right for us to escape together. It was too easy, too inces-
tuous. "Don't be sad," she said gently. "It doesn't become you."

They looked at each other and smiled.

Stephen had not gone to New York after all. He was making
progress on his dissertation. *Alarming progress,* he wrote. *Rapid,
astonishing progress. It consumes me. Maybe the answer was to give
in to the problem.* His postcards were filled with such enigmatic
declarations. They came regularly, beautiful little missives, colorful
and compact, awaiting in her mailbox like exotic birds. He tactfully
avoided any mention of his brother. She hadn't yet gathered the
courage to ask about Leo when they spoke on the phone.

But the person who had surprised her the most was June.

June showed up at the end of her last choir practice, standing in
the church with her hands clasped before her. Nora had not seen

her arrive. She had on her usual makeup, her hair perfectly coiffed, yet something seemed missing, as if a layer had been removed.

Nora stood there uncertainly, unsure of what to say.

June gestured toward one of the pews. "I've never been here, all this time." She gazed around at the church. "It's quite beautiful."

"Yes."

June didn't say whether she had heard them practicing. She didn't say how she had known when to come. She did not engage in her normal June pretenses. They were past that, it seemed, at least in this particular moment.

"I hated the suburbs, you know," she said suddenly. The sentence sat between them. Nora watched it settle, floating down like a feather. June seemed to be weighing her words. "You'd never think it now, but I was the rebel in the family. The black sheep, if you can believe it. Marrying a Jew! Living in Manhattan! New York in the seventies was not what it is today. I'm not exaggerating when I say that my parents feared for me." She smiled to herself.

"Michael and I must seem so settled to you, so—I don't know—established. But at the time, we shocked everyone. My friends from school thought I was crazy. Even Michael's colleagues. They all lived uptown, you know, the Upper East Side. They were such conservative WASPs. We were the wacky liberals in the Village." June laughed, and Nora realized it was a rare sound, the way it escaped from her. Later, Nora would wonder if June had truly called someone else a WASP.

"I wanted certain things for myself. I wanted to be around all that energy, not in a doorman building with gargoyles. I wanted to live a certain way—to see shows and experience art, to not give all that up. I wanted to not resent my kids. I wanted to be happy."

Nora was relieved that June wasn't yelling at her or discussing Leo; she wasn't attempting to convince her to rethink her decision.

The conversation had not taken a turn to Nora's actions. So Nora listened politely, as though it were completely normal that June should be there, in the church, sitting with her in a pew.

"You don't know it now, but for the rest of your life, there will be pressure to compromise. The pull of this will be a force. And it won't go away." June tucked a strand of hair behind her ear and then finally looked at Nora. "You will feel judgment, terrible judgment, for fighting this current." June's eyes held Nora's. Nora felt her mouth go dry. "But not from me." And at this June nodded, as though confirming that she had delivered her intended message.

Nora, mystified, nodded back. Wait, she wanted to say. What exactly are you saying?

But June was already standing, smoothing her skirt, and something slipped back into place. A bit of armor, her usual self. "Well," she said more formally, "we wish you the best of luck, Nora. We really do." With that, she turned on her heel.

Was it a pardon? A blessing? Nora, still sitting, felt immobilized, and for some time she continued to stare off in the empty church. Finally she rose, shaking off the conversation, not knowing what to make of it.

We of course don't expect you to fly out for this, read the note accompanying the invitation, in a neat navy script. *But know that you are welcome.*

The sixteenth had passed already, a warm Saturday in Milan. Nora had been ordering gelato, hunting through her wallet for change, when the date dawned on her.

Later, back in her flat, she sat by the balcony. She imagined the party as it would unfold. She imagined Michael and June waking on Delancey and making preparations. Stephen, resentful, would drag himself to his parents' town house. Her thoughts approached Leo. Would he bring someone new? Was he dating already? She shrank back from the idea, unable yet to face it.

Weeks later, approaching July, she has not yet talked to Stephen about how it went. "The same, it is always the same," he will say. The second anniversary of her mother's death looms, a black day on the calendar, but she has been consumed with finalizing an upcoming trip to Paris. A thousand details harangue her, swarm her like insects. She must follow up with the bus company, on strike yet again. She had persuaded the program director that they should stop for lunch at a spot she remembered fondly from when she made the same trip as an undergrad. The students will love it. The magical opera with its dramatic lights and cavernous sound. The daily lessons and classes might later be a blur; she could not remember her own vocal lessons from when she was here. But this trip—the trip would stay with them forever.

I don't know where it will all lead, she had written Stephen earlier that day. *I don't know what I'll do after this, how it will turn out.* The program director had suggested there might be a spot for her in New Haven in the music department. "You have a gift as a coach," he had said.

But I'm glad, she typed. *Even if it's all a little up in the air. For the first time in so long, I feel happy.* She had paused as these words came out onto the screen, paused and examined them, testing them out.

The cursor blinked, waiting.

It looked right.

She hit send.

Acknowledgments

It is a relief and a pleasure to finally be able to thank those who have helped me.

Miriam Altshuler, you are an extraordinary agent and a wonderful friend. I feel very fortunate to be your client.

Kara Watson, thank you for your exquisite editorial eye, your marketing brilliance, and for being so gifted at what you do.

Whitney Frick, you tended to these characters with me. You have been a fierce advocate of this novel from the beginning, and I'm so happy that this book brought us together.

I wish to acknowledge the Rona Jaffe Foundation and Bread Loaf Writers' Conference for their generous support. Beth McCabe, your belief in this project was a game changer. Michael Collier, I owe so much to Bread Loaf. Thank you, many times over.

To Helen Schulman, for being a remarkable teacher and for leading workshops exactly as they should be led. Teddy Wayne, for being unfailingly generous throughout this process. Dave Gilbert, for being so kind, and so cool.

Ron DeMaio founded an arts program at my public high school that made me think I could be a writer. Before that program, I didn't know that being a writer was feasible. Honestly, I didn't know that writers *existed*. Ron, the program you created and your inspired way of leading it changed the course of my life. You mentored me at fourteen, and you read a first draft of this novel nearly two decades later. In essence, this is all your fault.

Thank you to the magazines and editors who have believed in my work, especially *VQR*.

There are two people I wish to acknowledge who are no longer here. The first, Stan Hall, was my eighth-grade English teacher. A dazzling teacher, he promised he would forever scan bookstore titles for my name. He was certain this day would come, and I wish he could be here to witness it.

The second, Jared H. Miller, was a friend who died in 2005 after a courageous battle with cancer. Jared was in the middle of getting his MD/PhD, and his death came as a shock. I think of Jared often. I think of the example he set, the way he inspired those around him, and his immense generosity and drive. He never would have guessed it, being far too humble, but he influenced me tremendously, and his memory influences me still.

Thank you to Nan Graham, Katie Monaghan, and all of the outstanding people at Scribner. Thanks also to Bronwen Pardes for going to bat for me, Micaela Tobin for her musical expertise, and Reiko Davis for her extraordinary helpfulness throughout this process.

To my friends and family who have cheered me on and rooted for me; your support means more than I can say. I especially wish to thank Manish, Jen, Sofie and Serena Shanbhag. To my mother, Suhas Shanbhag: how lucky I am, to have been raised by you. You taught me more than you could ever know.

Finally, this novel is dedicated to Noah and Zoe Lang. Noah, this book would have been impossible without you. It is that simple.

Zoe, people sometimes ask how I wrote a novel while caring for a baby. They do not understand. I didn't write this book despite having you. I wrote this book *because* of having you. My daughter, you have inspired me to be a better person, raising me up simply by being you. Thank you for being exactly who you are.

Sources

Many resources proved useful in the writing of this novel. Joseph Allen Boone's *Libidinal Currents: Sexuality and the Shaping of Modernism* and Michael North's *Reading 1922: A Return to the Scene of the Modern* were both invaluable. Slavoj Žižek's *The Parallax View* illuminated the term, discussed in *Ulysses*. Michael's idea about insurance policy trades stems from "What's Your Life Worth?" by James Vlahos (*New York Times*, August 12, 2012). Jonathan Safran Foer's "Why a Haggadah?" (*New York Times*, March 31, 2012) was instrumental for Stephen's seder, as was *New American Seder*. Ann Patchett's *Bel Canto* offered a pleasurable and illuminating foray into opera.

Lastly, each chapter in this novel contains lines excerpted from its corresponding episode in *Ulysses*. For a list, please refer to the author's website at www.mayalang.com.